FLYAWAY VACATION SWEEPSTAKES!

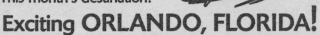

This month's destination:

Exciting ORLANDO, FLORIDA!

Are you the lucky person who will win a free trip to Orlando? Imagine how much fun it would be to visit Walt Disney World**, Universal Studios**, Cape Canaveral and the other sights and attractions in this area! The Next page contains tow Official Entry Coupons, as does each of the other books you received this shipment. Complete and return *all* the entry coupons—the more times you enter, the better your chances of winning!

Then keep your fingers crossed, because you'll find out by October 15, 1995 if you're the winner! If you are, here's what you'll get:

- Round-trip airfare for two to Orlando!
- 4 days/3 nights at a first-class resort hotel!
- $500.00 pocket money for meals and sightseeing!

Remember: The more times you enter, the better your chances of winning!*

*NO PURCHASE OR OBLIGATION TO CONTINUE BEING A SUBSCRIBER NECESSARY TO ENTER. SEE BACK PAGE FOR ALTERNATIVE MEANS OF ENTRY AND RULES.

**THE PROPRIETORS OF THE TRADEMARKS ARE NOT ASSOCIATED WITH THIS PROMOTION.

VOR KAL

P9-CRM-383

FLYAWAY VACATION
SWEEPSTAKES
OFFICIAL ENTRY COUPON

This entry must be received by: SEPTEMBER 30, 1995
This month's winner will be notified by: OCTOBER 15, 1995
Trip must be taken between: NOVEMBER 30, 1995-NOVEMBER 30, 1996

YES, I want to win the vacation for two to Orlando, Florida. I understand the prize includes round-trip airfare, first-class hotel and $500.00 spending money. Please let me know if I'm the winner!

Name_____

Address _____ Apt. _____

City   State/Prov.   Zip/Postal Code

Account #_____

Return entry with invoice in reply envelope.

© 1995 HARLEQUIN ENTERPRISES LTD.   COR KAL

FLYAWAY VACATION
SWEEPSTAKES
OFFICIAL ENTRY COUPON

This entry must be received by: SEPTEMBER 30, 1995
This month's winner will be notified by: OCTOBER 15, 1995
Trip must be taken between: NOVEMBER 30, 1995-NOVEMBER 30, 1996

YES, I want to win the vacation for two to Orlando, Florida. I understand the prize includes round-trip airfare, first-class hotel and $500.00 spending money. Please let me know if I'm the winner!

Name_____

Address _____ Apt. _____

City   State/Prov.   Zip/Postal Code

Account #_____

Return entry with invoice in reply envelope.

© 1995 HARLEQUIN ENTERPRISES LTD.   COR KAL

DUNLEAVY FARM
KENTUCKY

Dear Nan,

Permit me to introduce myself. I am your paternal grandmother, Octavia Whitworth Dunleavy.

When I think of the bitter circumstances under which your father and I parted company, I feel safe in guessing that you've probably never heard of me. So I imagine this letter will come as quite a shock, but please bear with me.

My dear granddaughter, I need to see you. I have a proposition to discuss that I hope you will find most interesting....

Looking forward to hearing from you,

I remain,
Yours affectionately,

Octavia Whitworth Dunleavy

ABOUT THE AUTHOR

Janis Flores has had a wide and varied publishing career. She's written several mainstream novels and more than fifteen romance novels. The Dunleavy Legacy, of which *Done Cryin'* is the second book, is her first trilogy. The three books—each one a complete romance—follow the fortunes of a new generation of Dunleavys. The stories are moving, emotional and dramatic, exploring the complex relationships among members of a wealthy, powerful family.

Janis is very excited about this trilogy. "It takes place in the thrilling world of Thoroughbred racing—a setting close to my heart." The author lives in California with her farrier husband, Ray, and a couple of dogs. She enjoys riding and training her Arabian horses.

Janis Flores
DONE CRYIN'

Harlequin Books

TORONTO • NEW YORK • LONDON
AMSTERDAM • PARIS • SYDNEY • HAMBURG
STOCKHOLM • ATHENS • TOKYO • MILAN
MADRID • WARSAW • BUDAPEST • AUCKLAND

ISBN 0-373-70658-8

DONE CRYIN'

Copyright © 1995 by Janis Flores.

This edition published by arrangement with Harlequin Books S.A.

® and TM are trademarks of the publisher. Trademarks indicated with ® are registered in the United States Patent and Trademark Office, the Canadian Trade Marks Office and in other countries.

Printed in U.S.A.

DUNLEAVY FAMILY TREE

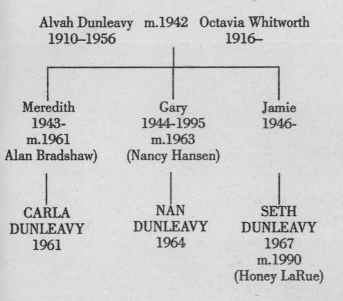

Alvah Dunleavy m.1942 Octavia Whitworth
1910–1956   1916–

Meredith   Gary   Jamie
1943-   1944-1995   1946-
m.1961   m.1963
Alan Bradshaw)   (Nancy Hansen)

CARLA   NAN   SETH
DUNLEAVY   DUNLEAVY   DUNLEAVY
1961   1964   1967
                                        m.1990
                                        (Honey LaRue)

PROLOGUE

As Octavia Dunleavy emerged from the main house at Dunleavy Farm, the stallion neighed loudly from atop the hill. Octavia smiled. Done Roamin' never failed to call to her when she brought his carrot at night; it was a ritual between the eighty-year-old woman and the twenty-year-old horse that had lasted for years.

This evening, Octavia's spirits were light. In the house behind her, her granddaughter Carla had just finished talking to Octavia's second grandchild, Nan, in Montana. Nan hadn't yet consented to come for a visit, but Octavia was hopeful. She had taken a chance all those months ago when she wrote to the three grandchildren she'd never met, but after Carla had answered and said she would come, look what had happened. Now not only was Carla here to stay, she and the farm's manager, Wade Petrie, had fallen in love.

Octavia chuckled. That was only one of the changes that had taken place since her headstrong oldest grandchild had arrived. With her blessing, Carla had taken over the farm's finances and was in the process of arranging a big loan from Trent Spencer, the investment banker who owned the farm next door.

It was funny how things worked out. When she'd first dreamed up the idea of asking her grandchildren to visit Dunleavy Farm, she had wanted a chance to get to know them—and to show them the farm. After all, she wasn't getting any younger, and if she was alone when she went, Dunleavy Farm would cease to exist. Before that happened, she hoped her grandchildren would get a sense of their family history. In its time, the farm had been one of the best.

She paused. "Be honest, you silly old woman," she muttered to herself with a shake of her head.

The truth was that she had hoped that one, two or all three of her grandchildren would decide to make the farm their home. But she had tried not to count on it, and even when she had wanted so badly for Carla to stay, she'd kept her promise to herself not to bring any pressure to bear on her granddaughter. If Carla wanted to stay on, it had to be her decision. Hers alone.

And now Nan might come to visit, Octavia thought as she began walking again. Nan, the daughter of her only son, Gary, who had left Dunleavy so many years ago. Thinking of Gary, she sighed. He'd had such a temper, not to mention an iron will as strong, or stronger, than her own. How they had battled over that girl he'd wanted to marry! How she had threatened and pleaded and cajoled . . . all to no avail.

Her steps slowed once more as she reflected on all those lost opportunities over the years. She had so much to make up for, she thought, so many mistakes to try to correct. She'd started the process with Carla and Done

Driftin', and to her relief, things had worked out despite the colt's accident.

Now Done Cryin', another of Done Roamin's offspring, waited for Gary's daughter. If Nan came to visit, would that colt work the same miracle for her as Done Driftin' had for Carla?

She hoped so. She hoped so with all her might.

CHAPTER ONE

"WHO WAS THAT CALLING, Nan?"

Far from Dunleavy Farm in Kentucky, on a mild—for March—day, Nan Dunleavy sat in the cluttered office at Saddleback Ranch, near Bozeman, Montana, her hand still on the phone. At the question from the ranch's cook and housekeeper, she looked up and saw Yolanda Bonney in the doorway.

Yolanda had worked at the ranch for years, first for Nan's father, and more recently, just for Nan. Gary Dunleavy had died six months ago after a long battle with cancer. His illness had cost almost more than the generous Nan had to give, both financially and emotionally. Nan was sure she'd cried so much, she'd never be able to cry another tear.

But then a new problem would arise—the ancient boiler would break down, or a cabin roof would spring a leak, or one of the few remaining horses on the ranch would take sick, and suddenly it would all seem too much. She'd break into tears again—she who hated to cry because it was such a waste of time.

Before she knew it, she'd turned thirty-two and her prospects for the future didn't look any brighter now than they had last year, or the year before that. If anything, they seemed grimmer.

But she'd been depressed enough lately, so she forced a smile for Yolanda and said, "It was the strangest thing. That call was from somebody named Carla Dunleavy." She paused because she still couldn't take it in herself. "Carla said she was my...cousin."

Yolanda's dark eyes widened. "But your dad always said you had no living relatives."

"I know. But Carla knew about...the letter."

Some months ago, Nan had received a letter from a woman in Kentucky who claimed to be her grandmother. Since Nan's father had told her he was an orphan with no known family, she'd thought at first that the letter had been sent to the wrong person. Still, she couldn't help reading it, and once she had, she'd been hooked. Now she'd read it so often, she could recite it from memory.

Dear Nan,

Permit me to introduce myself. I am your paternal grandmother, Octavia Whitworth Dunleavy. When I think of the bitter circumstances under which your father and I parted, I feel safe in saying that you've probably never heard of me.

My dear granddaughter, I need to see you. I have a proposition to discuss that I hope you will find most interesting...

Nan had been so shocked at the news that she'd still

been staring at the letter when Yolanda had come to ask what she wanted for dinner.

"Why, Nan, honey!" Yolanda had exclaimed when she saw Nan's pale face. "What's the matter?"

Nan didn't know how to explain. Her legs felt too weak to hold her, and she sank into a nearby chair. "I'm not sure," she'd said. "I just got a letter from someone who claims to be my... grandmother."

Yolanda had put a hand to her ample bosom. "My goodness gracious! Do you think it could be true?"

"I don't know. Dad always said we had no family. But this woman is so convincing. She calls Dad by name, and listen to this. She says that if I come to stay at her farm for a month, she'll give me my own racehorse."

"What?"

"I know. It sounds incredible, doesn't it?"

Yolanda was nothing if not down-to-earth sensible. Flatly, she'd said, "She sounds as crazy as a loon. You're not going to go, are you?"

"No, of course not." Nan had thrown the letter down on top of some old bills. "I can't just... pick up and leave. What about the ranch?"

"Not to mention what you'd find when you got there," Yolanda had said darkly. "What if this is some kind of prank, or something? What if it's someone playing a joke?"

Yes, but what if it wasn't?

Nan couldn't seem to stop herself from wondering. After all, the woman said her name was Dunleavy, and that was strange. Even more fascinating was the fact that Octavia owned Dunleavy Farm. Nan had always had a faraway love affair with Kentucky and the sleek Thoroughbreds for which the state was famous. But, stuck up here on a Montana dude ranch where sturdy quarter horses were the rule, the closest she had come to any of those magnificent runners was in the den, when the television reception was good enough to catch one of the Triple Crown races.

But that hadn't discouraged her from studying pedigrees until she was a walking encyclopedia on every significant bloodline in racing. And when, long ago, she'd read about Dunleavy Farm and its famous Triple Crown winner, Done Roamin', she'd asked her father if they were related to the Dunleavys. To her intense disappointment, Gary had denied any relationship. In fact, Nan remembered, he had been so angry that she hadn't pursued the subject.

But still, she had wondered. And wondered again, after she had received the letter from the woman who claimed to be her grandmother.

And now she'd had a phone call from a cousin she'd never heard of, who not only knew that Octavia Dunleavy had contacted her, but who also had the same surname. It seemed to be too much of a coincidence. Despite what her father had told her, *could* Octavia Dunleavy's claim be true?

Yolanda seemed to be following Nan's thoughts. Tentatively, she asked, "You don't think that letter was legitimate, do you?"

"I don't know. I thought at the time that it was a mistake, but now—" Nan broke off. "What do you think?"

Yolanda came in and sat down in the old leather chair by the door. She was a big, comfortable-looking woman in her early sixties, with steel-gray hair pulled back into a no-nonsense bun that matched her personality. Nan, who had lost her mother when she was two, regarded Yolanda as the mother she'd never known. Yolanda always seemed to have the answers. But it looked as if there were some things Yolanda wasn't sure about, after all. "I don't know, honey," she said. "If it was just the one thing, I could dismiss it. But a phone call, too? Now, that's a little bit much. I'd have to give that some thought."

Nan stood and walked to the window. She was a small woman, only five foot two, with dark hair cut utilitarian short and intense green eyes she had inherited from her father. Small-boned and slender, she knew she looked fragile, but underneath, she was as tough as steel—or so she liked to think. Hard work and too much of the bad that life had to offer had given her an edge; she moved and spoke as if wasting time and motion was the worst thing in the world. She had little patience with frills and fancy words, and even less tolerance for fools. She prided herself on getting things done.

At least she used to, she thought darkly, remembering the past lonely months when everything in her life seemed out of control. She had always been able to get a handle on things, but after her father died, she couldn't keep the ranch going no matter how diligently she worked. Yolanda said she was too hard on herself; after all, no one could have foreseen how much Gary's illness would cost, and no one had known about the mountain of other debts her father had totaled up without telling anyone.

But Nan did blame herself; she couldn't help it. She had loved her father deeply, but she hadn't been blind to his problems. Tall and handsome, and green-eyed like his daughter, Gary Dunleavy had always had time to help others; he'd been well liked by everyone. But he'd also been an irresponsible dreamer who, for reasons he'd never shared or cared to explain, drank too much. Nan always knew when a binge was coming on; he'd become withdrawn and taciturn, locking himself in his room for days at a time. On those occasions, which she had early come to dread, it was as though some inner demon took him by the throat and forced him to the bottle so he could forget. But forget *what,* he'd never told her, and she had never found out.

Gary Dunleavy should never have tried to run a business, she'd often thought, especially a dude ranch, where there were always so many details to worry about. Nan had known her father wasn't suited for it when she was barely seven years old and had to take the dude strings out. Visitors thought it was cute when they saw the small girl on the big quarter horse leading a group on a trail ride. Little did they know she was doing it because her father had had so much to drink, he couldn't stay in the saddle.

Nan had learned young what kind of man her father was. But it didn't matter, she thought. Despite the odds and obstacles, he hadn't given her up after her mother died, even though well-meaning neighbors had tried to convince him that a child so small—and a little girl, too—would be better off adopted or in a foster home.

"No, sir, she's staying with me," Gary had said to each one. "My daughter has lost one parent. I'm not going to have her lose the other."

It warmed Nan's heart to think of it. Her father had kept his word, even through the awkward times of early adolescence when, with Yolanda's help, of course, he'd had to deal with such feminine milestones as training bras and menstrual periods. And then he'd had to confront the reality of her going out with boys. She smiled, remembering those awful first dates. She didn't know who had been more uncomfortable: she, her date, or her father. He'd been so protective, some boys had been afraid to go out with her.

Her smile vanished. Too bad he hadn't scared off one of her older suitors—if "suitor" was what Lloyd Havermill could be called. Lloyd had been one of the guests at the ranch last fall. Dark-haired and dark-eyed, as good-looking as he was charming, he had swept the usually immune Nan right out of the saddle. The Dunleavys had a long-standing policy of not becoming involved with the guests; romantic dalliances, no matter how tempting, could cause difficulties and make things awkward for everyone. Nan had never had any real problems in that area; after all, how involved could she get with someone who was only going to stay at the ranch for a short while, and who would probably be saddle-sore most of the time, anyway?

But Lloyd had been different. She knew it as soon as she picked him up at the airport with a half-dozen or so other guests for the week. It was a look in his eye and the way he smiled. She'd felt herself being drawn to him even as they introduced themselves, and before the day was over, she'd been helpless to resist. She hadn't known he was married until his wife and two children made a surprise visit to the ranch to take him home.

"But you never asked," he'd reminded her during the brief snatch of time they'd had together on the pretext of settling his bill.

She'd prepared a blistering diatribe, only to bite it back at the last second. He was right, she thought bitterly. She hadn't asked. It was her own fault. The fact that he hadn't said anything seemed beside the point. What was done, was done. She had to face the fact that the one time she'd broken the Dunleavy rule, she had made a total fool of herself.

To this day, she couldn't understand it. Months after the fact, she was still wondering why she'd been caught up like that. It wasn't like her to be impulsive. As much as she had loved her father, dealing with the consequences of his irresponsible behavior had made her vow to be just the opposite. She had worked on being methodical and careful; she had tried to plan things every step of the way.

Until Lloyd came long. Now what haunted her was the possibility that she was more like her father than she wanted to admit.

It was a moot question, anyway, she thought, suddenly becoming impatient with herself. Even before Lloyd flew off in his private plane with his loving family by his side, she had taken an oath that she would never be caught unawares again. And at this moment, not long after Carla Dunleavy had called, she had other problems to worry about. The surprising phone conversation aside, she still had to figure out what to do about the ranch.

"Yolanda—" She turned away from the window. But just then, they heard the sound of an engine on the road up to the main house. Noise traveled far in this quiet country; in years gone by, it might have been the sound of wolves howling at night, or the occasional snarl of a mountain lion on the hunt. These days, those sounds were rare. City folks who came to the dude ranch on holiday had to be satisfied with the harsh cry of a hawk overhead, or the barking of coyotes.

This afternoon, it was only a car.

"Now, who could that be?" Yolanda wondered, getting up to look.

Nan looked out the window, and recognized the vehicle. "It's Wes Morton," she said.

Yolanda immediately looked displeased. "Huh," she snorted. "Now I'm glad I never got to those pies I was planning to make today. He don't deserve a piece of *nothin'*."

"Now, now," Nan said, but she was preoccupied. Wes was the loan officer of the bank in nearby Bozeman, where she had recently applied for yet another loan. The fact that Wes was coming all the way out here in person to tell her the decision could be good or bad; she had no way to judge yet. They had been friends since they were in school; if the news was positive, he might be coming to celebrate. On the other hand, he could be here to commiserate.

In silence, she and Yolanda watched as the car passed under the tall lodgepole pine sign welcoming visitors to the Saddleback Ranch. As he pulled up in front of the big porch, Yolanda gave Nan a look.

"You going to be all right?" the older woman asked.

Since Nan had told her about the need for the loan—as well as what they'd have to decide if she didn't get it—she knew there was no point in pretending. "As well as I can be right now, I guess." She tried a smile that turned into a frown. "We'll know soon enough, won't we?"

Yolanda gave her shoulder a comforting pat. "I mean it, don't you go worrying about it. One way or the other, we'll get along. We always have, haven't we?"

Yes, they had, Nan thought, tucking her T-shirt more neatly into her worn jeans. *But things had never been this bad.*

She grimaced at the thought. Summer bookings were almost nonexistent; inquiries about reservations had slowed to a trickle. Even if she got the loan, she didn't know how she was going to pay it back. Right now, she had only two couples reserved for June, normally one of the busiest months.

But she'd worry about that later. Right now, she had to deal with Wes, who was starting up the steps when she opened the screen door and came out onto the porch.

"Hi, Wes," she said. To her dismay, she had to struggle for control. The thought of what she would have to do if she didn't get this loan terrified her. Somehow she forced a smile. "How about a cup of coffee?"

Squinting up at her, Wes took off his Stetson and brushed a hand over his face. The day was cool, but he was sweating. It wasn't a good sign, but Nan managed to keep her expression neutral.

"Why don't we walk a spell?" he suggested.

Now she knew she was in trouble. Wes never walked farther than from his house or office to the car. He certainly wouldn't choose to take a walk when he could be sitting comfortably in the house. But Nan needed time to compose herself, so she nodded.

"Sure," she said, jamming her hands into her pockets so he wouldn't see how she'd started to shake. The suspense was too much. As she came down the stairs, she decided to make it easier for both of them. "You sound like a man with a lot on his mind."

"Well, I am, Nan," he said, falling into step beside her. He was of medium height, the same age as she was, with dishwater blond hair cut short and brown eyes behind black-framed glasses. "I came to tell you—"

When he broke off, she knew it was worse than she had anticipated. She stopped and looked up at him. "I didn't get it, did I?"

Genuinely distressed, he shook his head. "I'm sorry, Nan. I tried everything I knew, but the bank just won't extend any more credit to the ranch."

She looked away, telling herself she would not cry. She'd known this might happen; she'd tried to prepare for it. She just hadn't realized how... how *final* those words would sound. She felt so cornered.

As though he sensed her struggle, Wes turned to look tactfully at the hills that surrounded the ranch on three sides. Nan followed his glance, trying to distract herself by thinking of how much she loved the view. To her, the hills were like gentle giants, always there to offer comfort. She couldn't count the times she'd ridden up there to think, to dream... to cry.

Today, a few clouds moved majestically over the heights, huge balls of foamy white on a brilliant blue sky. The sight was enough to hurt her eyes.

"I'm sorry, Nan," Wes repeated into the silence that had fallen between them. "I wish there was something I could do. But you won't take a personal loan—"

"No, I won't, so don't ask me again, Wes. It's bad enough being in debt to a bank. I won't owe money to my friends, too."

"Aw, Nan, I thought we were more than friends."

At that moment, Nan couldn't help wishing they *were* more than friends. She knew Wes was in love with her; if she'd said the word, they would have married years before. He'd still have her, she knew. But she couldn't marry a man just to save a piece of land that wasn't hers in the first place.

She hadn't known until her father was very ill that Gary had mortgaged away most of the equity he'd once had in the Saddleback. With money so tight, and fewer and fewer guests coming to stay each year, Nan needed this loan to pay off the most pressing bills. Fixing up the ranch was something she couldn't even consider until her other problems were taken care of. Now it seemed that she'd run out of options.

"Now, don't start, okay?" she said gruffly. "You know I hate all that sentimental stuff."

"But I could help you, Nan. You know I'd do anything for you."

"I know you would."

"Then why don't you let me? We could—"

She couldn't let him go on or she might be tempted, after all. "No," she said. "You know I'm fond of you—"

He reached for her hands. "That's a start, isn't it, Nan? Oh, don't you see? I've got enough love for both of us, and in time, maybe you—"

Gently, she extracted herself from his grip. "It wouldn't work. I told you that. It wouldn't be fair to either of us, but especially to you. No, I mean it," she insisted when he opened his mouth to protest. "You're a kind, generous man, Wes Morton. You deserve better than a . . . than a wife who doesn't love you."

"But we could work it out," he said almost desperately. "If you would just give it a chance, I know we could be happy."

Once again, she wished it were true. Her mouth tight, she turned and looked in the direction of the horse corrals. The enclosures had once teemed with horses, but they now stood almost empty because she couldn't afford to feed all those hungry mouths. She glanced at the big barn beyond, the interior dim and dusty because most of the hay was gone. She looked at the rows of cabins, all of which needed painting, and felt even more weighted down. She had tried so hard, but in spite of her efforts—and Yolanda's, too—it was all coming to an ignominious end.

"Oh, Wes," she said with a weary sigh, "it's not that simple."

"Why not?"

"Because . . . because I've been thinking of leaving."

"Leaving! What, here?" He couldn't have looked more shocked if she'd said she had to get out of town because she'd robbed the bank. "But you were *born* here, Nan. You've lived here all your life! Where would you go? What would you do?"

Those were good questions, she thought. Until the words had slipped out, she hadn't even realized she'd been thinking of going away. But then, as she examined the idea, she realized it had been at the back of her mind ever since she'd heard from Octavia Dunleavy.

"I didn't tell you, Wes," she said, "but some time ago, a woman who says she's my grandmother contacted me." She couldn't keep the note of awe from her voice. "She owns Dunleavy Farm in Kentucky."

Wes looked completely bewildered. "What's that?"

"Only one of the most famous Thoroughbred horse-racing and breeding farms in the entire country!"

"Oh." He still seemed confused. Then he frowned suspiciously. "If that's so, why didn't your dad ever mention it? I know he didn't, because I would have remembered something like that."

"I don't know why," she said. "He just didn't. The point is that she's contacted me now, and I'm going to visit. If I like it there, I might even stay."

Wes stared at her as if she were out of her mind. And maybe she was, she thought, shading her eyes against the late-afternoon sun before turning away from him. She had to do something; she couldn't just sit and wait for things to happen. She'd been doing that too long, as it was…years. *I'm done cryin',* she told herself fiercely. It was time to get on with her life. She had given her all here, but no amount of hard work was going to bridge the growing gap between her dwindling revenues and all those bills.

"Nan," Wes said, "I know how stubborn and proud you are, but don't you think you're being a little hasty? Why don't you let me go back to town and talk to the board about the loan again? Maybe I can convince them to—"

Until that very moment, she hadn't made the final decision. Now it seemed crystal clear, and she said, "Thanks, Wes, but my mind is made up." He looked so unhappy that she touched his arm. "But I appreciate everything you've done. You've been a good friend."

"Oh, Nan," he said forlornly. He looked at her a moment longer, clearly hoping she'd change her mind. Then he gave her a quick hug and a kiss that just missed her mouth. After a moment, as if he was afraid he'd start to blubber, he climbed into his car and drove away.

Nan watched until he disappeared. Then she sighed and went inside to tell Yolanda she was going to Kentucky.

IN KENTUCKY, about a hundred acres or so away from Dunleavy Farm, Trent Spencer and his sixteen-year-old son, Derry, angrily faced each other in the living room at the Spencers' ChangeOver Farm. The argument had been going on for some time, and Trent had had enough. Logic had failed, reason had fallen by the wayside, tact and diplomacy were long gone. He'd tried everything to convince his son what was right. The only thing he had left was to use a defeated parent's last resort.

"You're going to because I'm your father and I said so!" he thundered.

His once-loving, eager-to-please boy who had suddenly metamorphosed into this rebellious, unknown man-child, glared at him defiantly. It seemed that all Derry did these days was glare, Trent thought. That was, when he wasn't locked in his room being completely uncommunicative. But this time, the matter under discussion wasn't trivial, like forgetting to mow the lawn, or leaving the refrigerator door open. It had to do with Derry's future, and Trent was adamant. After skipping nearly four weeks of school one or two days at a time, and forging his father's signature on various excuses for his absences, Derry was going to pay for his misdeeds by going to summer school and being grounded the entire time.

"Oh, yeah?" Derry said. He had the same wavy black hair—without the silver temples—as his father, but his eyes were blue instead of Trent's deep brown. He thrust out his chest. He had grown again this past year and was only about four inches under Trent's six-foot-two.

"And what'll you do if I don't go to summer school?" Derry sneered. His handsome face, so like his father's, was distorted and ugly with resentment and anger. "Put me in juvenile hall? Send me to a work farm? I know, since you're so into rules and regulations, maybe you'll enroll me in military school!"

"Don't tempt me," Trent warned.

"And don't treat me like a child! Aw, this is stupid. I'm going out!"

Derry started to brush past, but Trent grabbed him. "This is just like you," he said. "Running away from problems you can't—or don't—want to solve. Unfortunately for you, you can't escape this time. You're going to face it like a man."

"Let go of me!" Derry shouted, trying to jerk free of Trent's strong grasp. When he failed, he raised his hand in a fist. Trent was so surprised at the sight that he let go. Father and son stared at each other for a moment, Derry obviously just as shocked by his actions as Trent. The taut silence lengthened and held. Then Derry's face flooded with anger again.

"I never wanted to come here, anyway!" he shouted. "I didn't want to stay with you after Mom died. I was perfectly happy at Grandma's, but no, you insisted. Well, you know what? I hate this place, and I hate you. Now, leave me alone. I'm going out, and you can't stop me."

Trent was still so stunned at the idea that Derry might actually have struck him that he just stood there as his son stormed out the front door. Seconds later, he saw Derry flash by the front windows, furiously pedaling his bike toward the road. Trent didn't go after him. He couldn't move.

Where did I go wrong? he asked himself. He had never felt so defeated as he wondered, *How will I fix it? Will I ever get my son back?*

CHAPTER TWO

NAN LOVED KENTUCKY from the moment she entered it. She knew she was being silly to feel so strongly about it; after all, she'd been seeing the same tree-dotted, gently undulating hills for some time before she actually crossed the state line. But just knowing she was here made the long trip worth it. She'd dreamed about visiting the famed Bluegrass state most of her life.

Even the air smelled different, she decided, breathing in deeply from the truck's open window as she headed east on the interstate. On the seat beside her was a map. She glanced at the long, black line all the way from Montana to Lexington, and felt a thrill. She was almost at Dunleavy Farm. What would she find?

Now that her journey was nearly over, she wished more than ever that Yolanda was with her. Nan had sold Saddleback Ranch and asked Yolanda to come to Kentucky with her, but Yolanda had said no.

"I'm too old to make such a change, honey," Yolanda had said as they sat in the kitchen over coffee for the last time. The big main house was quiet; they were the only ones present. Miraculously, it seemed to Nan, the ranch had sold only a week after she'd put it up for sale. Some people from Southern California who wanted to leave the smog-filled air for the Big Sky country had bought the place, lock, stock and barrel. With *cash*. They were entranced with the idea of owning and operating a dude ranch. Nan wished them luck, and hoped they had as much stamina as money. It wasn't going to be as easy as they thought.

Still, it wasn't any of her business anymore, and after paying off her outstanding bills, she figured she had just enough to keep her for a couple of months until she decided what to do about her grandmother's invitation. If things didn't work out at Dunleavy Farm, she wasn't sure yet what she'd do. Scared by the thought, she wanted Yolanda to come with her.

But Yolanda had added, "I've lived in Montana all my life. Why would I want to go anywhere else now?"

"But you said yourself that the winters were hard on you now."

"Well, that's true," Yolanda agreed. "I can't seem to take the cold as well as I used to. But still... this is my home. I think I'd better just stay here."

And no matter what Nan had said, or how she'd begged, Yolanda stood by her decision. A bingo-playing friend of hers named Minnie Joss had an extra room at her house in town, and Yolanda moved in there.

"Now, don't you worry about me, you hear?" Yolanda had commanded when they said goodbye that last day. A little teary-eyed herself, she gave Nan a hug, then held her away again. "And you call me when you get there, promise? I won't sleep a wink until I know you're safe." She cast a skeptical glance at the old farm truck that was parked by the curb. Covered with spots of primer, rust and flaking ancient blue paint, it looked as if it had some kind of disease, but it was the only vehicle Nan had.

Nan saw the direction of Yolanda's gaze and smiled. "Now, don't start. I know you don't like that truck, but it's never failed me. It'll get me there, don't worry."

"It's not the truck I worry about, it's everything else. Now, I mean it, Nan, don't you go picking up strangers or thinking that everybody is as neighborly as we are here in Montana. It's a bad world out there, and I want you to be careful."

"I'll be careful," Nan promised. Then, before she could begin to sniffle, she gave Yolanda another hug and started on her way.

And now she was on the outskirts of Lexington. She'd taken her time on the trip, stopping and camping out once or twice, telling herself that it was because she needed a vacation, but really trying to delay the moment when she met her grandmother face-to-face for the first time. The idea that she had any relatives aside from her father was still too new to comprehend, and as the miles passed, she became more and more anxious. Octavia had invited her to stay at the farm. And now that Nan had burned all her bridges behind her by selling the ranch, she really didn't have any other place to go. The thought excited her and made her sick with apprehension at the same time.

What if she didn't fit in? she wondered. What if her grandmother didn't like her? What if *she* didn't like

Octavia Dunleavy? And, most nerve-racking of all, what if this was all a big mistake that she wouldn't discover until she'd been there for a while?

The closer she got, the more jittery she became. Finally, some miles after turning off the interstate, she pulled to the side of the road to get herself together. She tried to scoff at her fear—after all, it was too late to worry now. According to the directions Octavia had given her when she'd phoned to say she was coming, she was nearly at the gates to Dunleavy Farm. She couldn't turn around and go back now.

Stop worrying, she told herself impatiently. Her grandmother had sounded genuinely pleased at the news that she had decided to visit.

"Oh, I'm so glad you're coming!" Octavia had exclaimed when Nan had called. "You don't know how long I've waited for this. It will be wonderful!"

Despite Octavia's enthusiasm, Nan had felt reluctant to commit herself. Hopeful that she could find a job as a waitress or a maid somewhere—Lord knew, she had experience, filling in when the few employees the ranch had occasionally called in sick—she had tried to warn her grandmother not to expect too much.

"I can't promise I'll stay," she'd said. "I'm only coming for a while."

"Oh, yes, of course," Octavia had said blithely. "I understand completely." Then, sounding almost like a young girl, she had laughed. "But you know, that's exactly what Carla said when she first came. And now she's part of the family. In fact, I don't know what I would do without her. She's already made so many changes that I hardly recognize the place.''

Carla Dunleavy was another reason Nan had her doubts about settling in at the farm. She pictured her cousin as a bossy busybody who enjoyed ordering everyone around. She stiffened at the idea, but then told herself to stop being silly. She had only talked to Carla Dunleavy once. Carla might be a perfectly nice person, even if she *did* have that aristocratic-sounding English accent.

Well, it didn't matter, Nan decided once again. If they didn't like each other, she'd stay out of the way. And if they *really* didn't like each other, she'd leave. After making it clear that she was only coming for a visit, she certainly wasn't obligated to stay.

But now she was almost there, and what little confidence she'd had, seemed to have disappeared. She looked down at her worn jeans and faded T-shirt and grimaced. She should have stopped somewhere and changed, but the idea hadn't occurred to her. Quickly, she jerked the rearview mirror her way, but that made things worse. Her hair was windblown, and she looked pale. Oh, this was a great way to arrive, she thought, looking as if she'd just stepped out of a wind tunnel.

Hastily, she reached for her battered old purse that had fallen to the floor on the other side. She had a comb in it somewhere, and hopefully, that ancient lip gloss. She was rummaging through the clutter when she happened to glance at the outside mirror. Coming up behind her, his head down, was a teenage boy on a bike.

He was pedaling without looking where he was going, and she could see he was going to run right into the truck. Quickly, she reached for the door handle.

"Hey!" she yelled. "Look out!"

The boy looked up at the last second. His face blanched, and he slammed on the brakes—too late. The bike went into a sickening skid, and as Nan watched in frozen horror, he went right with it. Before she could move, he slid under the bed of the truck.

"Oh, no!" she cried. She was out in an instant, running in a crouch toward the back, trying to see underneath. Praying he hadn't been hurt, she shouted, "Are you all right?"

Brushing off gravel, he sprang up and was trying to pull the bike free from the undercarriage when she reached him.

"Oh, my God!" she exclaimed at his torn shirt and shredded jeans. His knuckles were scraped, and a small cut on his forehead was trickling blood. She grabbed him and tried to get him to face her. "Did you break anything? Do you hurt anywhere?"

He seemed more embarrassed than anything. "Naw, I'm okay," he said without looking at her. His attention was still on his crumpled and bent bike. "But I think the bike's had it. It seems to be stuck. Can you help me get it out?"

"Forget the bike, I want to know if you're all right! Look at me, you might have a concussion or something."

She reached for him again, but he shook her off. "I told you, I'm fine. If you want to know the truth, I feel like a jerk. I don't know why I didn't see your truck sitting there. I'm sorry."

"I'm the one who's sorry. Come on, at least sit down for a minute. I want to make sure you're okay."

He must have been feeling a little shaky, after all, for this time, he allowed her to lead him to the passenger side of the truck. As he sat sideways on the seat, she looked frantically up and down the road to see if anyone was around. But no cars were in sight, and the nearest structure that even looked as if it might be a house was at least a mile away.

She tried to decide what to do. She couldn't drive the truck with the bike tangled up underneath it, and she didn't want to leave the kid while she went running off to find assistance. Quickly, she searched his face. His eyes were clear and his color was good, but she was no doctor, and she didn't want to take anything for granted. One thing she could do was treat the small bleeding cut over his eye.

"Now, you stay here," she commanded. "I've got a first-aid kit in the back, and I'll get something for your face."

"My face? What's wrong with my face?" He put a hand to his forehead, and when it came away colored with a little smear of blood, he paled. "I'm bleeding!"

"Not much," she assured him. "It's only a little—"

She never got the words out. Before she could finish the sentence, his eyes closed and he pitched toward her.

Caught off balance, it took all her strength to catch him. He was much bigger and heavier than she was, and, unconscious, he weighed a ton. As she staggered back, trying to stop his fall, his arms flopped over her shoulders and his head lolled against her neck.

How much does this kid weigh? she wondered, gasping. And then, *What in the hell am I going to do now?*

She didn't have a choice. Bracing a leg, she threw her one hundred pounds into getting him onto the seat again. She was more successful than she intended. Momentum and his weight dragged her forward, and to her horror, she was pulled in after him as he fell back into the truck. Pinned under his arm, she was struggling to free herself when she heard the screech of brakes.

Thank God! she thought in relief. *Help was here at last!*

Panting from exertion, she looked over her shoulder and saw that an expensive black car had pulled up behind her. A man was just getting out, and she called to him, "I need some help here!"

The man ran toward her. When he saw the boy on the front seat, he stopped midstride. "Oh, my God, what happened? Is he all right? Is he hurt? Good grief, he's bleeding!"

"It's only... a surface... scratch," she gasped, still trying to battle her way free. Her position was awkward: half in, half out of the cab, with the boy pinning her down. And the man who was supposed to be assisting was just standing there, staring. What was the matter with him?

"Don't . . . just . . . stand there!" she commanded between struggles. "Get him off me!"

The man finally moved to help as the kid began to come to. When the boy opened his eyes and saw Nan's face not two inches from his, he reacted instinctively by jerking back. She was still caught under his arm and he pulled her with him.

"Hey!" she cried. "Let go!"

"Yes, for God's sake, let go!" the man exclaimed. He waded in, grabbed the boy's arm with one hand and pulled Nan out of the truck with the other. Setting her unceremoniously on her feet outside, he immediately turned to the teenager and asked, "Are you all right, Derry? What happened? Did this woman hit you?"

Nan was trying to straighten her twisted T-shirt when she realized the man had called the boy by name. "Do you two know each other?" she asked.

The man looked over his shoulder at her. Brusquely, he said, "This is my son. What did you do to him?"

After all she'd done—or tried to do, Nan bristled at his tone. "I didn't do anything to him! I was just sitting in my truck minding my own business—"

Apparently assured that his son wasn't bleeding to death, the man straightened and glared at her. Sarcastically, he said, "Oh, and I suppose he just came along and ran into *you,* is that right?"

Nan was about to answer hotly that that's exactly what had happened, but at that very moment, she saw the boy glaring at her from behind his father's bulk. She could tell he was reluctant to have his father know what had happened. Nan hesitated. She didn't want to get him into trouble, but if she didn't tell the truth, how was she going to explain the bike caught under the truck?

Now that she'd had a moment to catch her breath, she began to realize how the scene must appear. No wonder the father was angry, she thought guiltily. It certainly looked as if she'd hit the kid and run over the bike.

"Well?" the man demanded.

She caught another look from Derry. For some reason, she couldn't betray him, so she said vaguely, "Well, it's kind of hard to explain."

"Try," the man said flatly. "You'll have to explain this to the police, so you might as well—"

"The police!" Nan was horrified. She couldn't have the police dragged into this, not even to help Derry out of an embarrassing jam. She could just imagine what her grandmother would say if she had to call from the station to say she'd been . . . detained. Oh, how had this happened? She hadn't been in Kentucky five minutes, and already she was in hot water! She looked hard at the man. "You can't call the police," she said.

He stared right back. "What, are you crazy as well as careless? There's obviously been an accident and you're clearly responsible for it. It's a miracle my son wasn't hurt more seriously, or even . . . killed!"

Derry tried to intervene. "Dad—"

"You be quiet," the man snapped. "We have to get you to a hospital as soon as possible."

"The hospital! But Dad, I feel—"

"You don't know how you feel. You could have a head injury or—"

"Dad, I just fell!" Derry shouted.

"After *she* ran you down!"

"I didn't run him down!" Nan cried.

The man glowered at her again. "I think I've heard enough from you," he said. "Now, if you will be kind enough to get me your license and insurance numbers while I help my son to the car, we can—"

Derry jumped out of the truck. Despite her anger and aggravation, Nan was relieved to see that he appeared to be all right. She guessed that he was still mortified about fainting at the sight of his own blood, for he reddened as he looked quickly at her, and then away. He said to his father, "It wasn't the way you think, Dad. I'm okay, so let's forget it, all right? Can you do what *I* want . . . for once?"

"It's not a matter of doing what you want! It's a matter of—"

"All right, all *right!* It was my fault, okay? Does that make you happy?"

"What would make me happy," the man said angrily, "is to find out exactly what happened here!"

Derry's face was crimson. "I'll tell you later. Now, can we get the damned bike and go home? Can you do what I want for a change without giving me a giant hassle about it?"

Derry didn't wait for an answer but stamped around to the back of the truck. He was so enraged by this time that he jerked the bike free on the first try. The frame was bent and one wheel wobbled when he pulled it out. With a disgusted sound, he heaved the bike over his shoulder and started toward his father's car. Grabbing the keys from the ignition, he marched around, threw the bike into the trunk and got into the car. Slumping in the leather seat, he growled out the window, "I'm ready anytime you are."

Nan glanced at the man, who was clearly trying to hold on to his temper. She couldn't tell if he was more annoyed with her or with his son. Then she decided it didn't matter. She'd wasted too much time already, and she wanted to be on her way. She was going to be late, and how would she explain?

"Look," she said, "I'd like to know if he's really all right. If you'll give me your telephone number—"

The man gave her a coldly furious look. "Don't you have that backward? Derry can say what he likes, but we both know that *you're* the one responsible for the accident. I'll need your name and address and any other pertinent information."

She echoed, "Any other..." His son had told him that it wasn't her fault. The idea that this man was deliberately choosing to disbelieve the truth made her so angry that she lost her temper. Rashly, she said, "Well, too bad for you, because I'm just passing through. You see that Montana license plate? If you want me bad enough, you can trace me through that. Good day, Mr....whatever your name is. I'd like to say it was nice

meeting you, but it hasn't exactly been the most pleasant experience in my life.''

And with that, she whirled around, climbed into the
truck and started it with a roar. For once, the ancient,
temperamental engine caught the first time, and as she
drove away in a cloud of exhaust and dust, she checked
the outside mirror. When she saw that the man had actually pulled out a pen and pad and was taking down
her license-plate number, she frowned.

"You're not in Montana anymore, Dorothy," she
muttered dryly, throwing the truck into second gear
with a grinding noise that brought her back down to
earth.

She shifted more carefully the next time and tried to
calm down. But the rest of the way to Dunleavy Farm,
she couldn't get the man and his son out of her mind.
She told herself that it was because she was angry at the
father and pitied that poor boy for having such a parent, but the truth was, as obnoxious as he'd been to her,
she'd felt some kind of . . . pull toward the man.

No, that was crazy, she thought. The man had been
plain rude. And yet, she had to admit, if she'd been in
his place, she would have acted the same way. He'd had
a right to be upset.

But he didn't have the right to accuse her of trying to
hurt his boy, she thought with a toss of her head. Especially when Derry himself had admitted that the
whole thing had been *his* fault.

"Oh, forget it," she muttered. "You've already got enough to be concerned about."

And she did, for just then the gates to Dunleavy Farm appeared. After all her worry and wonder, she was finally here.

CHAPTER THREE

DUNLEAVY FARM WAS the most beautiful sight Nan had ever seen. The drive in, with its canopy of trees overhead, made her feel as if she were entering a land of make-believe; she couldn't stop staring. Huge pastures on either side were bordered by the famous straight-as-string fences, and when she saw a few glossy horses grazing inside, she felt as if she'd died and gone to heaven.

Then the house came into view, and she gasped. Awestruck, she hit the brakes. She'd seen a picture of the farm in a magazine once, but nothing prepared her for the reality before her eyes. Never in her wildest dreams had she seen anything like it.

The house—no, the *mansion*—was white with a roof of sapphire blue. Tall windows marched along the entire front; these were flanked by shutters painted the same color as the roof. There was also a porch—or was it called a veranda here? she wondered, and felt a moment's irrational panic when she couldn't remember. Then she pulled herself together. What difference did it make?

It made a *big* difference, she thought, jerking her gaze down to the leprous hood of the truck. Now she wished she had allowed Yolanda to talk her into painting it, no matter what the cost! How could she drive up to those front doors in this? She'd be too embarrassed to get out of the truck.

But she couldn't just sit here, either. She'd come all this way; it was now or never. So she put the vehicle in gear and was promptly rewarded with a grinding noise from the transmission that reminded her, belatedly, that she should have had it checked about ten thousand miles back.

Perspiration prickled her forehead. This was getting worse and worse, she thought. Now she wasn't even sure if the rattletrap would make it to the front door— or hold together long enough for her to think of an excuse to leave. It was clear to her that she didn't belong here. She'd just pay her respects and go. As soon as she was on her way again, she'd decide what to do.

She was so busy coaxing the truck into gear that it took her a moment to realize her arrival hadn't gone unnoticed. Someone had come out onto the porch.

Heart thudding with a fresh onslaught of nerves, Nan pulled to a stop by the front steps. True to form, the temperamental old truck backfired loudly just as she got out. The person standing on the porch jumped at the noise.

Trying to hide her embarrassment, Nan smiled. "Don't worry," she called. "It sounds mean, but it won't attack."

The woman on the porch laughed and came down the steps. She had beautiful chestnut-colored hair that shone in the sun and one of the best figures Nan had ever seen on a person outside a fashion magazine.

Or maybe, Nan thought, marveling, it was the way those slacks fit. She hadn't the faintest idea what the material was, but it looked soft and expensive and perfectly cut. All too conscious of her own disheveled appearance, she stuck out her hand.

"Hi," she said. "I'm Nan."

The woman returned the handshake briskly, her manicured nails flashing in the sun. Smiling with perfect white teeth, she said, "And I'm your cousin, Carla. Welcome to Dunleavy Farm."

Nan looked up into expertly made-up eyes whose green color was similar to her own. But that was about the only thing they had in common, she thought. With the feeling that she never should have come growing in her by leaps and bounds, she said, "Thanks, it's good to be here. It's magnificent."

"It is, isn't it?" Carla said with a note of possessive pride. She looked around, then back to Nan's face. "Is it what you expected?"

Nan looked around, too. "I don't know," she said honestly. "I didn't know what to expect." Her tone turned reverent. "But I'll say one thing. It's different."

"From Montana, you mean?"

Nan shook her head. "From anyplace I've ever been."

Carla laughed again. "I know what you mean. I felt the same way when I first arrived. So, come in! Grandmother has been on pins and needles, waiting for your arrival. She's so anxious to meet you."

Since she had come all this way just for this purpose, Nan knew it was silly to want to delay going inside. The farm, what she had seen of it, was lovely; Carla couldn't have been more welcoming. After what her cousin had just said, she had no reason to believe her grandmother would feel differently about her arrival. And yet...

"We're on our own, Nannie," her father had always said to her. *"With your mother gone, there's just you and me. And no matter what, we'll always be our own little family. Nothing's going to change that, ever."*

But something *had* changed it, Nan thought. The old familiar equation had been altered when her father died. And now, instead of being alone, she had discovered a *new* family...a cousin, a grandmother—and who knew how many others she hadn't heard of and didn't know existed. Was it any wonder she felt unsure of herself?

She glanced at Carla, whose polish and sophistication made her feel even more diminished. Nan knew just by looking that her cousin was the kind of woman who could walk through a pigsty in a white suit and shoes and emerge on the other side without a smudge.

"Appearance isn't everything," Yolanda had often reminded her during her teens when Nan was jealous of the way so many of the daughters of the ranch's well-to-do guests were dressed. Those girls made it seem so effortless, their long hair, usually blond and curly, their hands soft and well cared for, their nails painted pink. What did it matter if their name-brand jeans were so

tight they had to be almost lifted into the saddle, or their boots were so new that they could hardly walk? Nan saw the way the hired hands looked at them. She never caught approving glances like that—and it wasn't because she was the boss's daughter. She just didn't look like the others.

But why was she thinking about that now? Carla was waiting for her to say something, so she said, "I'm sorry I was late. I...er...ran into a little trouble on the road."

To her credit, Carla didn't even glance at the mottled old truck parked in front of the big house. Nan knew that it must have been tempting. Instead, Carla looked concerned.

"What kind of trouble?" she asked. "Was there an accident? You aren't hurt, are you?"

Nan wished she hadn't mentioned it. "I'm all right. It was nothing, really, just a . . . a road hazard that held me up for a while."

"Oh, that's good," Carla said, sounding relieved. She smiled again. "But speaking of being held up, we'd better go inside or Grandmother will come out and get us." Her voice dropped a notch. "I know it will be difficult for her not to be, but she isn't supposed to get too excited. I doubt she mentioned it, but a while ago she gave us quite a scare when she had a mild heart attack."

Nan drew in a breath. "She never said a word. Is she all right?"

"She's okay. But the doctor said it was a warning of sorts. He told us she has to keep quiet, rest and try not to do too much." Carla rolled her eyes. "It's like trying to tell a bee not to buzz."

"But isn't she in her eighties?"

"Chronologically, yes. But don't let numbers fool you. She and I went shopping once, and I, who could do Picadilly and the Left Bank and Monte Carlo in one whirl, was so exhausted when we finally got home that I had to take a nap. Grandmother, however, was still raring to go."

Nan laughed dutifully, but Carla had lost her somewhere between Picadilly and Monte Carlo. Her insecurities beginning to rise again, she said, "I won't have to worry about that, at least. I can't remember the last time I went shopping."

She hadn't meant to add that last part, and was embarrassed as soon as she said it. But cool Carla didn't blink an eye. Linking her arm through Nan's, she said with a wink, "Then we'll have to go soon—just you and me. So, are you ready? Oh, don't worry about your luggage. We'll have someone bring it in later."

Nan thought of her "luggage"—one battered suitcase and a box tied with string—and wanted to say it wouldn't be necessary. She wasn't going to stay long enough to unpack. She had already decided that she'd talk to her grandmother for a while, maybe stay for supper, then be on her way.

"I'm so glad you decided to come," Carla said just then. "It's going to be such fun, you'll see. And when . . ."

Carla started up the porch steps, pulling Nan in her wake as she chattered on. She was clearly trying to put her cousin at ease, but it wasn't working. What was she doing here? Nan wondered wildly. What had possessed her to come? She belonged in Montana, where—

Suddenly, from out of nowhere, it seemed, came a shrill neigh that made Nan stop in her tracks. She had never heard anything like it, proud and defiant and commanding all at the same time. She looked around.

"What was that?" she asked.

Carla smiled and turned to point, but Nan had already seen the magnificent horse standing high on the hill behind the farm. From this distance, the stallion—and it had to be a stallion, Nan thought—was silhouetted against the sky. For a second or two, it seemed that the afternoon sun struck sparks off the horse's blood-bay coat, surrounding him with fiery light. She blinked to dispel the illusion, but as though the horse somehow knew he'd caught her attention, he snorted and tossed his head. Unable to take her eyes off him, she asked, "Who in the world is that?"

"That," said a voice behind her, "is Done Roamin'. He's quite a sight, don't you think?"

Nan turned. She'd been so entranced by the stallion that she hadn't heard anyone come out to the porch. But when she saw the petite elderly woman with the fluffy white hair and bright green silk dress, she knew she was about to meet Octavia Dunleavy. Smiling, Octavia came forward on tiny feet, her cane making a staccato tapping sound.

"Hello, my dear," Octavia said, gazing at Nan with the Dunleavy green eyes. "I've waited a long time to meet you. Welcome to Dunleavy Farm."

On the trip down, Nan had carefully rehearsed what she was going to say when she finally met this woman. Now that the moment had come, she couldn't remember any of it. Like the farm itself, Octavia Dunleavy was so unlike anything she had expected that she was almost struck dumb. With an effort, she remembered her manners.

"It's nice to be here," she said awkwardly. She wasn't sure if she should give this small but somehow formidable woman a hug or kiss until Octavia opened her arms. It was such a welcoming gesture that she did both without thinking. When she pulled back from the unexpectedly tight embrace, she suddenly felt a little teary.

Don't you dare cry! Nan ordered herself. She was not going to humiliate herself further by bursting into tears when she'd been here less than ten minutes.

Fortunately, she remembered Done Roamin' and said, "That's a beautiful horse. I've read about him, but seeing him in the flesh is—" She broke off midsentence. Just as she'd turned to look in the direction of his paddock, Done Roamin' had started down the hill.

At first, Nan thought she was imagining things, or that the sun had dazzled her eyes—anything but that the famous Triple Crown winner was moving with such an awkward, shambling gait. It was painful to watch, but she couldn't take her eyes away. Once again, she found herself holding back tears.

As though Octavia understood, she touched Nan's arm. Her voice quiet, she said, "It's always a shock the first time. But even then, I don't think any of us who know horses ever get used to it."

On Nan's other side, Carla agreed. "Grandmother's right. I thought it wouldn't be so painful after a while. But it still is."

"I never read about an accident," Nan said. "What happened?"

Her fond glance still on Done Roamin', who was slowly picking his way down the hill, Octavia said, "We kept it quiet because we never did find out for sure. It was a stable accident, had to be. We came out one morning and found him that way. The only thing we can figure is that he cast himself during the night and smashed his hock trying to get loose."

Nan shuddered. "How awful!"

"Yes, it was. But there was never a question that we would try to save him—no matter what it took. And we did. Although, if it hadn't been for Wade, I don't know what I would have done."

"Wade?" Nan asked.

"Wade Petrie—my fiancé," Carla supplied, and blushed.

Octavia winked at Nan. "He *was* my barn manager, but now, because of your cousin, here, he might leave me to start his own training stable."

Carla recovered quickly. "Now, Grandmother, you're making it sound as if Wade's deserting you. You know he won't do anything until we find you another good barn manager.''

With another private wink at Nan, Octavia said, ''No one will be as good as Wade. But I realize that young lovers must have their way. I know you'll both doubt it, but I was young once myself.''

''You're still young,'' Carla said. ''Now, why don't we go inside.'' She took Octavia's arm and gestured to Nan. ''Grandmother asked Teresa, our cook and housekeeper, to prepare one of her famous teas. A welcome to Dunleavy Farm wouldn't be the same without that.''

Nan, who was accustomed to tea bags soaked in hot tap water because she never had the time or patience to wait for a kettle to boil, was unprepared for what awaited her when she entered the big, elegant front room. A silver service gleamed on a coffee table; it was flanked by china plates of hot, fluffy biscuits and tiny cold sandwiches with the crusts cut off the bread. Nan was so impressed with the sumptuous sight that it took her a few seconds to realize that she was surrounded by horse-racing memorabilia that had to date back fifty years or more. Wide-eyed, she halted midstep and looked around.

''This is unbelievable!'' she said. ''I never dreamed—''

She stopped again when she saw the glass case at one end of the big room. Quickly, she went to it. Inside was a postage-size racing saddle, a jockey's blouse in the farm's racing colors of royal blue and gold, and a saddlecloth emblazoned with a stitched number eight.

"Is that...oh, it can't be!" She turned to Octavia. "Is this the saddle Done Roamin' wore when he won the Triple Crown?"

"For all three races," Octavia said. "But how do you know about that? It was so long ago."

Reverently, Nan touched the glass. "I've loved horses all my life," she said. "Thoroughbreds—racing Thoroughbreds, most of all. We never had any at the ranch, of course, but I've followed racing since I was old enough to read the form books. Years ago, when I first came across a reference to the Dunleavys and Dunleavy Farm, I was so excited. I was sure we had to be related, but when I asked my father—"

She stopped with a painful flush. "I'm sorry. I shouldn't have mentioned Dad."

"Nonsense. Of course you should talk about your father. He was..." Octavia's voice faltered a bit before she went on, "He was my son, after all."

Nan glanced at Carla, then back to her grandmother. She wasn't sure if she should say it, but then she decided she might as well. She was so tired of secrets. Her father must have had a good reason for lying to her all these years, but she couldn't imagine what it was— and right now, she didn't much care. If these women were to be her new family, she didn't want any more mysteries or puzzles to create misunderstandings. She wanted everything to be out in the open.

But when she began to explain, she suddenly realized she didn't know how to address this woman. Helplessly, she said, "I...er...I'm sorry, I don't know what to call you."

Octavia sat down in a beautifully upholstered wing chair. "Call me whatever makes you feel comfortable. Carla calls me Grandmother, but if you prefer, you may use Octavia."

Nan thought about it, then said shyly, "I'd like to call you Grandmother, too, if you don't mind."

Octavia smiled with pleasure. "I'd like that most of all. Now, you were saying something about your father...?"

Nan came to sit near Octavia's chair. She knew what she was going to say would be hurtful, but there was no other way. "I'm sorry to have to tell you this, but Dad always denied that we were related. He insisted the name was just a coincidence, and that he was an orphan with no known family."

"I...see." Octavia's shoulders slumped momentarily, then she straightened and said briskly, "Well, it's no more than I expected, I guess. And certainly no less than I deserved."

Nan hated to ask. "What do you mean?"

"It's a long story, my dear, and something I'd rather not get into right now. We'll talk about it at another time. Let me just say that the reason your father felt so strongly was that we quarreled his last day at home. He wanted to quit college to marry a girl he hardly knew—"

"My mother..."

"Yes, your mother." Octavia looked pained. "Gary was so hot-tempered and stubborn. He wouldn't accept that I didn't disapprove of Nancy. After all, I hardly knew her. The truth was that I didn't want him to abandon his education. He only had a year left to complete, and he had such a bright future—"

Nan couldn't disguise her bitterness. "But instead, he married an ignorant Montana girl and ruined his life on a going-nowhere dude ranch, is that it?"

As soon as she saw Octavia's expression, she regretted having said the words. She'd spoken before she thought, and now she had hurt this old woman, and for what purpose? Her grandmother might have made mistakes in the past, but Nan knew that her father hadn't been innocent or perfect, either.

She remembered Gary's drinking and suddenly wondered if he had come to resent the fact that he'd never finished college, or that his life hadn't turned out the way he'd planned. Maybe he'd even secretly wished he hadn't married her mother. Was that why it hadn't seemed to matter to him when he'd been diagnosed with cancer?

Sadly, Nan realized that she'd never know for sure now. The only one who could have told her was gone, and he'd taken his secrets with him.

"I'm sorry," she said, reaching for her grandmother's frail-looking hand. "I shouldn't have said that."

"I understand," Octavia replied softly. "From what little you told me on the phone, my dear, you've endured a lot this year. It's been a sad time for you—losing your father and your home at the same time."

Not to mention making a fool of myself over a married man, Nan thought, but didn't say aloud. She'd already said too much.

"How about some more tea?" Carla suggested. "Grandmother says that a cup of tea always makes things seem better, and since I've been here, I have to agree with her. Although," she added with a wink at Nan, "sometimes there's nothing like a glass of champagne to make a picture brighter. What do you think?"

Nan, who rarely drank anything stronger than soda, was thankful for her cousin's efforts to put her at ease. But now that she had regained some of her equanimity, she realized that she had a splitting headache. She was just wondering how she could excuse herself without appearing rude, when they all heard a car outside.

"Now, who can that be?" Octavia asked with a significant glance at Carla.

Carla got up and went to one of the front windows. "Would you believe it?" she said brightly. "It's Wade." She turned back toward Nan to explain, "He had to go into Louisville this morning and we didn't think he'd be back so soon. Now you'll get to meet him before dinner."

"Dinner?" Nan said.

"Oh, yes," Carla said blithely. "I know you must be tired, but we're having a dinner for you, and one of the neighbors is coming over. You can rest for a while and freshen up later, but in the meantime, let me introduce you to Wade. He'd like to meet you."

Nan didn't know what to do. The idea that a dinner had been planned in her honor made her feel awful. Since she was going to leave soon, she didn't want special treatment. Already, she felt guilty about not announcing her imminent departure; if these kind people went to any more trouble for her, it would be harder to leave.

But she could hardly refuse to meet Carla's fiancé, so she said, "And I'd like to meet him. Are you coming, Grandmother?"

"Indeed I am," Octavia said, waving away Nan's offer of help. She used her cane for leverage, and got to her feet. With Carla in the lead, they trooped outside.

Wade had arrived in a truck-and-trailer combination that made Nan gasp when she saw it parked in the driveway. There was only one word to describe the rig—magnificent. Painted in the farm's colors of royal blue and gold, the outfit gleamed from stem to stern. She was still gazing in appreciation, when a horse whinnied impatiently from inside.

The horse's call was immediately answered by a chorus from around the farm, the loudest of which belonged to Done Roamin'. Nan was smiling at the imperious stallion as a man got out of the truck and came around the front. He was tall and rangy, with intense blue eyes that immediately sought Carla. His long-lipped mouth curled in a smile for her before he turned to Nan.

Like so many Montana men, he was wearing a Stetson, and when he tipped his hat to her, Nan grinned. Because of those eyes, and that smile, and that hat, she immediately felt a kinship to him.

"Nan, that cowboy there is Wade Petrie," Carla drawled. "Wade, this is my cousin, Nan."

When Nan heard the lilt in Carla's voice, she smiled again. It amused her to see that, right before her eyes, her cousin changed from a sophisticated socialite to a woman obviously in love. But then, as Carla ran lightly down the steps and into Wade's welcoming arms, Nan felt a twinge. *Wouldn't it be nice,* she thought, and averted her eyes from the sight of the lovers' eager reunion.

Fortunately, she was distracted by another loud whinny that shook the trailer. It was clear that the horse felt he'd been inside long enough; he wanted out.

The sound was impossible to ignore. With an exaggerated gasp, Wade broke away from Carla and grinned at Nan once more. "Sorry I missed your arrival," he said. "I wanted to be here, but I ran into a road hazard on the interstate that held things up."

Thinking that road hazards seemed to be the norm around here, Nan came the rest of the way down the steps. She held out her hand and Wade took it. "That's okay," she said. "It's nice to meet you. I've already heard a lot about you."

Wade smirked at Carla. "All good, I know."

"Oh, absolutely," Carla retorted. "We started with your good qualities because we knew it wouldn't take long."

They all laughed, then Wade went around to the back of the rig and let down the ramp. As he went inside the trailer to get the horse, Nan wondered why he was letting it out here, in front of the house, when the barn area was in back. She was just deciding that maybe they did things differently in Kentucky, when the horse emerged with another blasting challenge that nearly raised the shingles on the roof.

As soon as Nan saw that horse, she became oblivious of everyone and everything else. As the colt stood there in leather halter and trailering bandages, all she could do was stare, openmouthed. She'd never imagined such an exquisite creature could exist.

"Like him?" Wade asked.

Like him? Nan tried to speak, but couldn't. For a horrible moment, she thought she might burst into tears—this time from the sheer overpowering presence of this horse. She looked around. Everyone seemed to be waiting for her to say something. She swallowed over the lump in her throat.

"He's... beautiful," she whispered.

Carla smiled. "You know, I bet I looked that way when I first saw Done Driftin'."

"You mean, sort of goofy with stars in your eyes?" Wade teased. "Yeah, you did."

Nan hardly heard them. Her eyes on the horse, she took a hesitant step forward. "May I... touch him?"

she asked almost reverently. She felt like a child who had been transported to a wonderland. Even so, she had to be careful. She knew how temperamental these highly strung animals could be, and no horseperson ever took anything for granted about someone else's horse—especially a young stallion.

"Touch him?" Wade looked at Octavia, trying not to grin. "What do you think, Mrs. D.?"

"I think you'd better stop teasing the girl," Octavia said with mock asperity. "Both of you."

"Teasing me?" Nan said. She didn't understand. "What do you mean?"

Carla's eyes were sparkling. "She means," she said, "that Wade didn't go all the way to Louisville just to bring back any old horse. Did you, Wade?"

"No, ma'am, I didn't. This one here's special."

"I can see that," Nan breathed. She couldn't look away from him. The colt's reddish-bay coat glistened in the sun, and when she finally got up the courage to touch him, he felt as soft as satin. Gently, she ran her hand over his shoulder and top line, feeling the smooth strength of conditioned muscle. At her touch, the colt's skin quivered, and he turned his imposing head with the wide-set eyes to look at her. She reached out a hand and he gently nuzzled her palm.

"Well, that settles it," Wade said. "He doesn't take to that many people. Here, you'd better hold him."

"Me?" Nan pulled back. "Oh, I couldn't!"

Wade took her hand and slapped the end of the lead into it. "Well, you'd better," he said. "Because I've got things to do right now."

Nan was in heaven. After all these years, she was actually holding on to one of the glorious racing creatures she had always dreamed about. "What...what do you want me to do with him?"

Octavia came forward. Softly, she said, "Anything you want to, my dear. His name is Done Cryin', and he's yours if you'll have him."

If she'd have him? *If she'd have him?* Nan looked from one smiling face to the other, wondering if it was a joke—or a dream from which she would awake to find that she was in her own bed.

Then Octavia said, "Welcome to Dunleavy Farm," and Nan knew that if this was a dream, she never wanted it to end.

CHAPTER FOUR

HIS MIND on other things, Trent Spencer finished the knot in his tie and stepped back from the mirror. When he saw that the small end of the tie hung about six inches lower than the wide end, he muttered a curse and ripped the thing off. Ready to assist as always, Trent's houseman, George, stood by; when Trent saw the inscrutable face reflected behind him in the mirror, he scowled.

"Don't say it," he warned. He and George had been together a long time. In fact, the Basque had worked for Trent's grandfather in the old feed store, nearly fifty years before. Then, his name had been Gilamu Llorentz, and he'd been a ten-year-old orphan from the Basque country. George was still Basque at heart, but long ago he had anglicized his name to George Lawrence. Trent often wondered what he would do without the efficient houseman who, with a staff of two, handled all the household chores.

He wasn't wondering what he would do without George tonight, though, and he glowered again before he snatched up the tie and put it around his neck for a second try.

"Don't say what?" George asked innocently. He reached for Trent's suit coat that hung in readiness on the wooden valet and brushed away an imaginary speck.

"You know what," Trent replied. This time he managed a double Windsor knot that would have to do. He wasn't going to stand here all night trying to tie this thing until he got it right. He had a dinner party to attend, and he didn't want to be late. Still frowning, he reached for his tie tack. As he jammed the point through from front to back, he looked at George again.

"I know you disapprove of the way I'm handling Derry," he said. "But I'm at my wit's end. If I don't keep my thumb on him, he'll turn out to be a hooligan." His jaw tightened. "His mother—God rest her soul—spoiled him rotten."

George came to stand behind him again, holding the coat out for him to put on. Eyes cast downward, he murmured, "It isn't proper to speak ill of the dead."

"I'm not speaking ill of her. It's the truth."

"Perhaps."

Normally, Trent could handle the houseman's oblique comments, but tonight he wasn't in the mood. Impatiently, he said, "And what does that mean?"

"Nothing. Nothing at all." George took a brush from his pocket and began to ply it industriously across the back of the coat.

Trent resisted the urge to grab the thing out of George's hand. "Don't give me that. I know when you have something on your mind."

"I have many things on my mind."

"And so do I. Now, either say what you have to say or stop insinuating that I'm some kind of monster because I expect my son to behave like a civilized human being."

"A civilized human being is one thing," George observed. "A son is something else."

"Are you suggesting that they can't be one and the same?"

"Most assuredly they can. But probably not when one is a sixteen-year-old boy."

"His age is not an excuse."

"No, but it's a fact."

Trent sighed. This was getting them nowhere.

"What are you trying to say, George?" he asked bluntly. "Surely you don't condone Derry's behavior."

"You are inquiring about my opinion? Because you know that I would never intrude when I have not been asked."

Trent counted to ten. "Yes, yes, I know how unassuming you are," he said. "Go ahead. Even though I probably won't like what you have to say on the subject, I'm asking, anyway." He sighed again. "Lord knows I need some kind of advice."

With only the fleetest of satisfied smiles, George repocketed the clothes brush. "All right, then, since you ask..."

Trent knew he was in for a lecture. Refusing to glance at his watch, he leaned against the marble sink counter, his long legs crossed, while he waited for George to tell him where he was going wrong with his son.

"Derry does not mean to cause trouble," George began.

"You could have fooled me. Since that's what he's done ever since he arrived."

"He is a good boy. He does not intend for his actions to cause problems. It's just that he is so unhappy now. In the space of a few months, he has had to deal with many changes. First, he lost his mother, and his entire life changed. Then he came to live here and was forced to leave all his friends behind. Add to that, a father he barely knows, and it is a perfect prescription for trouble."

"And all that is my fault?"

"Did I say it was? I know how you fought for your son's custody. I remember how hurt you were when you lost—"

"I wasn't hurt. I was angry."

"You were hurt *and* angry," George corrected calmly. "But that is not the point, is it? The point is, no matter whose fault it was, you and your son are strangers to each other. In the best of circumstances, it would take time to remedy that. But you have the additional complication of the boy's grief."

"I know, I know. Sandra's death was a blow to all of us..." Trent paused a moment, thinking of his ex-wife. It seemed so strange to know she was gone; even at her most annoying, Sandra had been so vital and alive.

She'd never told him about the cancer. He hadn't even known she was ill until a few days before she died; not even their son had known her true condition until she'd been forced to go to the hospital. And that's when Derry had finally called him—when it was too late.

But it had always been too late, he thought with a heavy heart. The doctor had told him that even if he'd been aware of the dire diagnosis, there was nothing anyone could have done. By the time the cancer was detected, it had spread so far that the only thing medicine could do was keep Sandra comfortable until the end.

But damn it! he thought angrily. He could have been with her, at least. No one should have had to go through something like that alone. Their divorce hadn't been amicable, but Sandra should have known he would have been there if she'd wanted him. They had once loved each other; together, they had produced a son. What really rankled was that in the end, she hadn't trusted him to do the right thing. He'd do anything to change that if he could, not only for Sandra's sake, but because of Derry.

Because the sad, frustrating truth was that Derry blamed him. Blamed him for not being there when his family needed him, but most of all, because Trent hadn't been able to save Sandra. It was irrational, Trent knew, but it didn't help his relationship with his son.

The problem now, he thought, as he had so many times, was how to handle it. He'd tried everything, it seemed, from allowing Derry to have his way to making him toe the line. Nothing had worked. And now, this business with the school. He hadn't known what to say when the school principal had called to ask why

Derry was missing so many classes; that was the first he'd heard of the truancy. He had told the woman he'd speak to his son and straighten it out.

"I'm afraid *speaking* to Derry isn't going to be enough," the principal had replied. "The fact of the matter is that your son has missed so much school this year that it's possible he will be held back to repeat the grade."

He was shocked. It was even worse than he'd thought. Trying to remain calm, he'd said, "I'd rather it didn't come to that, Mrs. Evans. Surely there must be something we can do."

"I appreciate your feelings, Mr. Spencer, but—"

"Look," he'd said almost desperately. "I don't know if you're aware of it or not, but Derry's had a rough time this year. First, he lost his mother, then he had to leave the only home he'd known so he could live here with me. It's been a tough transition for him."

"Mr. Spencer, I sympathize with Derry's loss and subsequent upheaval, but we're still dealing with the problem of how much school he's missed."

Then Trent had seized on an idea. "How about summer school? Derry may be unhappy and rebellious right now, but he's an intelligent kid. I know he can make up the time if he tries."

The principal was silent. Trent had waited with mental fingers crossed until she said, "That's a possibility. I'll check into summer classes and see how feasible it is." She paused. "But if this office agrees to Derry's making up the classes, you'll have to see that he attends the school. If he doesn't—"

"Oh, he'll attend," Trent had promised grimly. He was thinking that his son would go to class every summer day, if he had to accompany Derry to school himself. "And thank you for calling, Mrs. Evans. I appreciate your time and concern."

"Yes, well, it's my job."

And *his* job, he'd thought as he hung up the phone, was to convince his son that agreeing to attend summer school was the most important decision he could make at this time in his young life.

That's when they'd had that fight and Derry had pedaled off on his bike. Trent hadn't been able to go after him right away; he'd needed a few minutes to pull himself together. But finally he'd taken the car and gone out to look for him. He would never forget the sinking feeling he'd had when he'd come upon that rickety old truck down the road and recognized Derry's bike caught in the undercarriage.

Just thinking about it scared him all over again. But he knew now that he'd badly overreacted. He should have waited to find out what had happened before flinging around wild accusations.

Still, he had to admit that the driver of that broken-down truck had given as good as she'd got. Those eyes of hers had flashed like green rockets, and as angry as he'd been, he could see that she was holding on to her own temper by a thread.

"What are you smiling at?" George asked. "I thought we were having a serious conversation, and here you are, laughing at me."

Trent came back to the present. "I'm sorry, George. I wasn't laughing—not at you, anyway. I was thinking about the woman Derry ran down this afternoon. Lord, she was mad!"

"I don't blame her," George said, still miffed. They'd both finally heard the whole story after Trent brought Derry home and calmed down enough to listen. "She must have been frightened, as it was, having someone run into her like that. And then, for you to accuse her of running him down..." He *tsk-tsked*.

"I was upset. I didn't know what the hell had happened. What would *you* have thought if you'd seen Derry's bike under that truck and him bleeding on the front seat?"

"At first, I would have thought the same thing. But then, when he tried to tell you it was his fault, you wouldn't listen."

"I suppose now you're implying that I never listen to him."

"Well, do you?"

"Yes, I do. In fact, I—" He stopped. They'd had this discussion before and it hadn't solved anything. Resignedly, because he knew George would tell him, anyway, he said, "All right, what do you think I should do?"

"Give him time."

"Time! He's had months. How much more time does he need?"

The houseman handed him his keys and wallet. "He needs to know that you won't leave him."

"Leave him? But that's ridiculous!"

"Is it?" George's wise dark glance rested on Trent's face. "His mother did."

"That's different. Sandra—"

"To a boy whose world has just turned upside down, it's the same thing."

Trent wondered if George could be right. Unfortunately, he didn't have time to argue about it; if he didn't leave now, he was going to be late.

"We'll talk about this another time," he said.

George nodded. "Whenever you wish."

Before Trent went out to the car, he stopped to see Derry, who, as always, was holed up in his room. When he saw his son sprawled on the bed, eyes closed, headphones clamped to his ears while he beat out the time to some mercifully inaudible music, his jaw tightened. Derry was supposed to be doing his homework. Resisting the urge to rip the headphones off his son's head, he tapped Derry on the shoulder. Derry was so far into the music that it took him a moment to realize that someone in the real world wanted him.

"Oh...uh...Dad," he said when he finally looked up and saw his father standing beside the bed. He sat up, pulling one of the headphones away from his ear. "What can I do for you?"

Once again, Trent silently counted to ten. It seemed that's all he did lately. A few of Derry's schoolbooks were scattered over the bedspread—obviously for effect. It was clear from their pristine condition that they hadn't been used much.

"You can get cracking on your homework," Trent told him. "If you remember, after our discussion this afternoon, you promised to study."

Derry glanced distastefully at the biology book that was closest. "I know. But that stuff's boring. I learned all that last year in my old school. I don't know why I have to take it again."

"All right, then. Maybe you should ask the teacher for an extra-credit assignment." Trent paused, but then he couldn't help himself. "God knows, you need it."

"I *said* I'd go to summer school, didn't I?" Derry stated, immediately sullen. "What more do you want from me?"

Trent thought of about a dozen things right off the bat, but this was not the time to go into it, so he said, "Right now, I want you to turn off that stereo and finish your homework. I'm going out, but I'll be back by eleven."

"Gee, I can hardly wait," Derry muttered.

Trent pretended he hadn't heard. Closing the door behind him, he left the house.

AT DUNLEAVY FARM, Nan was trying to get ready for dinner. Her suitcase and the twine-tied box she'd brought with her had been waiting inside when Carla showed her to the guest room where she was going to stay. Forgetting that she hadn't wanted her cousin to see her pitiful pieces of luggage, she looked around at the lovely green and white furnishings and exclaimed, "What a lovely room!"

"It is, isn't it?" Carla agreed. "The house has several guest rooms, but we thought you'd like this one. It's so restful."

Nan didn't know how much resting she was going to be doing—not with that colt in the barn. At the thought of Done Cryin', she felt her heart swell. Impulsively, she said, "You know, I'm still not sure if I'm going to stay or not, but now that I've seen Done Cryin'—"

"I know," Carla said with a grin. "You want to see him run, don't you?"

"How did you know?"

"Because I felt the same way about Done Driftin'. Once I saw him, I had to stick around for a while. And now I'm here to stay."

"You really like it that much?"

"I love it here," Carla said simply. "I've been all over the world, but there's something about Dunleavy Farm..."

Nan wasn't sure if she should ask. Hesitantly, she said, "When we talked before, you mentioned that something had happened to your colt. Would you like to tell me about it, or is it too painful to talk about?"

"Both," Carla said. "But you have to know. It happened after his first race this year, which he won, wire to wire."

"What a thrill!"

"Yes, it was. But then . . . he had an accident. The groom was walking him, and the colt got scared and ran. He injured himself so badly that he'll never race again."

"Oh, Carla, I'm sorry," Nan said with true sympathy. "It must be awful for you."

"It is. But it's even harder for Done Driftin'. He was in racing condition when it happened, of course, and ever since he's been cooped up in a stall. He's climbing the walls."

"Poor fellow! Can't you hand-walk him, or something?"

"I wish I could. If he could get even a little exercise, it wouldn't be so bad. But according to the vet, it's not time yet. We had to bring him home from the track because every time he heard the call to race, he'd go crazy, thinking it was time to run."

"How sad!"

"Yes, it is." Carla made a determined effort to smile. "But soon as he's able, I'm going to try to make things up to him. Meanwhile we've got Done Cryin' in race training, and he's showing the same promise as my colt did. They were both outstanding two-year-olds, and now that Done Cryin' is three, he's blowing them away. He won another race a while ago and nearly set a track record doing it."

"He did?" Nan's eyes shone.

"He did indeed," Carla said proudly. "Wade says that if he keeps on like this, he could go to the Derby."

"The *Kentucky* Derby?"

"Is there another?" Carla teased. "And who knows? Maybe he'll go all the way and take the Triple Crown, just like his daddy did so many years ago."

"Oh, Carla, do you really think . . . ?"

Carla laughed at Nan's expression. "Let's not count our races before they're run, okay? Right now, we've got to get ready for dinner. Oh, and by the way, we don't get fancy here. Something simple—slacks or a dress will do."

Nan held her bright smile until Carla went out, closing the door behind her. Left alone in the elegant guest room, she looked in despair at her so-called luggage. Inside were cotton blouses that had been washed so many times the material was threadbare, and jeans she'd worn so long they were almost like gauze instead of denim. But dresses? She didn't have a single one to her name.

She tried to laugh at the thought that she was one woman who could truly say she didn't have a thing to wear, but at the thought that she'd have to appear downstairs soon for dinner, she felt like crying instead.

Unfortunately, her wardrobe was going to be the least of her worries, she thought as she stepped over the suitcase and went to the window. The bigger problem, she knew, was how she was going to make her excuses and leave.

At the question, she wrapped her arms around her waist and gazed out at the farm. Her guest room was on the second floor, and from her vantage point she could see some of the paddocks and the immaculate barn area. Her glance went to the place where she imagined Done Cryin's stall to be, and she bit her lip. The horse was going to stay at the farm tonight; tomorrow morning, she and Wade were to take him back to Louisville so she could meet his trainer, Dwight Connor.

Tomorrow she'd be introduced to the man who had trained so many famous runners. She shivered with anticipation. She'd fantasized about such things all her life; to think that her dreams might be coming true was more than she could absorb at once.

Maybe she could stay just until she and Wade delivered the horse to the track and came back, she thought. What harm would there be in that? Then, duty done, she could make her excuses and leave. She'd think of a reason for her abrupt departure—say she had a job offer, or had to meet some friends in Florida...something.

Because one thing was certain, she knew bleakly, and that was that she didn't belong here. She could dream about it all she liked, but the facts were that she was a Montana girl and these people here were Kentucky born and bred. Or in her cousin Carla's case, she *looked* the part even if she wasn't a Kentuckian.

I, on the other hand, Nan thought, *wouldn't look like I belonged in Kentucky if I stayed here the rest of my life.*

But if she left, that would mean she'd have to leave Done Cryin' behind, too, and even now she wasn't sure she could do that. Just the idea of that magnificent colt was enough to give her a thrill. She couldn't describe her feelings when Wade had put that lead rope in her hand. With his intelligent eyes and bold presence, that colt was her fantasy horse come to life.

Feeling foolish, she turned away from the window to get dressed. Ten rushed minutes later, she was standing in front of the mirror, grimacing at her appearance. She'd done what she could to fancy up her single pair of half-decent slacks and white blouse with the scarf Yolanda had given her, a long, crinkled-silk rectangle in autumn colors to complement her skin and eyes. But instead of arranging it around her neck—a feat of feminine skill she had never mastered and doubted she ever would—she'd tied it around her waist like a cummerbund. With a pair of flats and the little gold earrings her father had given her for her last birthday, she was as ready as she would ever be.

She still felt shaky, and as she gave herself one last check in the mirror, she touched one of the earrings and thought about her father. Would he be happy or displeased that she'd accepted her grandmother's invitation to come to Dunleavy Farm? she wondered. Would he approve of what she was doing, or not? And most important, what would he have felt about her selling the ranch?

"I'm sorry, Dad," she whispered, trying to remember him, not as he'd been at the last—a sick, emaciated man old before his time—but as the robust young father who used to toss her up into the air and laugh. "I did what I thought was best."

But had she? Nan looked at her reflection and wondered if in reality she'd only done the expedient thing in selling the Saddleback and coming to Kentucky.

"This place is all I have to give you, Nannie girl," her father used to say about the ranch. "Your mama and I worked hard to make a go of it so that one day you'd have it as a nest egg..."

But the egg had cracked and the nest had crumbled and in the end, Nan thought sadly, she'd had to sell it, anyway. She'd told herself she hadn't had any choice, but as she stood in the guest room at Dunleavy Farm tonight, surrounded by luxury in an elegant old house filled with mementos of its racing past, she wondered what she would have done if the letter from her grandmother hadn't arrived when it had.

Before she could answer the question, the doorbell chimed. The sound startled her out of her introspection and made her jump. Whoever the dinner guest was, he had arrived. She had to go down; she'd run out of time.

A MAN WAS STANDING in the front room when Nan came in. His back was to her, but even so, she thought there was something vaguely familiar about him. Then she told herself she was being silly. The only man she knew in the whole state of Kentucky was Wade Petrie, and even though Wade had dark hair, he wasn't as tall or as broad-shouldered as this man. The stranger was talking to Octavia, but when Nan entered the room shyly, her grandmother saw her and immediately smiled.

"Oh, Nan, do come in," she said. "I'd like you to meet our neighbor, Trent Spencer. Trent, this is my granddaughter, Nan Dunleavy. She just arrived from Montana today and—"

Even before he turned around and Nan saw his face, her mouth was forming a silent, *"Oh, no!"* of recognition.

It couldn't be! she thought frantically, and in the few seconds left to her, she wondered what she was possibly going to say to this man.

Nothing came to her, and when Trent turned completely toward her, her last faint hope that he wouldn't recognize her vanished when she saw his dark eyes widen. Oh, he knew her, all right, she thought. But then, it would be hard to forget the woman he'd accused of running over his son. To make matters worse, she had practically told *him* to go to hell when he'd asked for her identification. When she remembered how she'd challenged him to trace her through her Montana license plate, she cringed. What must he think of her?

Before either of them could say anything, Carla earned Nan's undying gratitude by coming in behind her. As soon as she saw Trent, she said, "How nice to see you, Trent. Have you met my cousin, Nan?"

The only thing to do, Nan decided, was to brazen it out. Hoping he wouldn't make a scene in a house where he was a guest, she said stiffly, "We've met."

Carla looked puzzled. "But you just got here!"

Nan hoped that by taking charge of the conversation, she could avert disaster—or at least keep Trent quiet until she figured out how to explain this. Quickly, she said, "I know. It was quite a coincidence, actually. You see, I happened to meet Mr. Spencer's son, Derry, on the road today, when he was...uh...having a problem with his bike. We were just getting acquainted when Mr. Spencer came along." She turned to stare at Trent, daring him to contradict her. "Isn't that right, Mr. Spencer?"

Trent's handsome face gave nothing away. Nan held her breath until he said, "Oh, absolutely." Then he stared at *her* and added, "But *Nan*, I thought we agreed that you would call me Trent."

"Oh...yes...right," Nan said, glaring at him. What was he up to? Why had he agreed so readily to her tale?

"Well, you can call *me* confused," Carla said. "Why didn't you mention it, Nan?"

Still trying to figure out his motives, Nan jerked her glance away from Trent. "We had so many other things to talk about that it just slipped my mind, I guess."

"What happened to Derry's bike?" Octavia asked. She looked up sharply. "He didn't fall off, did he?"

"Oh, no, nothing like that," Nan said before Trent could respond. "It was just some problem with the...frame."

Octavia looked doubtful. "I see. Then he wasn't hurt?"

"Probably just his pride," Trent said neutrally. He was still looking at Nan. She could *feel* his eyes on her, and she refused to look his way. "You know how teen-age boys are."

"Yes, I do," Octavia said with a laugh. "In fact, I remember *you*, Trent, when you were Derry's age. You were, as they say, a holy terror."

"Now, Octavia, you know that isn't true," Trent said. "And anyway, even if it was, I grew up to be a respectable businessman, didn't I?"

"You certainly did," Carla agreed. "I don't know what we would have done without you lately."

Trent seemed embarrassed—or pretended to be, Nan thought suspiciously. He said, "I didn't do that much. Besides, it was to my benefit, too."

Nan couldn't help herself. "What did you do?"

She hadn't meant to ask something so personal; she could feel herself flushing bright red. Quickly, she said, "I'm sorry. I shouldn't have asked. It's none of my business."

"But of course it is," Octavia declared. "You're one of the family, Nan, so you might as well know, too. You don't mind if I tell her, do you, Trent?"

Modestly, Trent shook his head—*but of course he would*, Nan thought in annoyance. Clearly, Octavia was about to praise him for some good deed he'd done, and he was pompous enough to want everyone to know just how wonderful he was. Well, it wasn't going to work on her, she decided. No matter what the news was, she wasn't going to change her mind about the man. She hadn't liked him from the moment he got out of that big, black car earlier this afternoon, and nothing she had observed since had altered her opinion. He was arrogant and opinionated and so sure of himself that he didn't listen to anyone, not even his son. *Especially* his son. He was everything she detested in a man.

"I know Trent doesn't like being complimented," Octavia said, "but I'll never be able to thank him enough for his help. If he hadn't arranged for loans to keep the farm going, Dunleavy Farm would have ceased to exist."

NAN KNEW that the dinner served that evening was excellent, but later when she tried to recall what had been on her plate through the many courses, she couldn't think of a single item. She remembered picking at what was put in front of her, but for all the attention she paid it, she could have been eating cardboard.

Fortunately, Octavia and Carla directed the conversation; she knew that if it had been left up to her, silence would have reigned throughout the entire meal. She hated to admit it, but she was so intensely aware of Trent Spencer sitting across the table from her that it was impossible for her to relax. To make matters worse, he kept *staring* at her. Every time she looked up, she seemed to catch yet another intense glance.

What was he thinking? Was that a smirk on his face? Did he know how uncomfortable she was? Was he amused at how annoyed she was that *he* seemed to be responsible for rescuing Dunleavy Farm? Nan wasn't sure just why it irked her, but it did.

Why did it have to be Trent Spencer, of all people, who had arranged for the loan? she wondered irritably. Now she had to be nice to him whether she wanted to or not. Because she was a Dunleavy, she was obligated to him. The thought made her squirm.

At long last, the evening ended. Using the excuse that she'd had a long day, Nan said her good-nights and escaped to the guest room. She *was* tired, but even so, she tossed and turned half the night. Finally, almost in a rage, she got up and untangled the sheets and blankets before throwing herself down again. She'd told herself that as soon as she and Wade dropped off the colt and returned to the farm again tomorrow, she'd say good-bye and head out. But was that really what she wanted to do?

Already, the farm was exerting a pull on her that she wouldn't be able to resist for long. And as for how she felt about Carla and her grandmother, there was no question.

And Done Cryin'?

There would never be another horse like him again, she knew. But she had to face the facts. She didn't belong here, and it had been a mistake to come. She had to get out while—as Yolanda would have said—the getting was good.

But it was another hour or more before she slept, and when she did, her dreams were mixed up with vistas of rolling hills and lush blue-green pastures and fast horses. And the arresting dark glance of a man named Trent Spencer.

CHAPTER FIVE

NAN WAS up and dressed early the next morning. The house was quiet when she crept downstairs in jeans, boots and T-shirt, and she glanced longingly in the direction of the kitchen because she wanted a cup of coffee. She didn't want to disturb anyone and was passing by, when the connecting door swung open. She and Teresa stared at each other in surprise.

Then Teresa exclaimed, "Why, Miss Nan! What in the world are you doing up at this hour?"

"I'm sorry, I guess I'm used to getting up before six. Did I disturb you?"

"Heavens, no. I was sitting reading the paper and having a cup of coffee." Teresa held the door open a little wider. "Would you like something to eat?"

Yolanda had always been after her for not eating breakfast, but Nan couldn't make herself look at food in the morning. "No, thank you. But if there's enough, I would like some coffee."

"There's always enough coffee. Come on in and sit down. I'll have it for you in a jiffy."

Nan didn't want Teresa to wait on her, but the housekeeper insisted. "No, you sit right there," Teresa said when Nan offered to get the coffee herself. "Cream and sugar?"

"Just black, please."

"Hmm," Teresa said with gentle disapproval. "I should have known a little thing like you wouldn't want to sweeten her coffee. Well, I'm just going to have to fatten you up another way. How about one of those cinnamon rolls? I put 'em up last night so they'd be fresh this morning."

Nan glanced at the plate Teresa indicated. As delicious as the rolls looked, they made her stomach lurch. "If you don't mind, I think I'll wait until a bit later."

Teresa rolled her eyes. "Oh, *I* don't mind, not at all. I should just get used to you girls watching your figures all the time. Miss Carla is the same way. She tells me she can't resist my beaten biscuits, so please don't make 'em or she'll get fat. As if *that* one would ever put on any weight. It's just a lost cause around here, a lost cause..."

As the housekeeper fetched a cup and saucer and poured the coffee, she kept up a running grumble that made Nan smile. Teresa sounded so much like Yolanda that it was like being back in the ranch kitchen. She felt homesick, but she resolutely brushed away thoughts of the Saddleback. The ranch was gone, and she had to forget it.

"You look a little sad, Miss Nan," Teresa said when she brought the cup to the table. "Is anything wrong?"

"I guess it's just a little difficult getting used to the farm," she said. "It's so different from what I'm used to."

"Is that so? Tell me about it. I've never been to Montana." Teresa smiled. "In fact, the farthest I've ever been out of Kentucky is Cincinnati—and that's just over the river out of Louisville. What was your place like?"

Nan wondered how best to describe the Saddleback. She certainly didn't want to portray the ranch as it had been right before she'd sold it—tacky and run-down—so she chose to characterize the place as it had been when she'd been young and she'd believed that all things were possible. At that time she couldn't imagine living anywhere else in the world.

"Well, it was prettiest in the spring when all the wildflowers were in bloom," she began. Her eyes took on a faraway glaze as she pictured the hills behind the ranch. In the fall, they turned brown; during winter the trees poked up disconsolately through the snow toward the gray sky. But when it turned warm again, those slopes became great spans of color that made the place come alive.

"In the spring," she continued, "the horses shed their winter coats and turned glossy, and even the air had a different taste and smell. The grass turned green—a pure, deep green, not the blue tint it has here, and the sky was so blue, it could hurt your eyes." She smiled. "I guess that's why they call it Big Sky country."

"It sounds so wonderful," Teresa said, her eyes on Nan's expressive face. "Go on."

But Nan was embarrassed by her poetic description and shook her head. "There's not much to go on with. It was just a dude ranch where city folks came for vacation. When I was young, I thought it was the best place on earth."

"And now?"

Nan finished the last of her coffee and stood. "And now it doesn't belong to me," she said. Once again, she felt a pang. Had she done the right thing in selling the ranch? Maybe she could have tried harder, she thought. Maybe she could have—

"Well, good morning." Wade Petrie came in the back door and stopped in surprise when he saw Nan standing there. "What are you doing up so early?"

Nan glanced at the clock on the wall. It was already six-thirty. Did everyone but these two sleep in around here? But she didn't want to be rude, so she said, "I wanted to be ready when you decided to take Done Cryin' back to the track."

"Oh, I see." Wade nodded to Teresa as he headed for the coffeepot. "Well, that'll be a while. I've got a few chores left to do before—"

"I'll help," Nan offered eagerly. "What can I do? Muck out stalls? Clean tack?"

Wade laughed. "Hold on. We've got John and Charlie to do things like that."

"But there must be something I can do."

Wade obviously heard something in her voice, for he asked, "Are you any good at medicating horses?"

Nan thought of all the doctoring she'd done over the years for the ranch horses and grinned. "I've medicated a few in my time. What do you need?"

"I was about to rewrap Carla's horse. Maybe you'd like to help."

"I sure would."

In fact, Nan couldn't think of anything she'd like better. Carla had told her briefly what had happened to the colt, but Nan wanted to find out more. She hadn't wanted to ask her cousin, who had been reluctant to talk about Done Driftin's accident, but this might give her the opportunity to get some answers.

She and Wade both thanked Teresa for the coffee and went out. It was a beautiful day, and Nan breathed in deeply as they took the path toward the barns. It really was lovely here, she thought. She was going to hate leaving.

"So," Wade said after a short silence, "what do you think of the farm?"

She didn't hesitate. "It's the most extraordinary place I've ever been. Like Disneyland and all the wonders of the world rolled into one."

"Gee, I'm sorry you don't like it."

Embarrassed, she said, "I didn't mean to rhapsodize. It's only—"

"Don't apologize. I felt the same way when I first came. In fact, I still do. No matter what you've done or where you've been, Dunleavy Farm is still quite a place."

Nan agreed fervently. "It is that."

Wade laughed. He had a wonderful laugh, she thought. She could see why Carla had fallen in love with him. There was something so strong and honest about him; just by looking into his eyes, she could see that he was at ease with himself and the world.

"I never had a chance to thank you for bringing Done Cryin' to the farm yesterday so I could see him," she said. "It was a wonderful, thoughtful thing to do."

"Well, ma'am, I'd like to take credit," he drawled, "but the truth is, it was Carla's idea. She thought that since her colt helped her to make up her mind about staying, Done Cryin' might do the same for you."

"How did Done Driftin' convince her to stay?"

"It happened the first time she saw him. We were out riding—having an argument, actually," he explained with a rueful chuckle, "when Done Driftin' came thundering up to the fence. One look, that's all it took for Carla to fall in love. With the horse, I mean," he added with a wink. "I'm afraid I didn't have such an instant effect on her."

Nan laughed. Then she had to confess, "I'm sorry, Wade, but I think I know how Carla felt. It was the same for me yesterday when Done Cryin' came out of that trailer. I don't think I've ever seen a more wonderful horse in my life."

Wade snorted in mock disgust. "You Dunleavy women! You're all the same."

Nan felt comfortable enough to tease him. "Think of it this way. Your competition is well-bred. After all, Carla's colt *is* a son of Done Roamin'."

"Oh, that makes me feel a *whole* lot better."

Nan laughed again. She didn't know if Wade was being silly for her benefit or not, but she was grateful. Her spurt of homesickness had disappeared, and as they entered the sweet-smelling interior of the barn, she felt better than she had in months.

Her smile dissolved a few minutes later when she got her first glimpse of Done Driftin', Carla's colt. He was in a stall bedded so deeply with straw that at first it was difficult to see the bandage around his front leg that covered it from knee to hoof. She was still staring when a young man poked his head out from a stall farther down.

"Are you ready to treat Done Driftin'?" the groom called to Wade.

"Yes, but I've got help," Wade called back. He looked at Nan. "Are you up to it? Normally, this colt is pretty easy to handle, but he's been cooped up for so long now that he's a little fractious. I can ask John to assist, if you like."

"I think it'll be okay," she said. "What do you want me to do?"

"Just hold him while I change the bandage and check that leg underneath. Do you want a twitch or a lip chain?"

"No, let's just try it simple at first."

In Nan's calm, competent hands, Done Driftin' was an angel. The hot-tempered colt towered over her as she held the lead rope, but she kept up a chantlike murmur that seemed to have the horse mesmerized. She waited until she was sure the colt was relaxed before she started asking questions about his accident.

"Carla didn't say much about it, and I didn't want to ask, but what really happened, Wade?"

Wade was squatting carefully beside the horse's front feet, his hands sure and quick as he unwrapped the bandages. "It's not a pleasant story..." he said. He stopped a moment to inspect the colt's grotesquely enlarged fetlock, then reached for the medication that had been prescribed to reduce the swelling. "Someone got onto the backside with a motorcycle and took a run at him—"

Nan gasped. "Deliberately?"

Wade's voice turned hard. "That's what we figure."

"Was the driver caught?"

"No, unfortunately. But maybe it's a good thing. Because if I ever get my hands on the SOB, I'll probably kill him."

"Poor Carla," Nan said. She looked up at the horse and stroked his forelock. "And poor Done Driftin'."

"Right on both counts," Wade agreed grimly. He took fresh bandages and began rewrapping the horse's leg.

Nan was silent. There didn't seem to be much to say, and finally Wade finished and stood.

"That was great," he said. "I think I'll have you help me every day. He's never stood that good except for Carla, who can make him do anything."

"He's her horse," Nan said, pleased at the compliment and glad to get onto another subject. "They have a bond."

"Like you already have with Done Cryin'," Wade declared. He cocked his head. "Can you hear him down the way, pawing his stall because you haven't come to visit yet?"

Nan had heard her colt from the minute she'd come in. But she hadn't wanted to ask if she could go see him until they'd finished with Done Driftin'.

Or maybe, she thought, as Wade took the injured colt from her, she'd been trying to avoid the horse. She knew it was going to be difficult to say goodbye to him. Suddenly she wondered if it was a good idea to go with Wade when he took Done Cryin' back to the track.

She was still torn a few minutes later when Wade handed Done Cryin' over to her so she could put him in the trailer.

"He doesn't care for trailering, so it might be a little difficult to get him—" Wade started to say. He stopped as Nan calmly walked the horse up the ramp and inside, where the colt stood quietly, nosing the hay she'd already put in the manger. When he saw that, he pushed his hat back. "Well, that takes care of that," he said. "You got any other tricks up your sleeve?"

That had been the perfect time to say that she had to get back to the house and pack. But she hadn't said it, and before long, they were heading down the interstate toward the track. She was quiet on the way, and Wade seemed to sense that she needed time to do some thinking.

The only problem, Nan thought, after they arrived and were unloading the colt in front of Dwight Connor's training barn, was that she couldn't seem to make any decision at all.

The truth was, she didn't want to leave. She'd never been to the backside of a real racetrack, and the instant they drove through the gate, she'd felt the excitement here, the *hum* of the track. Horses were everywhere, some returning from the last workout of the morning, some already bathed after their work and being cooled out on the hotwalkers, others back in their stalls, either looking out or snatching at the huge hay balls hanging by their stall doors.

The place was a sea of colors and smells. Freshly washed racing bandages in rainbow hues hung from makeshift clotheslines, the smell of linseed oil was on the air as grooms cleaned tack. Now and then, one horse would call to another, and before long, there was a chorus of whinnies up and down the shedrows as other horses added their two cents to the din.

Nan loved everything about it.

She was even more impressed with Dwight Connor, who came out of his office so they could be introduced.

"It's a pleasure to meet you, Ms. Dunleavy," Dwight said, his big hand engulfing hers. "What do you think of that colt?"

"Please call me Nan. And I think he's wonderful. Don't you?"

"Well, he can run, I'll give him that," Dwight said. "He beat the pants off the competition a while back, but we'll see how he does next time out."

"When will that be?"

"Two weeks from Saturday. We already entered him, so I hope that's all right."

"You're asking me?"

"You're the owner, aren't you?"

"Well, not exactly," Nan said. "I mean, I'm not sure. But in any case, I know that whatever you decide is best."

Dwight looked at Wade. "This is my kind of owner."

Wade grinned. "Not like Carla, you mean, who had to know every intimate detail of her colt's life."

"Now, Wade, I never said—"

"I know, I know. But let me give you fair warning, my friend. From what I've seen of Nan, she's a real Dunleavy, too."

"Hey, Dwight," said a third voice that Nan instantly recognized. She whirled, hoping she was wrong. But no, Trent Spencer was standing in the aisleway right behind them.

"What are you doing here?" she exclaimed. Too late, she remembered that he had several horses in training with Dwight Connor. She felt like a fool.

He'd obviously noticed her tone. Stiffly, he said, "Dwight trains my horses, too. But I don't want to intrude. I'll come back later."

"No, that's all right," Nan said. "I'm the one who's intruding. I'll go wait in the truck."

"Oh, don't leave on my account."

Was he mocking her? Her eyes narrowed, she shot him a quick look. What a mistake. Last night, he'd been wearing a suit and tie; this morning, he had on jeans and a sports shirt. And, she had to admit, he looked handsome either way. His black hair shone in the sun, and the silvering at his temples was much too much of an attractive contrast with his lean face. The only thing that saved her, she realized, was the fact that he was wearing sunglasses. She had already experienced the intensity of that glance and didn't want to have to endure it again.

"Oh, it's not on your account, I assure you," she said with as much dignity as she could muster. "I know you probably have important business to discuss with Dwight. I'll just leave you men alone."

Was that a snicker she heard from Wade? She glanced quickly at him, but he sounded as innocent as could be when he said, "You might be sorry if you leave without seeing a few of Trent's horses. He's got some of the best in racing."

Nan looked again at Trent. "Is that true?"

Shrugging, he said, "You look at them and tell me."

As an invitation, it wasn't one of the most generous. But Nan was torn. If Wade was right, she would be

missing out on a golden opportunity. All her life she'd
wanted a chance to see racing Thoroughbreds up close;
now that she was here in the heart of Bluegrass, she'd
be a fool to walk away from some of the best because of
a little pride.

"Thank you," she said. "Where are they?"

Trent nodded. "Come this way." He took her el-
bow, polite as could be, to help her around a pile of
used straw in the aisleway.

She wanted to say that she could manage, but, as casual as the touch was, she felt a tingle all the way up her
arm. The fact that she was apparently susceptible to him
made her even more annoyed—with herself, with him,
with the entire situation.

Wishing she had never agreed to do this, she asked,
"How many horses do you have in training?"

For the first time he seemed more at ease. Ruefully,
he said what horse owners say the world over and rarely
mean, "Too many."

"Then maybe you should get rid of a few."

"You're right about that. The problem is choosing
which ones."

She understood what he meant a few seconds later
when they came to a stall where a nameplate listed the
name and owner of the horse. When she saw who it
was, Nan forgot how annoyed she was with Trent.

"Good Lord," she said. "Don't tell me that you own
a daughter of Champagne Sunrise!"

Trent was surprised despite himself. "How did you know that? Her nameplate only identifies her as Mimosa."

"Champagne Sunrise was a stakes winner who earned over a million dollars before he was retired with a bowed tendon. All his daughters have been stakes winners. Everyone who's interested in racing knows that!"

Trent was still staring at her in astonishment when the filly inside popped her head over the door. As Nan reached up to scratch the horse behind the ear, he said unwillingly, "You seem to know a lot about horses."

Nan still couldn't believe that she was this close to a horse she'd only read about. "Not really," she said. "It's been a—"

But just then, she happened to glimpse the nameplate of the horse in the next stall. Her eyes widened.

"Majnoon is supposed to be one of the fastest three-year-olds in racing," she said. "I didn't know you owned him."

"I bought him a short while ago. He's named after a legendary Persian hero, you know."

He was looking at her again; she could feel that gaze even behind the tinted lenses of his sunglasses. Suddenly nervous, she said, "He's beautiful."

"He certainly is, and he can run, too. Actually, he might be racing against your colt soon."

"Done Cryin' isn't my colt," she said immediately. "He belongs to my grandmother."

"But I thought she gave him to you."

"She wants to, but it's...complicated."

"I see."

How could he? she wondered. Suddenly, Trent's physical presence felt overpowering, and on the pretext of checking out the next stall, she moved on. He came with her.

"For a Montana girl, you seem to be mighty interested in Kentucky Thoroughbreds," he commented.

"I've loved horses all my life. In fact, I studied pedigrees and form books from the earliest I could remember. By the time I was ten, I—" Nan realized she was babbling and she stopped abruptly. "I'm sorry. You couldn't possibly be interested—"

"But I am."

She halted and faced him. Flatly, she asked, "Why?"

"Horse people are always interested in others who share the same hobby, don't you think?"

"Is that what you think horses are—a hobby?"

"What are they to you?"

Nan couldn't explain what horses meant to her, especially these exquisite, fleet, intelligent creatures who surrounded her right now. When that starting gate opened and the field thundered onto the track and began to run as no other creatures on earth could do...well, something took hold of her heart and wouldn't let go.

Until a while ago, she had never really dared to imagine that she might be part of it. Even now, it seemed an impossible dream, especially when she looked at Trent, with his big farm and his fancy car and his stable full of the best horses that money could buy. So she finally muttered, "I'll tell you one thing, they're not a hobby with me."

"Then why aren't you going to accept your grandmother's gift of Done Cryin'?"

Ah, that was a good question, wasn't it? The more she thought about it, the more she was tempted. But her father had had a reason for denying his kinship to Octavia Dunleavy, and she owed something to his memory. Gary Dunleavy hadn't felt he belonged here; after so many years of estrangement, how could she just forget all that and move in?

She didn't know. Right now, she didn't know anything. Except that she wished to hell Trent would take off those damned dark glasses.

"Not that it's any of your business," she said tartly, "but my grandmother's condition for accepting the horse is my staying here a month, and I never planned to do that."

"You're leaving?"

Was that a note of disappointment in his voice? Oh, of course not, she told herself acidly. When she left, he'd be just as glad to see her gone as she would be to see the last of him.

"As soon as Wade and I get back to the farm," she said.

"That's too bad."

She didn't want him to think it was too bad. She didn't want to believe he really felt that way, or that he felt anything at all for her except impatient dislike, which was certainly all she felt for him. To prove it, she said sarcastically, "Yeah, I can see you're real broken up about it."

He took off his sunglasses. "We didn't start out very well, did we?"

"No," she said. To her annoyance, her voice shook. "We didn't."

"It's my fault," he said. "I want to apologize for the way I acted yesterday."

She didn't want him to apologize. She wanted him to be nasty and mean and awful so it would be easier to carry on disliking him. But he'd turned this corner and now she was face-to-face with something she didn't want to admit.

I don't like him! she told herself furiously. *He's rude and obnoxious. I'm thankful that I'll soon be on my way and we'll never see each other again.*

So why did she feel so... bereft?

She didn't know. She didn't care. She just wanted to end this conversation and get out of here. But for some reason, she couldn't walk away—not when he was looking at her like that.

"You don't have to apologize," she said. "It was as much my fault as yours."

"No, I shouldn't have accused you like that. It's just..." He shook his head, and she saw the pain on his face. "I can't explain how I felt when I recognized Derry's bike under that truck. And when I saw him bleeding... well, I went crazy. Please, forgive me."

She hated him; she really did. How was she going to despise him when he looked so serious, so contrite?

"You were worried," she muttered. "I understand that. Forget it."

"I can't. I'd like to make it up to you. Would you... would you consider having dinner with me?"

She stiffened. Everything had been going so well. Now he'd put another spoke in the wheel. She didn't want to have dinner with him. She just wanted to go...

Where?

"You don't have to do that," she said quickly.

"But I want to."

"It's not necessary," she insisted. "The only thing I need to know is that Derry is all right."

"Oh, he's fine—physically, that is." Trent began to look grim again. "I guess I was hoping that a little conk on the head would knock some sense into him. But unfortunately, he's still the same maddening teenager he's been since he moved in with me at the start of the school year."

Nan wasn't sure what to say. "What about his mother?"

"His mother died last summer."

"Oh, I'm so sorry."

"I was, too, even though Sandra and I had been divorced for years. I fought for shared custody, but I lost. I think that's part of the problem with Derry. He's convinced I never wanted him."

Nan didn't know why he was telling her all this, but she was fascinated. "That can't be true. He must know what happened."

"I don't think he believes it. Lord knows what his mother told him. She was a little . . . bitter."

Nan definitely didn't want to get into that. "Maybe he just needs to adjust."

"Have you been talking with my houseman? That's what *he* says."

"Well, it could be true." Suddenly eager to help, she said, "We had all sorts of teenagers come with their parents to the Saddleback—that's the dude ranch my family owned. I'd say about ninety percent of them resented being there and did their best to make it as miserable as possible for everyone concerned. They didn't want to be away from their friends and what was familiar. It must be much more difficult for someone in Derry's situation."

"You mean when he's forced to live with a father he hates."

"You're exaggerating."

"I don't think so."

"Give him time."

"I'd like to, but I don't think I'll live that long."

"Maybe he needs someone to talk to, then."

Trent thought for a moment. "I realize I have no right to ask, but could you talk to him?"

"Me!" Her voice rose. "What could I say to him?"

"I don't know. More than I can, obviously. You seem to know a lot about teenagers—"

Nan was appalled. She'd let her guard down more than she should have. She hadn't meant to carry on the conversation this long, or to say the things she had. But there was something about him...

No, no there wasn't! What was she thinking? Not five minutes ago, she'd assured herself that she detested him. Now she was giving him advice. She didn't have time for this; she was going to be moving on. She wasn't going to get involved, even peripherally, with someone who would soon be a part of her past.

"When I suggested that Derry talk to someone, I meant a professional counselor," she said hastily. "You know, someone who—"

"He's already been through three counselors."

"Then maybe a psychologist."

Trent shook his head. "I know it's an imposition, Nan," he said. "But I'm at my wit's end. You seemed to have a good rapport with Derry yesterday—"

"I would hardly call that a *rapport!*" she protested. "He fainted in my arms."

"Yes, but he defended you afterward, don't you see? He's never done that for anyone, that I know of. So, please, won't you give it a try? I would be so grateful if you'd just talk to him for me."

"But what will I say?" As soon as she asked, she realized she'd committed herself. What was the matter with her? Why couldn't she just keep her mouth shut?

But she'd never been able to do that; why did she think she could start now?

Clearly, she couldn't, because a few minutes later when Wade walked over to see if she was ready to leave, she'd agreed to go to ChangeOver Farm later in the week for dinner.

"I don't know what I'll be able to do," she said to Trent, wondering if she could get him to change his mind.

"Just be yourself," he said. "I'll see you in a few days."

So now she had a dinner date and possibly a race to attend the week after that. Time was going by, and she was still at Dunleavy Farm.

I'll leave as soon as the race is over, she told herself again and again on the way back to the farm. *Bright and early the following Sunday morning, I'll be gone.*

CHAPTER SIX

NAN WAITED until the last minute to tell Carla and her grandmother that she was going to dinner at Trent's tomorrow evening. She wasn't sure why; it wasn't that she thought they might disapprove, or that she'd done anything wrong in accepting the invitation. She just felt . . . awkward about it.

Annoyed, she wondered why she should feel *awkward* about going to dinner at ChangeOver Farm. It wasn't that Trent Spencer was interested in her; he'd made that clear. He wanted her to talk to Derry; there was nothing more to it than that.

Maybe that's what was making her apprehensive. She didn't know what she could say to the boy, or what Trent expected. This was crazy, she thought. She was no counselor or psychiatrist; just because she'd helped a few kids over some rough vacation spots didn't mean that she was qualified to give advice to an unhappy teen who was having trouble communicating with his father. If things were that strained between them, Trent should seek professional advice, the three counselors Derry had already gone through notwithstanding.

She was about to call and tell him she couldn't make it after all, when Carla asked her if she had plans for the next night. They were at dinner, and Nan had been wrestling with her problem throughout the meal. Consequently, it was on her mind when Carla proposed a shopping trip or a movie, so she blurted it out.

"I can't," she said. "Trent Spencer asked me over to his place for supper tomorrow night."

Carla paused with her water glass halfway to her mouth. "Well, that was fast work."

Nan could feel herself turning red. "It's not what you think. The only reason I'm going is because of Derry."

Carla smiled slyly. "Isn't he a little young for you?"

"Carla!"

"I'm teasing. I know Derry's just a boy. But his father isn't."

"It's not a date with Trent!"

"Well, he's certainly good-looking enough, don't you think?"

"Now, Carla," Octavia murmured from her end of the table. "Nan's not used to your sense of humor."

"I'm being honest here," Carla said innocently. "Trent Spencer *is* good-looking, don't you agree?"

"Yes, I do," Octavia said calmly. "But I don't think that's the point Nan was trying to make. Besides, what would Wade say if he heard you talking about another man like that?"

"He'd just laugh. He knows he's the only one in the world for me."

"Then perhaps you should have gone with him to California to see those horses."

"Now, you and I discussed that, Grandmother, and we agreed this wasn't a good time for me to go. I'm still learning how to manage the farm, and now that Nan's admirer has—"

"Trent is not my *admirer!*" Nan exclaimed.

"Well, whatever he is, now that he's arranged that loan, it's more important than ever that I stay here and work closely with him and the new accountant. Don't worry, Grandmother," Carla assured Octavia. "Wade and I will have plenty of time together once he sets up his own training barn."

"Oh, you think so, do you?" Octavia said. "In case you're interested, miss, horses are a demanding business. Animals don't punch nine-to-five time cards, you know. They require around-the-clock care."

Carla's expression was serene. "It will be worth it to see him training horses again." She turned to Nan. "I've been meaning to tell you, but while Wade is in California, he's going to try and find our cousin, Seth."

"We have another cousin?"

"And a cousin-in-law, too, if there is such a thing. He's married to a woman named Honey."

"Honey... That's a pretty name."

"Yes, no doubt she'll be tall and blond with big blue eyes and we'll hate her on sight," Carla joked.

"Oh, not you!"

"Nor you, I might add."

"May I break into this mutual admiration society a moment?" Octavia asked. "I believe we were discussing Nan's dinner plans for tomorrow night."

Nan thought they had safely negotiated their way off the subject of Trent Spencer. Now that her grandmother had introduced it again, she knew Carla wouldn't let it go until she heard all the details. Sighing, she gave them a brief but detailed account of what had happened her first day in Kentucky when she and the Spencers had collided.

"Good heavens!" Octavia said when Nan came to the part about Derry sliding, bike and all, right under the truck as he tried to stop. "It's a miracle Derry wasn't hurt."

"Yes, it is," Nan said. Then she smiled. "The poor kid got such a shock. Don't tell him I told you, but he actually fainted at the sight of his own blood."

"Oh, men!" Carla exclaimed.

"It's a good thing teenage boys are almost indestructible," Nan said. "I'm convinced *something* protects them between the ages of thirteen and seventeen, since obviously they're too awkward to do it themselves."

Octavia laughed. "You sound as if you speak from experience."

"Well, there were quite a few teenagers who came—or I should say, were dragged—to the Saddleback by their parents. But once there, naturally the boys all figured they had to show off for the girls. And since most of them had never been near a horse, much less ridden one, it could be quite a rodeo at times. All of our dude string mounts were well trained, of course, but there's only so much even the most well-mannered animal will take. No one ever got injured, thank goodness. But at times, there were a lot of bruised egos and hurt pride limping around and trying to hide it.''

Carla and Octavia smiled at Nan's description, and soon after, Octavia excused herself to watch a television program in her suite, and Carla had some book work to do. But before her cousin headed to the office, Nan overcame her reluctance and asked a favor.

"Carla, would you...I mean, if you have time...do you think we could—'' she stopped, took a deep breath and finished the question ''—go shopping soon?''

Carla looked at her, a surprised expression on her face. "But I thought you hated shopping.''

"I do. But now that I'm staying—at least until Done Cryin' runs again, I need something other than jeans and T-shirts, and that's all I brought.''

"Say no more,'' Carla said. "It's too late to go tonight, and tomorrow I'll be tied up with the farm's legal business all day. And tomorrow night you'll be gone, so that's out.'' She tapped her teeth with a fingernail, pondering the problem. "I know. I've got more clothes than I could possibly wear in two lifetimes, so why don't you borrow what you like until we can get to the mall? We should be able to find time this weekend.''

"Oh, Carla, I couldn't borrow your clothes.''

"Why not?''

How could she say that she'd feel intimidated in anything Carla owned? The thought of trying to mimic her sophisticated cousin made her cringe. She'd look like a fool—worse than if she just wore jeans everywhere she went. She was trying to think of an excuse, when Carla snapped her fingers.

"I know what you're thinking," Carla said.

Nan looked at her cautiously. "You do?"

"Sure. You're thinking that nothing of mine is going to fit you, right?"

"Oh...right."

Confidently, Carla linked her arm with Nan's. "Well, don't worry. I'm sure with all I have, we'll be able to find something."

AND THAT WAS HOW, the next night, Nan found herself dressed in a cashmere skirt and silk blouse that had come from Carla's voluminous closet. Because of the differences in their heights, the skirt that on Carla was a mini became a knee-length on Nan. Nan had never felt fabric as soft and as fluid as the moss-green cashmere, or as luxurious as the blouse that matched it. But after giving both a longing touch, she had protested that she couldn't possibly wear them.

"Nonsense," Carla had said firmly, adding a necklace she selected from an overflowing jewelry case. "You'd be doing me a favor by giving these things some wear. I sent them to the dry cleaners, and would you believe it? I think the silly people did something to make them shrink. Now they're too small for me. It couldn't be," she'd added with a sigh, "that the real culprit is Teresa's cooking. I absolutely refuse to believe I could gain so much weight in so short a time."

"I know what you mean," Nan had said ruefully. "My jeans have been feeling a little tighter these past few days."

"So you see, it was meant to be," she'd said, shaking a finger in Nan's face. "But don't think this means wc arcn't going shopping. There's a party coming up—"

"A party?" Nan was horrified.

"Don't look so petrified." Carla had laughed. "It'll be fun."

"Fun!"

"You're not going to be put in a snake pit, you know," Carla had teased. "Besides, you worry too much. And we want to do Grandmother proud. She's shown me what she's going to wear, and we can't do less. On that night, the Dunleavy women are not only going to present a united front, we're going to look smashing while we do it."

The Dunleavy women. Nan thought about the conversation on the way to dinner at Trent's. Carla had pressed her to take the little sports car she had leased, but on that, Nan had been adamant in her refusal. Her cousin had done too much for her already; she would drive the truck, no matter how it looked.

But as she drove through Dunleavy's gates on the way out, she glanced back over her shoulder. The mere thought of a party was enough to inspire terror in her, so she decided not to think about it. Besides, she probably wouldn't even be here then, so she didn't have anything to worry about.

Still, the idea of leaving this beautiful ranch—no, *farm*, she corrected herself, remembering her grandmother's mock horror the other day when she'd referred to Dunleavy as a ranch—made her feel sad and depressed. It was beginning to feel like home.

The Dunleavy women, Carla had called them. Could she be one of them? Or would it just be better to leave now, before she became inextricably entwined?

"That's what Dunleavy can do to you," Wade had told her when they were taking the colt back to the track. "It gets into your heart and your blood and then it's impossible to leave behind."

"Is that what happened to Carla?" she'd asked.

Wade had grinned that wonderful grin of his and said, "Well, I'd like to think it was me. But I know, deep down, it was the farm."

The farm. Was Dunleavy where she was meant to be? Suddenly, she felt a longing to talk to Yolanda, who always gave the right advice. Because she hadn't wanted to run up any long-distance phone bills, Nan had written to Yolanda the very first night she'd arrived. But a letter wasn't the same as a conversation, and she decided that she would call Yolanda the next morning.

Right now, she had to deal with the current situation. The gates to ChangeOver Farm were dead ahead, and somehow she had to get through this evening. Why on earth had she accepted Trent's invitation? Judging by the churning of her stomach, she should have dredged up any excuse to get out of it. Now she was here and it was too late.

The house was lit up like a Christmas tree when she stopped the truck in the driveway that circled a spouting fountain. As she got out of the truck, her heart pounding with nerves, the fountain's cycle changed. Up shot three different-colored streams of water that seemed to float in the air for a moment before they all cascaded down. Normally, Nan would have been entranced by the impressive sight; tonight her mood made her critical. It was all so ostentatious.

Already she didn't like this place, she decided; it was so like its owner—brash and arrogant and insufferably superior.

Was that true?

She didn't care to answer. Her indignation carried her up the wide steps to the big brass front door. Or *doors,* she amended, realizing there were two, each of which could have been the entrance to a grand cathedral. Irked by that sight, as well, she rang the bell. A loud *bong!* reverberated inside, making her jump. Her irritation increased. She decided that if she'd had any doubts about who or what Trent Spencer was, they were confirmed now. He was just another well-heeled businessman who loved to show off his wealth.

Was that really all he was?

Before she could form an answer to *that* inconvenient question, the door swung open. A man only slightly taller than Nan appeared. He was wearing a dark suit and tie; when he saw her, he bowed.

"Ah, Miss Dunleavy," he said. "Good evening."

Nan forgot her irritation. The little man was smiling so engagingly at her that she had to smile back. "You must be Mr. Lawrence," she said. "It's nice to meet you."

"And you," he said, gesturing her inside. "Please, call me George," he said. "Everyone does."

"And everyone calls me Nan."

"As you wish," he said, with another charming bow. "Please, will you follow me to the living room? Mr. Spencer will be down directly. May I get you something to drink in the meantime?"

Nan was tempted to ask for a glass of something strong—a *big* glass. The house was so imposing and so beautifully decorated, that she felt overwhelmed. And, try as she might to walk quietly across the smooth, polished tiles of the foyer, her heels still sounded like firecrackers exploding as she followed George to the living room. By some unlucky chance, she happened to catch a glimpse of herself in a huge ornate mirror hanging over a glossy cherry-wood table and grimaced. She should have put on more makeup; she looked as white as a sheet.

Calm down, she ordered herself. This wasn't an interview; she didn't have to impress anyone. She was an invited guest, so it was her host's responsibility to entertain her.

That resolved, she looked cautiously around and had to admit that, if possible, the living room was even more elegant than the entryway. Her feet sank about two inches into the thick, beige-colored carpet, and she was still staring at the overstuffed furniture in a color scheme of ivory and apricot, when she realized that George was waiting for her reply. She hadn't answered his question about what she wanted to drink.

"If it's not too much trouble, I'll take a glass of—" Appalled, she realized she'd almost said *beer.* It seemed almost blasphemous to think of drinking anything other than wine in a room like this, so she amended her request to, "A glass of white wine, please, George."

"White wine it is. What kind would you like? We have Chardonnay, Chablis, Gewürztraminer..."

"Oh, anything is fine," she said quickly. At the moment, it was hard enough for her to remember her own name, much less what kind of wine was what. She'd thought that Dunleavy was luxurious, but it was nothing compared to this. Even the air seemed scented with a subtle fragrance, and it took all her resolve to stay where she was and not run out to the truck.

George disappeared, presumably to fetch her wine. Left alone, Nan took a deep breath, and then another. *You're acting like an idiot,* she told herself. She might not be as cosmopolitan as her cousin, but certainly, she was more sophisticated than this.

"Hi," a voice said sullenly from behind her.

She turned around. Derry was standing there—at least, she thought it was Derry. He looked so different in his shirt and tie that she knew immediately that Trent had established the dress code for tonight. Derry, it seemed, hadn't dared disobey.

"Hi," she said. "It's nice to see you again. How's the—" she almost said *head,* but remembered just in time how embarrassed he'd been about fainting, so she substituted "—bike?"

"Totaled."

"Gee, that's too bad."

"Yeah, well, things happen."

"I guess they do."

He looked so much like his father that she said, "You look nice tonight."

He scowled. "In this getup? I feel like a jerk."

This wasn't going well. Lightly, she said, "Well, we all have to suffer at social occasions, it seems."

"Why?"

"That's a good question. To tell you the truth, I'm much more comfortable in jeans, myself."

Shoving his hands into his trouser pockets, he slouched over to a couch and threw himself down.

Nan knew it was up to her to keep the conversation going, so after a pause, she asked, "So, how are things going?"

He shrugged. "How they always go. Sh—I mean, okay, I guess. Listen, Dad said I had to ask if I did any damage to your truck. I'm supposed to pay for it if I did."

"Thanks, but it won't be necessary. That old thing has been through so much it's never going to die. It's going to hang on so long I'll have to shoot it to put it out of its misery."

"At least you've got a vehicle," he said sulkily. "Dad won't even let me have a bike."

"But you have a bike—"

He looked at her impatiently. "No, I mean a *bike*. You know, like a motorcycle?"

Nan wasn't sure what to say to that. She wasn't going to get into the middle of *that* argument between Derry and his father, so she said, "If your father doesn't want you to get a motorcycle, he must have a good reason."

"Yeah, he hates me."

"Oh, that's not true!"

He sneered. "How would you know?"

Not about to tell him what she had sensed in Trent's voice when he'd talked about his son, she copied Derry's earlier gesture and shrugged. "I wouldn't. Perhaps you can tell me."

Maybe in the hope of shocking her, he said, "Look, all I did was skip a few days of school this last semester. What's the big deal about that?"

"I don't know. Were you sick?"

He laughed obnoxiously. "Yeah, of school."

She ignored that. "How many days did you skip?"

This time, his look was defiant. "Almost a month."

"That's a lot of school to miss," she said as noncommittally as she could. "Were you just bored with class, or what?"

"Class was the pits, the kids got on my nerves and the teachers were pathetic. I couldn't stand it, so I cut out."

"What did you do? Shoot pool and ride motor-cycles?"

She'd been half teasing, but to her dismay, anger flooded his handsome face and he shot to his feet. His expression turning ugly, he said, "What do you know about that?"

She drew back. "About what? I was just joking. You said your father doesn't want you out on a bike."

They were facing each other like wary combatants when Trent entered the room. As soon as Derry saw his father, he turned away and threw himself down on the couch again.

"Good evening, Nan," Trent said, glancing at his son, and then away when Derry glowered at him. "It's so nice to see you."

Nan decided to ignore Derry's display of bad manners. "Thank you for inviting me," she said to Trent. She made herself add, "You have a lovely home."

"Thanks. Would you like to see more of it?"

The last thing she wanted was to extend the evening by adding a tour of the house. She hated to admit it, but as soon as Trent came into the room, she was so aware of him that even her skin felt tingly.

Get a grip! she told herself sternly. She was allowing her imagination run away with her. This . . . feeling she had, had nothing to do with Trent's imagined power or presence; it was simple nerves. She just didn't like being here.

"Maybe another time," she said, and was relieved when George arrived with her wine. He carried it in on a silver tray, with a highball glass for Trent and another filled with juice for Derry.

"Oh, great," Derry said peevishly when he saw it. "Just what I needed—a Shirley Temple. Take it back, George. I don't want it."

"Not so fast, young man," Trent said. "I want to make a toast, and I'd like you to join us."

"Then give me something real to drink," Derry muttered. But at another look from his father, he got to his feet and took his drink from the tray.

Trent raised his glass. "To Nan," he said. "Welcome to Kentucky."

Flustered, Nan raised her glass to theirs, and they all clinked rims. "To Kentucky," she murmured, "and the fine horses it raises."

"I'll drink to that," Trent said.

"You would," Derry said under his breath.

Trent tensed, while Nan buried her nose in the bouquet from the excellent Chardonnay and hoped no one would explode. Trying to mitigate the increasing tension, she asked, "Don't you like horses, Derry?"

"Oh, they're all right, I guess." He shot a quick look at his father. "I don't have much to do with them. Dad has all the stable help he needs—not that I'd be caught dead mucking out stalls, mind you. But the really good ones are at the track, anyway, and I never get to see them."

This seemed to be a safe enough subject, Nan thought. At least the conversational ball was rolling. "Don't you go to the races?" she asked.

"Oh, yeah. When I have to—or when Dad wants to make sure I'm not out robbing and murdering people."

"Derry," Trent said tightly.

Quickly Nan asked, "Aside from that, what are your interests?"

"I like motorcycles," he said with a sneer. "But Dad won't let me have one."

That was Trent's cue. "I told you, not until your grades improve."

"Yeah, yeah, I know. You've said it enough times, haven't you?"

Out of the corner of her eye, Nan saw the muscles tighten along Trent's jaw. Before she could think how to defuse this newest minefield, Derry turned to her.

"What do you think?" he asked. "Don't you think I should have a motorcycle if I want one? I told Dad I wouldn't even take it outside the farm for a while. I'll just ride around here. It's private property, and my driving it won't bother anyone."

Except your father, Nan thought, and wondered how she could wriggle out of this one. She didn't want to say she agreed with Trent, because then Derry would think she was copping out. But she also remembered how she'd pestered her own father when she was even younger than Derry was now, to let her practice driving the tractor. And then the old truck. And then Yolanda's car. By the time she was thirteen, she could drive anything at the ranch with wheels.

But that was in Montana, she thought, where things were different. There, it was accepted that kids helped out on the farms and ranches. All too often, the only extra pair of hands that could be found in those outlying areas belonged to a child.

"I really don't think I should offer my opinion," she said diplomatically. "This is obviously a matter between you and your father."

"Well, thanks a *lot*."

Once again, George rescued her by announcing that dinner was ready. Wondering how she was going to get through the rest of the evening, Nan followed the houseman into the dining room.

An hour later, filled to the brim and beyond, Nan sat back from the table. She'd tried her darnedest to finish the excellent chocolate mousse that had been served for dessert, but she just couldn't manage it.

"That was wonderful," she said. "But I can't eat another bite."

"I'll finish it, if you don't want it," Derry said.

"Go ahead," she said.

"Oh no you don't," Trent said as Derry reached for Nan's dessert plate. "If you want another, I'll have George bring one from the kitchen."

Sullenly, Derry sat back. "Aw, lighten up, Dad. I was just kidding."

It had been like this all evening. Nan had tried her best to guide the conversation into safe areas, but she couldn't seem to find any. These two could argue or disagree about anything, it seemed. She'd been nervous on the way over; now she was so tense, she had a fierce headache. She was just wondering how soon she could politely leave, when Derry asked to be excused from the table. Trying unsuccessfully to hide his relief, Trent immediately gave his permission.

"It was nice seeing you again, Derry," Nan said as the teenager started out of the room without saying good-night to either of them. "Perhaps one day, if you like, you can come over to Dunleavy Farm, and we'll go riding together."

That stopped him. Already at the dining-room threshold, he turned around. "Riding? As on a bike?"

"Riding, as on four feet," she said pointedly. "I meant, on horses."

"Oh, that. Well, I don't know. I don't know how to ride."

She was genuinely surprised. "You don't? Here in the middle of Bluegrass country?"

"Yeah, well, I didn't always live here, you know. When I was with ... my mom, we lived in Chicago."

Nan noticed the change in his voice when he mentioned his mother and didn't press the subject. Instead, she said, "I suppose there's not much opportunity to ride in Chicago, is there?"

"No, not much."

"That's too bad. It can be a lot of fun."

"If you say so."

After his son had gone, Trent sighed.

Now that they were alone, Nan felt a new level of anxiety. It was time to leave, she thought, and said, "Thank you for a lovely evening—"

"You're not going yet, are you?"

"Well, I—"

"It's a nice night. Why don't we have coffee on the terrace?"

It must have been that heartfelt sigh that convinced Nan she couldn't leave, not just yet, anyway. Cautiously, she said, "All right."

The "terrace" that Trent directed her to was almost as big as a football field—or so it seemed to Nan. Flower boxes defined the edges; beyond was a long expanse of perfectly manicured grass that sloped down to a pond where several species of ducks and geese made their home. It was dark by this time, but cleverly hidden floodlights cast an ethereal glow on the outline of a swan floating peacefully on the unruffled surface of the water. For a moment, Nan was so caught up in the absolute beauty of the scene that she felt a lump in her throat.

For heaven's sake! she told herself impatiently. *It's just a bird on a pond!* She started to turn away only to realize that Trent was staring at her.

"What is it?" she asked.

"I was just thinking how good you are with Derry," he said.

Nan knew she had no reason to feel disappointed, but she did. Wondering what she had expected him to say, she shrugged and said, "I don't think I reached him at all tonight."

"At least he didn't leave the table in a rage."

"Does he do that often?"

Trent looked grim. "Not as often as he might like. Sometimes, though, I have to admit, it's easier to let him go sulk in his room than to try and deal with his attitude."

"He's just going through a stage."

"Easy for you to say."

"Well, I'm not his father."

"So where is it written that he and I can't get along?"

"He's a teenager. I was the same way with my dad when I was his age, weren't you?"

"No. I respected my father. I wanted to please him."

"Derry wants to please you. He just doesn't know how."

"I don't believe that. I think he wants to make things as difficult as possible for me."

Nan was beginning to get irritated, and her headache seemed to be getting worse. "Why are you so willing to believe the worst of him?"

"Because he never disappoints me."

"What an awful thing to say!"

"Well, it's true. You can't imagine how impossible life has been since he's come to live with me."

"He's your son!"

"Remind *him* of that."

"I think you do that all the time."

"And that's a bad thing?"

She was going beyond irritated into the dangerous territory of losing her temper. "Maybe we'd better not talk about this anymore."

"Maybe you're right."

They lapsed into silence for a moment. Finally, Nan couldn't stand it. "You know," she said, "you think Derry needs to talk to someone. But maybe you're the one who needs counseling."

Trent looked at her. "Oh, so now you're the psychiatrist."

"I just meant—"

"You meant that I don't know how to handle my own kid."

Nan took another grip on her temper. "I didn't say that."

"You might as well have."

That was the last straw. "No, but isn't that what you've been saying?" she asked. She turned to look at him. "Wasn't that why you asked me to come to dinner tonight—because you didn't know what to say to your son and you wanted me to help?"

He looked away. "That was one reason," he muttered.

"There was another?"

His jaw tightened. "Well, yes."

"Go on."

He was silent a moment. Then he said, "Oh, hell. I'm out of practice at this."

"At what?"

She tensed. He'd turned to gaze at her. When she met his eyes, she felt the hair at her nape stir. It was as though the air had suddenly turned on edge, the way it did on the Montana range when an electric storm was on the way. In the reflected glow from the torches near the pond, his eyes looked almost black. The shadows on his handsome face seemed to focus her gaze and hold it.

"At telling a woman how beautiful she is," he said, and took her into his arms.

It was so long since she'd been held by a man—especially one as compelling as this—that for an instant she felt herself giving way, surrendering to the impulse to press against him and put her arms around his neck and bring his mouth down to hers. Longing flashed through her like a fever, and in a daze, she looked up at him, her lips parted.

His voice turned hoarse. "Let's not talk about Derry anymore," he said. "Oh, Nan, I—"

"Coffee, anyone?" said a cheerful voice from somewhere in another universe.

Nan and Trent sprang apart. Standing in the open French doors that led to the terrace was George. He was holding a tray with a carafe and coffee cups.

Nan wasn't sure if George realized he'd interrupted something or not; in the few seconds it took for her to regain her composure, Trent changed back into the distant man he'd been all evening. The moment was past, the air was ordinary again, the swan long gone. The last thing she desired was coffee; right now, all she wanted was to be on her way home. How close she'd come to making a total fool of herself!

"Not now, George," Trent said meaningfully.

Nan couldn't let the houseman get away. Without looking at Trent, she said, "Thanks, anyway, but it's late, and I should be getting back."

Nan didn't know whether or not to be disappointed that Trent didn't try to argue her out of going. When he told her he'd walk her out to her car, she knew it was for the best, so she said good-night to the houseman.

"I hope you come back soon, Miss Dunleavy," George said. "Good night, now."

If she needed any more convincing that her coach had turned into a pumpkin, all it took was the sight of her truck sitting outside in the curving driveway by the fountain. The multicolored paint job looked even more leprous than ever under the porch lights, and she grimaced at it before she turned to Trent.

"Thank you for a lovely evening," she said. "Perhaps I'll see you again sometime."

"We'll see each other sooner than that if you're going to stay for Done Cryin's race."

She could handle talk about horses; it was a safe subject. "I said I'd stay. I really would like to see him run—once."

Trent seemed glad to be on a safe topic, too. "It should be quite a contest. He and my colt Majnoon are competing against each other."

She forced a smile with lips that felt stiff. "Then may the best horse win."

"The best horse," he repeated.

She had to get away from him. The longer they stood together, the more she began to wish that George hadn't interrupted them. Before some midnight madness inspired her to find out what it was like to kiss this man, she turned and went down the steps.

"Good night," she called over her shoulder.

"Good night. And thank you for coming."

He sounded so...sad? Wistful? She stopped and turned to look at him. "I...didn't really do anything."

Even from that distance, he had the power to hold her gaze. "Yes, you did," he said. "You seem to have both the Spencer men in your debt."

Nan wasn't sure what he meant. Was he joking? Teasing her? Just being polite? She wondered about it all the way to Dunleavy. She was still thinking about it later, after she got ready for bed and turned out the light.

It took her a long time to get to sleep that night, and when she finally fell into a restless slumber, her dreams were all mixed up. She and Trent were both wearing jockeys' colors, racing horses across a field of flowers, when they heard the sound of a big motorcycle coming fast. Nan looked behind her just as a grinning Derry roared up.

"No!" she cried as her horse swerved violently, unseating her.

But Trent caught her in midair, and suddenly, they were both riding the motorcycle, speeding away from... Danger!

With a strangled cry, Nan sat upright. The covers were tangled; her hair was plastered with sweat to her face. It took her a moment to realize where she was.

But it took her even longer to stop trembling.

It was only a dream, she told herself. But she couldn't get back to sleep, for despite her own reassurances, the danger had seemed much too real to dismiss.

CHAPTER SEVEN

MEREDITH DUNLEAVY returned to Dunleavy Farm the week before Done Cryin' was scheduled to race.

Nan and Carla had been out on an errand and were just driving up to the house when Carla suddenly stopped talking and stared straight ahead.

"Oh, Lord," Carla muttered. "Mother's here."

"How do you know?" Nan asked.

Carla pointed. When Nan glanced in the direction her cousin had indicated, she saw that a big silver-colored car was parked in front of the house. "That's your mother's car?" she asked. "How do you know?"

"It's her style."

"I didn't know she was expected."

"I didn't, either. I thought she'd gone back to England. And Grandmother obviously didn't know she was coming or she'd have told us."

Nan hesitated. "You sound as if this is...bad."

Carla pulled in behind the silver car and tapped her fingers on the steering wheel. "I don't know if it is or not yet. It depends on why she came, and what mood she was in when she got here."

Nan didn't think that sounded too promising, but since she'd never met Carla's mother, she decided the safest course was to say a noncommittal "I see."

Carla turned to her. "You might as well know that Grandmother and my mother have been at odds for years."

"Well, that certainly sounds familiar—except my father never told me about the farm, and in fact denied that we were related to any Dunleavy anywhere."

"My mother did the same, but at least your parents stayed married despite Grandmother's disapproval. My mother's marriage was annulled and I never knew my father."

"Annulled? How can that happen?"

"I don't know. Grandmother pulled some strings or something."

I'm sorry, Carla. I didn't know."

"Well, as you can imagine, it's not something I'm keen to discuss, especially since Mother and Grandmother are still carrying on a war of attrition."

Nan looked at the big car again. "But if that's true, why is your mother here?"

"I don't know. Let's go and find out."

Nan would have known Carla's mother anywhere. Meredith Dunleavy was standing by the window when they entered the living room, and as soon as she turned in their direction, Nan saw the striking resemblance between Carla and her mother. They both had the same chestnut hair and what Nan had learned were the trademark Dunleavy green eyes. Even allowing for the obvious difference in their ages, Nan marveled that they could have been sisters.

Like Carla, Meredith was tall and slender with a grace she demonstrated in every gesture. Her pale peach-colored suit was without a single wrinkle, and she looked as if—what was the saying Yolanda always used? As if she'd just stepped out of a bandbox. Beside her, Nan wished she had at least run a comb through her hair—especially when, after greeting Carla with a hug and a kiss, Meredith turned her perfectly made-up glance in Nan's direction and said, "Hello, Nan. I'm your Aunt Meredith."

Nan took a couple of steps forward, trying to combat the sudden shyness she felt. "I know," she said with a smile. "It's so nice to meet you after all these years."

Meredith surprised her by looking a little misty-eyed. "You resemble your father so much," she said. "It's been a long while since I last saw Gary, but I would have known you were his daughter."

Touched, Nan said, "It must run in the family. I was just thinking how much you and Carla look alike."

"It does seem to be a curse, doesn't it?" Meredith said. But she smiled when she said it.

"So," Carla said briskly, "now that the introductions are completed, why don't we sit down so you can tell us what brings you here, Mother."

Meredith looked at her with eloquent reproach. "Why, darling, I thought you'd be glad to see me. As I recall, the last time I was here, you didn't want me to leave. Now you wonder why I came? I don't seem able to please you."

"Oh, Mother, you know what I mean. You were supposed to be in London."

"Yes, I know," Meredith said with a sigh. She sat down on the couch, crossed her long legs and reached for her purse. Nan watched, fascinated, as Meredith pulled out a gold cigarette case and took a cigarette from it. Her hands were so graceful that she could have been filming a commercial. Nan was so intrigued that she forgot how much she disliked the smell of smoke.

"So," Carla prodded after Meredith lit her cigarette and sat back.

"It's really not complicated, my dears," Meredith said, including Nan. "I got to New York and changed my mind, that's all." She smiled at Nan through a wreath of smoke. "After all, it's not every day that I get a chance to meet my only niece. When I heard that Nan was going to visit the farm, I decided I had to come back."

"You came here just to meet me?" Nan asked.

"It's about time, don't you think?"

"*I* think it would be interesting to know exactly how you found out about Nan," Carla said. "I don't recall mentioning before you left that she was going to visit."

"Didn't you?"

"No, Mother, I didn't. So how did you know?"

"Well, I knew you had called her, darling, so what's the difference?" She smiled again, dazzling Nan, but, judging from Carla's expression, not fooling her daughter for a minute. Then she continued, "But why are we wasting time on such trivial details? Isn't the point that we're all here?"

"I'm not sure what the point is," Carla said. She looked keenly at her mother. "Does Grandmother know you've arrived?"

Meredith laughed. "Sweetheart, this house is big, I grant you. But it's not so large that people get lost in it. Of course she knows I'm here. I called this morning from the airport."

"Why didn't you let us know sooner?" Nan asked. "We could have come to pick you up."

"Oh, I didn't want to bother anyone."

"It wouldn't have been a bother!" Nan exclaimed.

Meredith ashed her cigarette in a nearby crystal ashtray. "Well, the last time, Carla forgot all about me. When she finally remembered that my plane had arrived, she was so late that I thought I'd have to hire a taxi. I decided it was easier to provide my own transportation this time."

"Very funny," Carla muttered. "I should have known you'd never let me forget that."

"That's what mothers are for, aren't they?" Meredith said serenely. She turned to Nan with a solemn expression. "I'm so sorry I didn't see my brother before he died. I wanted to, and I know I should have, but we hadn't spoken in years. I didn't know how he'd react to me after all that time."

"I guessed that," Nan said. It pained her to add, "I'm sorry to say that my father never told me about you. In fact, he never told me we had any other family at all.''

''That sounds like Gary.''

''That sounds like you, too, Mother,'' Carla told her pointedly. ''Remember, until Grandmother wrote to me, I didn't have a clue about any family other than you.''

''Yes, that's true,'' Meredith agreed calmly. ''But let's not allow past history to spoil things so soon.'' She turned to Nan. ''How do you like the farm so far, Nan?''

''Oh, I love it,'' she said. ''Who wouldn't?''

Meredith's tone was dry. ''You'd be surprised.''

''But it's so beautiful!''

''I have to confess, my dear, that I've never appreciated its charm. So, tell me. Are you going to stay, like Carla decided to do?''

Nan looked away. ''I . . . haven't decided yet.''

''But that's ridiculous!'' Carla exclaimed. ''You know you want to. And what about Done Cryin'?''

''I know, I know—''

''Well, I think you should stay,'' Carla stated firmly.

''Oh, yes, it's quite obvious what you think,'' Meredith said. ''Since you're still here, toiling away.''

''Don't make it sound like hard labor, Mother.''

''No, just pointless in the extreme.''

''Oh, please. I know you don't appreciate it, but things are changing here. We're getting a lot done.''

Meredith raised a well-sculpted eyebrow. ''Is that so?''

"Yes, it is. Isn't it, Nan?"

"Well, *you're* getting things done," Nan said. "I can't say the same for me. Sometimes I feel like a fifth wheel around here."

"Join the club," Meredith commented. She stubbed out her cigarette. "Well, I'm off."

"You're leaving already?" Carla asked.

"Not, I hope," a new voice said, "before we have a chance to talk."

They all looked toward the doorway, where Octavia was standing. As soon as she saw her mother, Meredith straightened. An immediate edge to her voice, she said, "Talk, Mother? Now, when have we ever done that?"

"There's a first time for everything," Octavia replied calmly. "And since you're here, we do have a few things to discuss."

"And those are . . . ?"

"Why don't you join me in my suite and see?"

"If you insist," Meredith said. She rose gracefully. "I'll see you later, darling," she said to Carla. And then to Nan, "You are staying long enough for us to get to know each other, aren't you?"

"I'll be here at least until Done Cryin's next race."

"And when will that be?"

Eagerly, Nan sat forward. "Next week."

"Well, then. We might have time, after all."

"How long will *you* be here, Mother?" Carla asked.

Meredith smiled. "Oh, I think I'll stay to watch Nan's horse race. I've heard through the grapevine that he's showing a lot of promise."

"What grapevine is that?" Carla asked.

Meredith tut-tutted. "You're so suspicious, daughter of mine. You know I took an interest in your colt. And now that Nan is here after all these years, should I do any less for her? Ta-ta, girls. Wish me luck with Mother."

CARLA HAD some book work to do so Nan took the opportunity to go riding. Incredibly, she hadn't ridden a horse since she'd come to Kentucky. Thinking how ironic that was, since she was here in the heart of the Bluegrass country, she went out to the barn and selected one of the riding horses Wade had told her he kept around just for such occasions.

She chose a bay mare that was more spirited than trained. She'd never ridden English before, but she figured a saddle was a saddle, and sure enough, once she was aboard, it was like coming home. With no clear idea of where she was going, she headed the mare out and up the hill behind the farm.

It was a beautiful afternoon, sunny and clear with just a hint of a breeze. She looked back as she crested the hill and then reined in the mare so she could stare down at the farm. The view was spectacular. Dunleavy Farm was spread out below her, and as she gazed at it, she felt excited and lucky and very glad to be here.

But for how long? she wondered. She couldn't just drift like this, hoping something would come along, or that her decision to stay or go could somehow be indefinitely postponed. It wasn't like her to vacillate, and she didn't like it.

Decide! she told herself. *One way or the other, make a choice!*

But it was so hard to know what to do. She loved it here; she couldn't deny it. But she couldn't stay without having some kind of job; no matter what her grandmother said, it wouldn't be right. She'd never been the kind to depend on anyone, and she wouldn't sponge off anyone, either. If she couldn't make her own way, she'd move on.

Unhappily, she urged the mare forward. She saw the trees up ahead and remembered Carla telling her about a creek there, so she started in that direction. She and the horse were beginning to thread their way through some low-hanging branches, when she heard a noise.

The horse heard it, too. The high-strung Thoroughbred stopped suddenly, ears pricked forward. Nan listened, trying to identify the sound. Incredibly, it sounded like a motorcycle. What would someone on a bike be doing up here?

If she'd been on foot, she might have explored the source of the noise. But as the sound of the bike grew steadily louder, the mare began to get nervous. Nan could feel the horse dancing underneath her, and she knew that if the motorcycle came any closer, she was going to have trouble controlling her mount. She was just turning toward home, when bike and rider burst through the trees, scaring the hell out of the mare and making Nan instantly angry.

"Whoa, now!" she cried as the horse whirled and leaped forward at the same time. The motion was so violent that she was almost unseated. But she'd been riding since childhood, and she wasn't easily thrown. In fact, during those few tense seconds as the animal frantically fought to get away from her, she wasn't worried about herself as much as she was concerned about the horse getting hurt. She was so preoccupied with trying to control the mare that at first she didn't notice that the strident sound of the motorcycle had stopped. But finally, when the horse stopped fighting her and came to a trembling, sweaty halt, she had time to push the hair out of her eyes and look to see who had caused all the commotion.

"Derry!" she exclaimed when she saw the teenager on the bike.

He was wearing a helmet. With a glance down the other side of the hill toward ChangeOver Farm, he turned back to her, his blue eyes hard behind the clear plastic visor. "You're going to tell Dad, aren't you?"

Nan was upset enough to say, "I don't know. I might. You could have caused a serious accident."

"Yeah, well, I'm sorry," he said, not looking sorry at all. "How was I supposed to know you were up here?"

"Isn't this Dunleavy property?"

"Oh, so now you're going to accuse me of trespassing?"

"I'm not accusing you of anything at all. But now that you mention it, just what *are* you doing up here—

and on a motorcycle? Didn't you tell me your father doesn't want you riding a big bike?''

"It's not mine," he said, as if that excused him. "I borrowed it from a friend. I just wanted to see how it felt to ride it. You can understand that, can't you?''

"I suppose, if I try hard enough. But I also understand how both of us could have gotten hurt, not to mention my horse. That's not a dirt bike, Derry. You shouldn't be riding up here. What if you'd flipped it?''

"I know how to ride a bike," he boasted.

"That may be," she said tartly. "But it's also beside the point. This little stunt of yours could have had serious consequences.''

"So you *are* going to tell Dad.''

"No," she said, and waited until relief flooded his face before she added firmly, "You are.''

Instantly, he tensed. "Oh no I'm not.''

"Yes, you are. If your father doesn't want you riding a motorcycle, you shouldn't be riding one, and you know it.''

"It's stupid. He has no right to tell me what to do.''

"He's your father.''

"He's not my jailer.''

"Is that how you think of him?''

"He won't let me do anything.''

"He's concerned about you. He doesn't want you to get hurt.''

"I *told* you, I won't get hurt. I know what I'm doing.''

Nan could see that this wasn't getting them anywhere. She was trying to think of a different approach, when he said, "Aw, just forget it! I should have known you'd take his side."

"I'm not taking anyone's side—"

"The hell you're not!" he shouted, and started the bike with a roar that made Nan's mare leap into the air. Before she could get the horse under control again, Derry had turned the motorcycle around and was heading down the hill—but away from ChangeOver Farm, she noticed.

Cursing, and sweating almost as much as her mount, Nan finally got the horse to calm down. Still angry, she watched Derry disappear. Then she started back the way she had come.

NAN DIDN'T WANT to mention her meeting with Derry until she had a chance to think about it. Fortunately, she didn't have to worry about her sharp-eyed cousin or her grandmother noticing her preoccupation. They were too excited about Wade's arrival home from his trip to California.

Nan and Octavia were out by the paddocks giving Done Roamin' his nightly carrot when the big rig pulled in, and even though Carla had been in the office going over the books, she came flying out of the house before Wade could climb out of the truck. When Nan saw them embrace, she unconsciously sighed.

"They look so right together, don't they?" she said to her grandmother.

"They do, indeed," Octavia agreed. "They've both changed since Carla came to the farm. Falling in love has been good for them."

"I guess they'll get married soon."

"I expect they will. Won't that be something? After all these years, we'll have a wedding here."

"It's the perfect place for a wedding."

"It is, isn't it?" Octavia agreed happily. She took Nan's arm. "Come along. Let's go and find out how things were in California. Maybe Wade will have news."

Nan knew that this was a reference to Octavia's grandson, Seth, and his wife, Honey. Carla had told her that their grandmother had written to all three of them at the same time, but so far, there had been no word from the couple. At the thought, Nan felt guilty. She had postponed answering her grandmother's letter herself. In fact, she still didn't know what she would have done if Carla hadn't called that day and asked if she was coming to visit the farm.

She knew how much Octavia was counting on seeing this last grandchild of hers, so she said encouragingly, "I'm sure Wade will have something good to tell us."

The two lovebirds broke apart when Nan and Octavia approached them. Looking a little dazed from his welcome, Wade said, "Howdy, Mrs. D.... Nan. Boy, it's good to be home."

"So we gathered," Nan teased.

He grinned, pushing his hat back and appearing boyishly handsome. "Hey, I've been gone a long time."

"Not that long," Octavia retorted. But her eyes were twinkling when she looked at the blushing Carla.

"So how was California?" Nan asked.

"Different. Why don't we go in and I'll tell you all about it?"

In the living room, Wade got right to the point. "I know you're interested in what I found out about Seth and Honey, Mrs. D., but I'm afraid it isn't much. They took their string on the fair circuit, as you thought, but they had to leave a while ago when Seth had an accident."

"An accident!" Octavia put her hand on her chest. "Oh, dear. Was it serious?"

"I'm not sure. It seems a horse blew up in the crossties and fell over backward on Seth. I think Seth broke his leg, or something. You know how track people are—they're long on rumors, but sometimes not much on details. Anyway, he and Honey had to lay over, but no one is quite sure where they are."

Nan saw how dejected her grandmother looked and tried to be supportive. "Don't worry. We'll find them."

"I hope so," Octavia said. "There isn't much time."

"What do you mean, not much time?" Carla asked. She exchanged quick glances with Nan. "Grandmother, you're not holding something back from us, are you?"

Octavia laughed. "My goodness, you girls are suspicious. No, I'm just fine, in case that's what you're asking. I just meant that we're running out of prep time for the Derby. Now that Never Done Dreamin' has won all her races down in Florida, she'll be coming back for the big race. I just hope that Seth and Honey will be here to see it.''

Nan knew about the horse with the magical name. She'd even seen tapes of the filly's races. If it hadn't been such a betrayal to her own Done Cryin', she would have said that no horse in the country could touch this last daughter of Done Roamin'. On fast tracks or sloppy, from any post position, once the gate opened and the dark bay filly was free to run, she went to the front. No horse could catch her, and some of the best colts and fillies in the country had tried.

''Won't that be something, when she comes back?'' she said, her face glowing as she thought about it. ''Oh, I can't wait to see her!''

''Yes,'' Carla said brightly before anyone else could mention it. ''If Done Cryin' goes to the Derby, too, we'll have not one but *two* of the horses entered. It will make history, won't it?''

In the short silence that fell, Nan knew that they were all thinking that Carla's magnificent Done Driftin' would have been racing, too, if it hadn't been for the still unexplained ''accident.'' She understood how her cousin must be feeling. ''I'm sorry Done Driftin' won't be there.''

''It's no one's fault that Done Driftin' won't be running,'' Carla said. ''That's just the way it happened.''

''It didn't just happen,'' Wade said. He put an arm around his fiancée. ''But don't worry, we haven't forgotten. We'll find that SOB on the motorcycle and have him arrested.''

''Let's concentrate on Nan's colt and the filly,'' Carla said bravely. ''They'll give the field a run for their money.''

''That they will,'' Nan agreed. ''And when Done Cryin' wins—''

''What makes you think *he'll* win?'' Wade teased, helping to lighten the mood. ''Never Done Dreamin' has never been headed.''

''Aren't we forgetting something?'' Carla asked. She looked slyly at Nan. ''What about Trent Spencer's Majnoon? He's raced well so far.''

Nan didn't want to talk about Trent Spencer. ''It's too soon to be discussing winners,'' she said. ''As I recall, Done Cryin' has a race or two to run before the Derby.''

''And maybe he won't even qualify,'' Wade said, trying to keep a straight face when Nan looked at him indignantly.

Carla laughed and pushed his shoulder. ''Stop teasing her,'' she said. ''Of course, he'll qualify. And when he does—''

''And when he does,'' Nan interjected, ''we'll see what happens. Until then, I'm not even going to think about it.''

No one believed that, not even Nan. They all laughed, and then Wade and Carla went off by themselves while Octavia retired to her room. Not long after that, Nan went upstairs herself. Now that she was alone, she thought again about what had happened with Derry today, and she knew she should call Trent and tell him about the motorcycle. But she wanted to give the boy a chance to confess to his father himself.

"He'll do it," she assured herself as she got ready for bed. "In the meantime—"

In the meantime, she decided to think about Done Cryin', and how much she was looking forward to seeing him race. Would he win? she wondered, and then knew it didn't matter if he did or not. Whatever the outcome, it would be a thrill, one she knew she would never forget.

CHAPTER EIGHT

DONE CRYIN' WON his race. For Nan, it was the thrill of her life to see the colt burst out of the gate and never look back. Not even Majnoon could do more than run in Done Cryin's wake. When it was over, Trent's horse was in second place by three lengths.

The crowd went wild, and cheers erupted again when the spectacular time was posted. Like his brother, Done Driftin', Nan's colt had set a track record.

"I *knew* he'd win!" Carla exclaimed over and over again as she hauled the dazzled Nan down to the winner's circle. "Oh, he's just as good as Done Driftin' was—maybe even better!"

Nan was still in a daze at what she'd seen. Of course, she, too, had never doubted that Done Cryin' would win, but the way he'd run had been something to behold. If ever a horse had wings on his heels, she thought, it was he.

The race over, the grandstand crowd was surging back to the video screens, the snack bar and the betting cages. The throng was so thick that Nan and Carla got separated. Nan was standing on tiptoe trying to spot her cousin's bright hair, when she found herself looking at Trent Spencer.

He was standing about five feet away from her, impatiently waiting for a break in the crowd so he could pass. He looked so angry that Nan drew back. She was wondering if she should turn and walk the other way, when he saw her. As fate would have it, the crowd parted at that moment, leaving them alone.

She couldn't just stand here, so she said, "Hello, Trent."

He looked at her abstractedly. His voice clipped, he said, "Congratulations."

Was he angry because Done Cryin' had beat his Majnoon? "You, too," she said. "Your colt ran a great race."

He was still distracted. Scanning the crowd, obviously looking for someone, he said, "Thanks."

"Is something wrong?" she asked.

He brought his eyes down to her face. "I'm sorry. I thought I saw Derry here a minute ago." He forced a laugh. "But of course that isn't possible, is it? I mean, how would he get here?"

How indeed? Nan wondered uneasily, suddenly remembering one of Derry's methods of transportation. But she didn't want to bring it up just then, so she said, "Well, I'd better—"

"Nan, can we talk?"

She looked at him in surprise. "About what?"

He took her arm, intending to draw her out of the way, but people were wall-to-wall, and they couldn't move.

"Damn it," he muttered, and looked at her again. "I had envisioned a better setting than this madhouse, but I suppose it will have to do. I've been wanting to apologize for Derry's behavior the other night, Nan. And for mine. I'm afraid I didn't make you feel...welcome."

How could she tell him that the problem was just the opposite? She'd felt *too* welcome the other night. In fact, if George hadn't interrupted them, she wasn't sure *what* she would have done.

"Apologies aren't necessary," she said. "I understand that you and Derry are having problems right now. As I saw with my own father, being a single parent is difficult."

"Then you forgive me?"

"There's nothing to forgive."

When he smiled, her heart swelled despite herself. Oblivious to the throng, he clasped her hands. "Good. Then can we just forget it and start all over again?"

She smiled, too. "I'd like that."

"Nan, I—"

"There you are!" Carla exclaimed at that moment. She pushed her way through the crowd and came to Nan's side. "I've been looking all over for you." She realized Trent was standing there and added, "Hi, Trent. Sorry about Majnoon. Better luck next time."

Trent looked wry. "Thanks. But next time I'll make sure he won't be running against Done Cryin'."

Carla laughed. "Good idea. Now, I don't want to rub salt into the wound..."

"Oh, really?"

Carla grinned impudently. "You're right. I can't deny it, I'm delighted. But as you know, Mr. Spencer, that's horse racing. Now, as much as I hate to break this up, I'm going to have to take Nan away. She's wanted . . . elsewhere."

"In the winner's circle, you mean. Go ahead. I'll just follow my second-place finisher to the barn where we belong."

"Why don't you come with us, Trent?" Nan asked. Now that they were friends again, she thought the celebration would be better if he was included.

Regretfully, he said, "I'd like to, but I can't. I came for this race only, then I have to get back to work." He paused. "We still have a lot to talk about. Maybe we can get together for dinner again."

"I'd like that," she said.

"How about tonight?" he asked.

"Tonight? You mean, for dinner?"

"Yes, we could go to the Charter Club—or anywhere else you like."

"The Charter Club is fine," Nan said. She'd never heard of the place.

"About eight?"

Nan nodded, wondering how this had happened. She'd spent all this time convincing herself—or trying to—that she wasn't going to get involved, but now, after a single apology, she was accepting another date with him.

"Well, I'm glad *that's* taken care of," Carla murmured after Trent left and they started toward the winner's circle once more.

Nan wouldn't look at her. "I don't know what you mean."

"Don't act so innocent. You've been moping around, but now there's a smile on your face that won't quit. I may be slow, but that glow seems to have something to do with Trent."

"Ridiculous," Nan said haughtily. "I'm just thrilled that Done Cryin' won his race."

Fortunately for the red-faced Nan, Carla didn't have a chance to say more—then. In the winner's circle, Ian McKenzie, the jockey, was just bringing the victorious Done Cryin' back. As though he knew what he'd done, the big bay colt was blowing and jigging around so much that two grooms had to hold him. At the sight, Nan reached up to give the horse's sweaty neck a heartfelt pat.

"You were wonderful," she said, while the photographer positioned everyone for the win picture. "You, too," she said to Ian, who grinned.

Done Cryin' snorted as though he, for one, had never doubted it.

NAN WAS ECSTATIC all the way to the farm. In her mind's eye, she saw the race a dozen times. In fact, she was so bedazzled and bemused that Carla finally laughed at her.

"Hey, come back to earth, cousin!" Carla exclaimed. "It was only a race."

"Yes, but he set a track record," Nan said dreamily. "Just like he did twice last year."

"Oh, I see you've already looked up his stats."

"Yes, I did. And did you know that he won the Woodview Memorial Juvenile just like his sire did? Of course," she conceded, "Done Driftin's times were just as impressive as a two-year-old's. And as for Never Done Dreamin'..."

Carla looked at her in amusement as Nan rattled off statistics she had memorized about the Dunleavy horses. But finally, she held up a hand to halt the flow.

"Whoa!" she said. "Give mercy. No wonder Trent Spencer said you sound like a walking encyclopedia of racing material."

"He said that?"

"He surely did."

"When?" she asked.

"Oh, the other day when he called about something to do with the farm."

"What else did he say?"

"So you're interested again, are you?" Carla said slyly. "I thought you didn't like Trent."

"Did I say that?"

"Well, you did mention that you and he had exchanged a few words about Derry the other night."

"That's forgotten now. He apologized today."

"Oh, I see. Then by your accepting his dinner invitation, am I to assume that all is forgiven?"

"I don't know. I'll have to see how it goes."

"Well, I knew as soon as I saw those great cheek-bones and those big green eyes of yours that you'd be trouble. I'll bet Trent knew it, too."

"I doubt it," Nan said dryly. "Considering how we met."

"That was an interesting touch, I have to admit. But I'll bet he saw possibilities even then. And you probably did, too."

Nan looked at her indignantly. "How can you say that? Besides, I've never really liked his type."

"And what type is that?"

"Oh, you know, the kind who thinks money can solve all problems."

"What makes you think he believes that?"

"Well, you should see his house—"

"I have."

Nan hadn't realized how she sounded until she saw her cousin smile. Ashamed of herself, she said, "I didn't mean—"

"Yes, you did," Carla said cheerfully. "And you're right. There are people like that. I've known some of them. In fact, I used to *be* one of them."

"No, not you."

"Oh, yes, me. But hopefully, I've learned a few things since I came to Dunleavy Farm. And one of them is that Trent isn't like that, Nan. He's kind and honest."

Nan didn't want to hear Carla extol Trent Spencer's qualities; it would make it even more difficult for her to keep her distance. Grumpily, she said, "You make him sound like an Eagle Scout."

"I mean it. I've told you how he arranged those loans for the farm. If he hadn't helped, things would be pretty bleak about now."

"That's what he does. It's his job."

"Yes, but in our case, he wouldn't take anything for it."

"So what? He already has more than he needs."

"Does he?" Carla asked.

Nan was silent a moment. Then she said, "We're talking about more than money here, aren't we?"

"You tell me. Why are you so hesitant about him, Nan? You know you like him—no, that you're already pretty fond of him. And we both know that he's falling head over heels for you."

"What? We don't know that!"

"Yes, we do. It's obvious—especially today."

"He was just glad we're friends again."

"Oh, really? And what about you?"

"I'm glad, too."

"Is that all?"

"I don't know." Nan looked out the window. "I *do* like him. But I'm not sure it would ever work."

"Why not?" Carla looked at her in exasperation. "Don't tell me it's his money!"

"That's part of it but not everything."

"Then, what?"

"It's Derry."

"Derry! You mean because he's been such a brat lately? He's a teenager, Nan. That should explain everything."

Nan hadn't told Carla about meeting Derry on the hill behind the farm the day he'd borrowed the motorcycle. What purpose would it serve? she'd asked herself. She didn't want Carla to get the wrong impression about the boy, especially when she was sure—wasn't she?—that he was just stretching his wings, acting like a typical teenager.

But it wasn't only the problem with Derry and the motorcycle that ate away at her; it was Trent's intractable manner involving his son. He'd dismissed everything she'd said, or tried to say, about Derry; he'd closed her off or shut her down when she'd tried to talk to him about his son—after he'd asked her to help. She knew that if she and Trent were to become more than friends, he'd have to be more open about his son with her. He'd have to be willing to hear her out.

"I'M GLAD you agreed to come," Trent said when they got to the restaurant and were seated. There was a candle in a round holder on the table; in the flickering light, he looked more handsome than ever.

"I'm glad, too," she said. She forced her gaze away from him and looked around the room. "This is a lovely place."

"I'm glad you're here to share it with me."

"So am I," she said with a smile. "Are you sure you aren't mad at me over Done Cryin's victory today?"

"No, not at all. As Carla so succinctly pointed out, that's horse racing. Those of us who are involved just have to accept that unless it's a dead heat, there's only one first-place finisher in every race." He smiled back at her. "If it had to be any horse, I'm glad it was Done Cryin'. I know what a thrill it was for you."

"I have to admit, I've always loved watching the horses run. But today was an experience I'll never forget."

"None of us forget the first time we witness our horse win a race."

This seemed a safe enough subject, so she relaxed. "You know, I was really surprised when Carla told me the number of people involved in racing who don't even ride."

"Or know how to," he added. "But that reminds me. Were you riding in the hills behind Dunleavy the other day?"

Instantly, she tensed again. Why were they suddenly talking about this? How much did he know about her meeting Derry the day she'd gone riding? This was her cue to mention it, she knew, but she didn't want to get into a quarrel, not when things seemed to be going so well.

"Yes, I was in that vicinity," she said cautiously. "Why?"

"I was doing some work in the office at home and thought I heard a motorcycle going that way."

"A...motorcycle?"

"Yes." He looked grim for a moment, then he forced a smile. "But if you were up there and didn't see anything, I was probably mistaken. Anyway, who would risk riding there? Not only is it private property, but no one I know would take a bike out there for fear of scaring the horses."

Damn, Derry didn't tell his father. *Maybe I should,* she thought, then rejected the idea. *It has to come from Derry or things will just get worse. I'll speak to the boy about it.*

To Trent, she simply nodded. "Yes, that's right."

Fortunately for her, the waiter came just then to take their orders. After the man had gone, Nan steered the conversation away from horses and motorcycles. "Grandmother says that you're responsible for saving the farm."

Trent laughed. "I wouldn't go that far. I only arranged a little financing. It's what I do, and I was glad to help."

"Carla told me you were an...investment banker? I'm not sure I know what that is."

"It's someone who puts people with money and no imagination together with people who have imagination and no money."

"How did you get into that?"

"I don't know, I just gravitated toward it. I always had a head for figures, and when I discovered that I also had a talent, not necessarily for making money, but for seeing how it could be made, I decided to put the two together."

"Very successfully, too."

"I've been lucky," he said with a deprecating shrug.

"So was the farm, when you decided to help out."

"Well, as I told your cousin, I owe a debt of gratitude to Octavia. She accepted the Spencers into racing when no one else around here would. Before that, my father and grandfather were just...merchants."

"What's wrong with that?"

"Nothing at all. But there are tradespeople, and then there are racing people. In the old days, especially in these parts, it was 'never the twain shall meet.'"

"That's silly."

"I agree. But it's not quite like that now. Economics has made strange bedfellows of us all."

"*That's* certainly true," Nan said, before she thought. She could feel herself reddening as she hastily added, "I mean—"

"I know what you meant." Before she realized what he was about to do, he placed a hand over hers. "Nan, you seem tense. Is something wrong?"

"Nothing's wrong," she said. "It's just that things have been so exciting lately, I'm feeling a little overwhelmed. It's all so different from my life in Montana."

"From what I've seen, you certainly seem to fit right in at Dunleavy Farm. And now that your horse has won—"

"Done Cryin' isn't really my horse."

Surprised, he said, "But I thought Octavia gave him to you."

"She wants to."

"You don't sound very happy about it."

"It's not that. Owning a horse like that is something I've dreamed about all my life, but I can't... accept a gift like that."

"Why not?"

"Because I haven't done anything to deserve it."

"But you're her granddaughter!"

"And my father was Octavia's son. He did everything he could to distance himself from his family. In fact, he vehemently denied there was even the remotest tie to anyone from Dunleavy Farm."

"That was his problem, not yours."

"It's not that simple."

He withdrew his hand and sat back, his dark eyes studying her face. His scrutiny made her nervous, and she quickly reached for her water glass. He was still staring at her when she put the glass down, and she asked, "Why are you looking at me like that?"

"I wasn't looking at you any way. Or... yes, I was. I was thinking..." He leaned forward suddenly. Startled by the quick movement, she pulled back. The candle on the table flickered, causing little flames to dance in the dark depths of his eyes. Despite herself, she felt mesmerized.

Softly, he said, "I was thinking how lovely you look tonight." He reached for her hand. She wanted to withdraw it, but she seemed helpless to do so. His fingers curled over hers. "I was thinking how much I wanted to kiss you."

He hadn't moved, but as though something was tugging her forward, she felt herself bending toward him. She couldn't take her eyes off his face. The desire she had tried so hard to ignore, the longing she felt for him overwhelmed her; the need to be in his arms could no longer be denied. It demanded release like a breath held too long. The air seemed electric with sudden tension; goose bumps rippled down her arms.

And then the waiter appeared.

"Will there be anything else, sir?" the man asked.

Just like that, the mood vanished. Nan came back to her senses at the same time that Trent looked up at the intruder. If she hadn't felt a lingering of that spell, she would have laughed at Trent's expression. *If looks could kill*, she thought, *the waiter would be pushing up daisies*.

"Nan?" Trent asked.

"No, thank you," she said. She hadn't realized until then that her plate had been taken away, and that she was sitting there with a half-finished cup of coffee in front of her. Had she eaten dessert? Had she even touched her dinner? She couldn't remember doing either. "I've had enough."

Trent apparently felt the same, for a few minutes later, they were on their way out of the restaurant. As he took her arm, Nan shivered.

"Are you cold?" he asked. It was a mild night, almost warm, and he had a right to sound surprised.

"No, I'm fine. Thanks for dinner. It was—"

She broke off at the look in his eyes. They were standing in the middle of the parking lot, the light from a dozen halogen lamps shining down on them, pinning them in an orange glow. She'd never seen him look more handsome.

"Nan," he said. "We didn't talk about...us."

"Trent, I—"

He put his arms around her and pulled her close. Quietly, he said, "You can't deny that something is happening here, can you?"

Yes! her mind shrieked. But her mouth answered, "No, I can't. But Trent—"

Gently, he pulled her closer. "Then kiss me..."

With her last ounce of common sense, she tried to pull back. "Trent, this is...I can't...I don't want..."

His mouth covered hers, drowning out her half-hearted protests. The instant she felt the touch of his warm lips, she was lost. She'd known she would be; she'd tried to fight it all night. But right there in the parking lot, she succumbed, leaning against him, pressing her body tightly into his, opening her mouth to kiss him more deeply, wishing they were anywhere but here.

"Umm...excuse me," someone said.

With a gasp, they pulled apart. An older couple was standing behind them, and the man gestured apologetically with his keys. "I'm sorry, but you're blocking my car."

Nan looked at the big Lincoln the man indicated. Sure enough, they were standing right behind it. Her face flaming, she sprang back. "I'm so sorry."

"That's all right, dear," the woman said. "It's hard to believe, but we were young once ourselves."

Nan was so embarrassed, she couldn't look at Trent. But he laughed easily and said, "I'm glad you understand."

The woman gave him an approving look. "I have to say, I don't blame her a bit."

"Now, Martha," her husband said. But he looked at Nan and whispered to her, "I have to tell you, though. I'm a mite envious of your fella myself."

Nan smiled at the compliment, but as soon as the couple climbed in their car and drove away, she headed toward Trent's car, which was parked a few spaces down. She wanted to get out of here. After what had happened a moment ago, it was obvious that she couldn't trust herself. Who knew what she might have done if she and Trent hadn't been interrupted?

"What must they have thought?" she murmured.

"Who cares?" Trent said. His eyes twinkled. "Besides, that old guy was right to be envious. I wish I could invite you to come home with me, but Derry is there tonight."

Thank God, Nan thought, and said, "That's all right. It's been a long day, and . . ."

"And what?" He touched her face, and she closed her eyes.

She couldn't pretend any longer; it was futile to try to fool herself. He was right. Something *was* happening between them; she'd be crazy to deny it. But she'd been impulsive before; she wanted to move more slowly now—to make sure that this was right.

"Trent, I'm so... Can we take it one step at a time?"

He pulled her to him again. This time, his kiss was feather-light. "We can take it any way you like," he whispered. "Just as long as we take the first step."

CHAPTER NINE

OCTAVIA'S PARTY took place on a perfect Kentucky night. The moon was full, the air was soft and sweet and the sky had a glow about it that other twilights lacked.

Of course, Nan thought nervously as she rubbed her hands together that night, the glow could be due to the electric torches and lanterns lining both sides of the driveway. If she hadn't been so apprehensive about meeting all those strangers in a few minutes, she would have enjoyed the sight. It was as though a thousand giant fireflies had joined hands to light the way to the house. She'd never seen anything like it.

She hadn't experienced anything like the past few days, either. Work crews had come to mow and clip and spruce up the outside, while an army of hired help cleaned the house from top to bottom. Everything gleamed and sparkled and shone, even the horses.

Nan had felt out of place amidst all the activity. She knew how to cook, but the kitchen was always full, presided over by a beaming Teresa, who had proudly declared that this was like the "old days" when Dunleavy parties were the talk of Kentucky.

Nor had she really been needed in the barns, where stalls were being cleaned and walls swept down and all the horses were being groomed within an inch of their lives. She felt more comfortable out there than in the house, but she had hardly picked up a brush before her cousin had found her.

"There you are!" Carla had called. "I've been looking all over for you. What are you doing out here?"

"I felt in the way, so I thought I'd come and help with the horses."

"Someone else can do that," Carla said firmly, taking the brush out of her hand. "We're going shopping."

"Shopping!" She had hoped that Carla would forget that plan. She tried to pull back. "Carla, I can't go!"

"Why not?"

"Because I...I..." She couldn't use lack of money as an excuse not to go. She knew Carla well enough by this time to know that her cousin would offer to buy her a dress, but she wasn't going to accept charity. All she had for the party were the black slacks and white blouse with the scarf cummerbund she'd worn the first night here, but it would have to do. She had to be careful with the funds she had; until she decided how to support herself, she had to plan ahead.

"I don't want to shop," she said. "There's too much to do here."

"Nonsense," Carla declared. "We're just in the way. And you won't have to buy anything if you don't want to. All you have to do is help me find something new for the party."

Nan thought of the evening gowns she had glimpsed in Carla's closet. "But you have dozens of things."

Airily, Carla waved her hand. "None of them are right. Now, are you coming or not?"

It seemed she had no choice. Carla had barely given her time to change into something a little more suitable for a shopping trip before they were on their way into town. During the drive, Carla had said casually, "You know, if *my* horse had recently won a big purse like Done Cryin' did, I'd celebrate a little. Maybe buy a new dress, and some shoes to go with it, have a facial— something!"

Nan had never had a facial in her life. She didn't think she'd care for one, either. She didn't like the idea of some stranger peering at her through a microscope and then fussing over her with creams and gels and lotions she wouldn't have bought even if she could have afforded them.

But Carla's nonchalant mention of the racing purse had caught her attention and she'd said, "That money isn't mine."

"Of course it is. Done Cryin' is your horse, isn't he?"

"Not yet. I haven't been here for a month."

"That doesn't mean anything. You know Grandmother would give him to you in an instant."

"I don't want her just to *give* him to me. It wouldn't be right to take him if I couldn't afford his training or upkeep. And the way things are, I don't know if, or when, I'd be able to."

Carla took her eyes off the road long enough to say, "You're just as proud and stubborn as the rest of us Dunleavys seem to be. Of *course* you can pay for his training. Don't you realize how much money that horse just won?"

Embarrassed, Nan said, "I never thought to ask."

Carla rolled her eyes. "Well, trust me. It's enough to pay for his training, and then some."

"But that money rightfully belongs to Grandmother. She's the one who raised the horse and absorbed all the expenses so far."

"Well, that's true. But she did it for you." Carla looked at her again. "Grandmother wants you to have the horse, Nan. Why don't you make her happy by accepting her gift? It's her way of . . . of making up for all the years lost."

Nan was silent a moment. Then she said, "Did you have second thoughts when Grandmother wanted you to accept Done Driftin'?"

"Second and third and fourth thoughts. But the first time I saw him, I fell in love with that horse. In fact, I wanted him so badly that I made the mistake of offering to *buy* him." Carla laughed ruefully at the memory. "Was Grandmother angry at that! She told me in no uncertain terms that while I might fancy myself a woman of the world, I had a lot to learn about the art of gracious acceptance."

"So what did you do?"

"I accepted the horse," Carla said, and smiled wickedly. "And decided I was going to repay Grandmother in another way."

"By taking over all the farm accounts," Nan said. "Well, that's fine for you, Carla. But what can I do for her?"

"You came, didn't you? That's a start."

"It's not enough. Besides, I can't think of anything I could do for Grandmother that isn't already being done."

"Have you asked her about that? She's delighted that you're here. She wants you to stay, Nan. You know that."

"I know."

"We'll give it some thought," Carla said. "But in the meantime, we're here. Let's go shopping!"

And go shopping, they did. To Nan's dismay, she was no match for Carla's enthusiasm and persuasive powers.

"It's *perfect* for you!" Carla exclaimed, after she'd practically manhandled Nan into trying on a froth of forest-green satin and gold lace. Nan wanted to see the price tag, but Carla whispered that places like this boutique didn't have them.

"Then what are we *doing* here?" Nan whispered back, appalled. She wanted to grab her jeans and run, but Carla was blocking the doorway to the dressing room.

"*This* is what we're doing here," Carla said, and turned Nan to face the mirror.

For a few seconds, Nan didn't recognize the lovely creature who stared back at her. Her eyes widened. The form-fitting deep green bodice made her waist look a mere hand span, while the bell-shaped knee-length gold lace skirt swayed gracefully at the slightest movement. Her expression marveling, she looked at Carla, who grinned.

"Like it?" Carla asked.

"It's beautiful, but—"

"No buts," Carla said briskly. She gestured to the hovering sales assistant. "We'll take it. Put it on my account, please. And yes, Nan," she said as Nan opened her mouth to object, "you can pay me back when we get home. Right now, as soon as you've changed, we're going to look for shoes!"

Now the big night was here, and Nan was supposed to be waiting in the front room with the rest of the family to greet the first guests as they arrived. She wasn't even dressed, and the way her hands were shaking, it didn't look as though she was going to be able to manage doing it by herself.

She had to do it, she thought. She had the dress, the shoes, everything she needed—except the courage to go downstairs and face all those strangers.

"What's the matter with you?" she asked herself fiercely. She couldn't understand it. At the Saddleback, she'd never had any trouble confronting strangers; she'd been required to greet newcomers to the ranch every week from early spring to late fall.

But this was different. In Montana, she'd been in her element; in Kentucky, she felt out of place. Carla and her grandmother and Wade—even her aunt Meredith in her own way—had done everything possible to make Nan feel welcome, but she couldn't rid herself of the feeling that she would always be a misplaced Montana girl.

Pull yourself together, Nan Dunleavy, she told herself. She knew she couldn't cower in her room all night. Her grandmother was expecting her to join the party. She could pretend for one night. All she had to do was get through this evening and everything would be all right.

She had finished dressing and was just adding the last touches to her makeup and hair, when she paused with the lipstick halfway to her mouth. She was fooling herself, wasn't she? she thought, staring at her wide-eyed reflection in the mirror. The real reason she felt so reluctant tonight was that she didn't want to face one particular guest.

Slowly, she recapped the lipstick. How *did* she feel about Trent? She wanted to confide in Carla, but every time she tried, she couldn't find the words. What was she going to say? That she'd developed some kind of schoolgirl crush on Trent Spencer? It sounded ridiculous even to her. Besides, she knew it was no crush.

Then what is it? she asked the pale reflection in the mirror. Was she in love? *Falling* in love? But how could it happen so fast? She hardly knew Trent; she knew even less about his marriage to Derry's mother. For that matter, she didn't know much about his son—and it seemed that if Trent had his choice, she never would. And that was a problem. How could they have a relationship that didn't include his only son?

Maybe she should just leave, she thought. It would make everything so much simpler. But when she looked around the room, at the floral and striped wallpaper, and the matching comforter on the bed, and the beautiful old armoire in the corner, she wondered how she could ever leave Dunleavy Farm now.

But it wasn't the room, she knew, getting up from the dressing table and wandering over to the window so she could look out. It was this place, the farm where her father had grown up. The ranch in Montana had its own history for her, but there was something special about this land. Her grandmother was part of it. So was the stallion Done Roamin', who never failed to inspire awe in her, and the brave Done Driftin', who would never reach his racing potential. And, of course, Done Cryin'.

But it was also Carla, and her aunt Meredith, and Wade. *They* were all family to her now, and the thought of moving on left her with a physical pang. The only thing that could possibly make this existence any better was if Yolanda was here to share all this with her.

At the thought, she sighed. Always mindful of her dwindling funds, she had started to write a letter to Yolanda the other day, but then had called, after all. She hadn't talked to Yolanda since she'd arrived, and she needed to hear that calm, quiet voice.

"Hi," she'd said, when Yolanda answered the phone at Minnie Joss's house. "It's Nan. How are you?"

"Is that really you?" Yolanda exclaimed. Nan could almost see her placing a hand on her chest, a gesture she used when she was surprised or startled, or wanted to make a point. "Oh, my goodness. Why are you calling? Is something wrong?"

Nan had laughed. "Nothing's wrong. I just wanted to talk to you. The last time I wrote, Done Cryin' hadn't run yet. But he raced a few days ago and...he won! Isn't that wonderful?"

"It certainly is. My, my. It's hard to believe after all your studying of Thoroughbreds that you actually own a racehorse."

"Well, I haven't decided if I'm going to take him," she reminded Yolanda. "After all, he's very valuable, you know. I'm not sure Grandmother should give me such an expensive gift."

"From what you've said in your letters, I'd say that your grandmother knows what she's doing," Yolanda said dryly. "She sounds like she's got a lot on the ball."

"Oh, she does," Nan agreed. "In fact, she's giving a big party soon. It makes anything we ever threw at the Saddleback pale in comparison."

Yolanda knew her too well. There must have been something in her voice, for the woman said, "You don't sound too happy about this party."

There was no sense in denying it. "I wish I didn't have to go," Nan said honestly. "To tell the truth, I still don't feel I fit in too well with these people. Oh, not

Grandmother and Carla and Wade. But . . . other people.''

Yolanda had immediately bristled. "Has anyone said anything to you? Because if they have, you just tell them right back that you're every bit as good as they are— better! And if they don't believe you, well, you just send them to me and I'll tell them flat out. Why, I never heard such a thing! Who do they think they are down there?''

"Hold on," Nan said, laughing again and feeling better already. "Before you get your dander up, let me say that everyone here couldn't have been more welcoming. It's *me* who feels out of place.''

"Now, why is that?" Yolanda demanded. "Why, you've got more character in your little finger than most people develop in a lifetime!''

"Thanks, but what I need more than character is a job, Yolanda. I've sponged off my grandmother long enough.''

"You're not sponging. You're visiting—at her invitation, I might add.''

"But I can't be a perennial visitor. Remember the old saying about overstaying one's welcome?''

"Lord, you're exactly like your father—stiff-necked with pride.''

"That's what Carla says. And maybe you're both right. But I can't help it.''

"So, what are you going to do?''

"I don't know yet.''

"Well, look here—and don't interrupt me now, I know how you are. I've got a little money put aside—"

"Oh, no—"

"I told you not to interrupt me. Now, I've been playing some bingo down at the church and I've won quite a tidy sum. And now that I'm sharing expenses with Minnie, I don't need much. After all, I've got Mac's pension, plus the social security income. So why don't you let me send you a little to help you get by—at least until you decide what you're going to do. I won't give it to you. We'll call it a loan."

Touched because she knew Yolanda was even more careful with her pennies than she herself was, Nan said, "I appreciate the offer, Yolanda, I really do. But you know I can't accept it. Besides, I've got enough to last a while. I'm not quite in the poorhouse yet. I even had enough to buy a dress."

"A dress?"

"Don't sound so shocked," Nan said with a laugh. "I've owned dresses before. Although, I have to admit, nothing as nice as this. No one is going to recognize me—especially not Trent."

She hadn't meant to mention Trent Spencer; she knew that Yolanda would immediately pick up on it, and she did.

"Trent?" Yolanda said, right on cue. "Now, I don't believe I've heard you talk about *him*."

"There's really nothing to tell, so don't get your antennas waving, like you always do. He's just a neighbor, nobody special."

"Oh, so it's like that, then."

"It's not like anything! We're just friends."

"I see."

Yolanda wasn't convinced, Nan could tell. She knew she'd just dig herself in deeper if she carried on, so she said, "I guess I'd better go. You take care of yourself now."

"Well, have a good time at that party, honey. And, even though I know it was expensive, I did so enjoy talking to you."

"Don't worry about the expense. It was worth it. I miss you, Yolanda."

"I miss you, too."

Reluctantly, Nan had hung up. Now it was party time, and already, she was late. She stopped to give herself a last check in the mirror, blotted the lipstick and went downstairs.

Wouldn't you know, she thought, that the first person she'd catch sight of would be Trent Spencer.

TRENT WAS JUST COMING in the front door when he saw Nan. She was standing by the steps. He couldn't take his eyes off the vision in green and gold lace. Never had he imagined that Nan Dunleavy could look like that!

"Good evening, Trent," a voice said as he stood staring at Nan. "Can I get you something to drink?"

He jerked his glance away, right into Carla's laughing green eyes. She had obviously seen him gazing at her cousin like an awestruck idiot. To his annoyance, she didn't even bother trying to hide her amusement.

"No, thank you," he said, dignified. "I just got here and have to pay my respects to your grandmother."

Carla glanced in her cousin's direction, then back at him. "Don't forget Nan," she purred. "Doesn't she look lovely tonight?"

He wasn't going to fall into that trap. Nonchalantly, he said, "Yes, she does. You're looking lovely yourself."

"Why, thank you, kind sir," she said throatily, laughter filling her eyes again. "I see you're alone. What a coincidence. So is my cousin." Before he could stop her, she raised her voice slightly. "Nan? Would you come here a minute, please? Look who just came in."

As Nan started toward them, Trent again couldn't take his eyes off her. It wasn't simply the dress, he decided, or the way her high heels showed her slim, shapely legs to advantage; the clothes simply accentuated how beautiful she was. Even more so than the night she'd come to dinner at his house. *Then,* she had looked soft and feminine. *Tonight* she looked like a siren.

And what had she done to her hair? he wondered. Or her eyes, or her mouth? She was still Nan, all right, but this new, different side of her dazzled him. What was she doing to him?

"Good evening, Trent," she said.

Even her voice sounded different, he thought distractedly. It was lower, huskier…sexier than usual. With an effort, he pulled himself together.

"Good evening," he managed to say, hoping he didn't sound like a cretin. "You look beautiful tonight."

Nan shot a glance at Carla, who smiled knowingly. "Thanks. You look very handsome yourself."

He was wearing a tux; it was nothing compared to the way her shoulders rose out of that green and gold dress, or how tiny her waist looked.

"Well," Carla said, sounding as if she was trying to smother another laugh. "Since you two are such scintillating conversationalists, I'll leave you. I have to circulate for a while. Then it's your turn, Nan."

To Trent's dismay, Nan said, "Let me come with you. I haven't seen Grandmother yet, and I want to make sure she's not overdoing it."

Trent didn't want to let her go. If she disappeared into the growing crowd, he might not find her again—or worse, someone else would. He had to talk to her before she got away. He wanted to say... what?

He didn't know. He'd think of it when the time came. Right now, he said quickly, "I haven't spoken to Octavia yet, either. Why don't I go with you?"

"All right."

They began to thread their way through the guests to the living room. He'd hoped Octavia would be here, sitting in her favorite chair, and she was. Like a queen, she was holding sway, but when she saw them, she smiled and gestured them closer.

"There you are! Nan, darling, how beautiful you look!" Octavia said as Nan bent down to give her a quick kiss. "And Trent—" She held out a hand for him to take. "Thank you for coming. Oh, I do love social occasions! Isn't it nice to see everyone here again?"

"It is indeed, Octavia," he agreed. "It's been a while, but I still remember how famous Dunleavy Farm was for its parties."

"Those were the days, weren't they? But perhaps they'll come again, now that two of my grandchildren are going to live here. Isn't that right, Nan?"

"Oh, well, Grandmother, I—"

"I'm sorry to interrupt you, my dear, but I see another old friend coming in. Will you excuse me? Trent, make sure you and Nan find some champagne. I want everyone to enjoy themselves tonight."

Octavia's friend had brought a crowd, and as the group surged toward the tiny matriarch, Trent and Nan were nudged out of the way. When they found themselves up against the bar that had been set up at one end of the big room, Trent took the opportunity to ask for two flutes of champagne. He took a glass and handed her the other.

"It's a little close in here," he said. "Why don't we go outside where it's easier to breathe?"

Nan immediately looked anxious. "I shouldn't," she said. "Like Carla, I'm supposed to be circulating."

"I think Carla can handle things for a while. If you don't mind, I'd like to talk to you about something."

"What?"

"Not here."

But the porch was almost as packed as the house, and as he looked over the throng, he despaired. How was he going to talk to Nan alone?

Then he saw the shadowed gazebo in the rose garden to the side. "Let's go over there," he said.

Nan had obviously had enough of being herded about as though she had no mind of her own. "Trent, what's this about?"

"Nothing. I just want to talk to you alone."

Nan searched his face with those lovely green eyes. Then, with the tiniest smile, she said, "I don't think Grandmother will mind if we slip away for a few minutes. But only that, all right?"

"Only a few. I promise."

Nan led the way. As Trent followed her through the darkened garden to the white latticed gazebo in the center, the scent of early roses wafted up on the night air, adding to the fairy-tale atmosphere. It was one of those beautiful Kentucky evenings where everything came together to make it seem almost like heaven.

Or did he just feel this way because he had Nan to himself for the next few minutes? His pulse quickened at the thought, and before he gave in to the urge to take her in his arms and kiss her senseless, he took a hefty swallow from his glass. He wasn't much of a drinker, but tonight he wished he had something stronger than champagne.

The gazebo was dark and quiet, far enough away from the house so that the voices and the laughter and the music became a muted part of the background.

They climbed the three steps of the small structure and sat down. By chance or coincidence, a shaft of moonlight fell on Nan's face, making her look ethereal. Her eyes sparkled, and there was a shine on her lips that was increasingly difficult to resist.

I'm going to do something stupid, he thought. Before he could, he said, "I enjoyed dinner the other night."

She looked down. "So did I."

The sight of her made him forget just about everything else. Unable to think, hardly remembering to breathe, he said fatuously, "We'll have to do it again."

"Yes," she said softly.

The urge to take her into his arms and kiss her, to hold her tightly to him so that he could feel every inch of that slim, lithe body, was becoming irresistible. Desire for her made him ache; he knew that they had to get back to the party.

"Well, I guess we should—"

Just then, a shadow appeared on the gazebo stairs and a lazy voice drawled, "Oh, I should have remembered what a secret hideaway this is. Am I interrupting anything?"

"Aunt Meredith!"

Trent thought he heard something in Nan's voice, but before he could think what it was, Meredith came up the last step and sat down languidly on one of the benches. She was wearing a gown made of a silvery material; it caught what light there was and made her appear to shimmer.

"Hello, Meredith," Trent said. "I didn't know you were back."

"Not to stay, I can assure you." In the dark, it was difficult to see Meredith's face, but he could hear that note of bored amusement in her tone that had always irritated him. Her body shifted to face Nan. "I only came to see my niece, and to learn how *this* story ends. If it's anything like what happened to Carla, my mother and Dunleavy Farm will have captured yet another victim."

"Aunt Meredith!" Nan was shocked. "How can you say such a thing?"

"Just joking, darling. I'm sure Carla must have told you by now about my somewhat jaded sense of humor. I didn't mean anything by it."

Nan chose not to respond to her aunt's comment. Instead she said, "I haven't seen much of you, Aunt Meredith."

"No, I've been trying to keep out of the way." Meredith must have realized how clipped she sounded, for she forced a laugh. "And I do have friends to visit. Sometimes I stay overnight. It's easier on everyone that way."

Trent didn't reply to that. He had been a young child when Meredith Dunleavy had scandalized Lexington's racing elite by running off with the farm manager here. He knew there had been bad blood between Meredith and her mother ever since. He'd been surprised when Meredith had shown up a couple of months ago to see

Carla; until then, it had been thirty-five years since she'd set foot on Dunleavy property.

"And because I've been . . . absent," Meredith went on, "I never had the chance to congratulate you on your win the other day. I hear Done Cryin' ran a fine race."

"He did. It was quite a thrill," Nan said. "Trent's Majnoon ran well, too."

The silver sparkles on Meredith's gown glittered. "Then congratulations are in order for you, too, Trent."

"Thank you, Meredith," Trent said, wondering why she was so tense, or if it was just her manner. "I take it you weren't at the track?"

"Me?" She laughed nervously again. "Oh, I rarely go to the races, Trent. It's an aversion I developed when I was young and Mother insisted we all troop to the track whenever a Dunleavy horse was racing."

"I see," he said neutrally. "That's too bad."

"Oh, I don't know. We all have different interests, don't we? It's what makes the world go round, I guess."

Nan spoke up. "It's nice that you came to the party."

Meredith seemed to relax. "Only because Carla asked me to. But never fear. I intend to leave not long after I make an obligatory appearance."

"You're leaving so soon?"

"Just the party. Mother won't get rid of me quite so easily. Now that I'm here, I'd like to watch your colt race. He is showing a lot of promise, isn't he? Soon, the Derby will be here and—oh, I'm sorry, Trent. I suppose your colt is entered, too?"

"Yes, but after what happened the other day, I'm not sure that anyone is going to catch Done Cryin'."

"True." Meredith looked at Nan. Suddenly sounding intense, she said, "You'll have to tell Dwight to keep a close eye on that horse. You never know what can happen."

Nan was startled. "What do you mean?"

"Mean?" Meredith seemed to catch herself. "Well, of course I'm talking about Done Driftin'. We wouldn't want what happened to him to happen to your colt, would we?"

Nan shuddered. "No, we wouldn't."

"Well, then. I'll be seeing you." Sounding relieved—and something else, Trent thought uneasily—Meredith lifted a graceful hand in farewell and headed toward the house.

Left alone, Nan and Trent looked at each other. Then he said, "Do you have any idea what *that* was all about?"

Nan shook her head. "I don't know Aunt Meredith well enough to say."

Trent watched Meredith's figure disappear. Then he turned to Nan. It was a beautiful night, he was with a beautiful woman and—for a few minutes, at least—they were alone in the dark. Desire for her flooded through him like a river over a broken dam, and before he knew it, he was reaching for her, pulling her tenderly toward him. She was so small, so delicate, he thought in wonder. He commanded himself to be gentle, but the instant he felt her body against his, he began to tremble.

The intensity of his feelings took over, and all he could think of was how much he wanted to make love to her right here on the gazebo floor.

"Nan," he whispered.

She didn't answer, but raised her arms and pulled his head down to hers. The touch of her soft lips was the most exquisite sensation he had ever experienced. He lingered there for a moment, savoring the sweet taste of her, but she was like a flower opening in his arms, and when he pressed harder and she opened her mouth and their tongues met, he knew beyond a doubt that he was losing his heart, and everything else, to her.

CHAPTER TEN

"DO YOU REALLY feel useless here?" Carla asked Nan the morning after the party.

Nan should have known her cousin would remember that remark. "Well, I'm used to working," she said. "At the Saddleback, there was always something to do. But here..." She spread her hands. "I probably wouldn't be any use, anyway. I don't know much about Kentucky farms—"

"But you know about horses."

"Not Thoroughbreds."

"You could have fooled me. You were reeling off statistics like nobody's business on the way back from the track."

"Yes, but that's just pedigrees. Practical experience is something different."

"I don't know. Horses are horses, and Wade—"

"Did I hear my name?" Wade said from the doorway.

Carla's expression softened and she reached out a hand to him. "Yes, you did. I'm glad you're here. We were just talking about putting Nan to work."

Wade winked at Nan. "You'd better watch out. Carla intends to organize everyone and everything around here, or else."

Carla protested. "Now, Wade—"

"Don't worry, sweetheart," he said, giving her a quick kiss on the cheek. "That's just one of the many things I love about you." He straightened and looked at Nan. "If you're serious, I have a suggestion."

"You do?" Nan tried hard to keep the eagerness out of her voice. If she could get any kind of work, she thought, she might be able to stay here a little longer. "What is it? I'll do anything!"

"Hold on. You might not find this to your liking."

"Whatever it is, I'll take it!"

"Well, good. Tomorrow morning at five, you can start mucking out all twenty stalls—"

"What?" Carla said, horrified. "Wade, you can't mean it!"

He laughed and put his arm around her. "No, in fact, I accepted *that* job for you."

"In your dreams!"

Nan couldn't wait. "Wade, please!"

He took pity on her. "All right, it's this. You know that I've been thinking about setting up my own training stable again. Well, a few minutes ago I got off the phone with a prospective client named Ed Grenway. He's eager to get into racing and wants to buy some horses."

"But what does that have to do with me?" Nan asked.

"I want you to find the right horses for him—and any other clients who want to buy," he said. "I already know how good you are with pedigrees and just about anything else to do with racing stock, so if you want to, you could search out the sales and figure out what horses would be best, and I'll advise Ed which to buy. How does that sound?"

Nan couldn't answer for a moment; she was so overwhelmed. Finally, she managed to say, "It . . . sounds . . . like heaven."

"I warn you, it won't be much in the beginning, but I think it could work into a nice little sideline for you."

Nan thought of all the hours in the past she'd amused herself by studying stud books and racing charts and family pedigrees late into the night. Fervently, she said, "Oh, yes, I'll do it. I'll be glad to help in any way I can."

"Oh, you won't just *help*," Wade said. "You'll be part of the team. That's the whole idea, Nan. We're going to keep this in the family."

Keep it in the family.

Nan looked at Wade's handsome, smiling face, and at Carla's excited, expectant gaze, and was overcome with emotion. "How can I ever thank you?"

"Just do a good job," Wade said. "That's all I ask."

NAN WORKED HARD on the list of horses Wade had asked her to find for his new client. When she finally handed him the detailed inventory of potential candidates a few days later, he whistled.

"When did you have time to do this?" he asked.

"It's not as substantial as I'd hoped," she apologized, "but I only had those few catalogs that you gave me to work from. And I knew you were in a hurry. If I'd had a little more time, I could have put together something more comprehensive."

"This is good enough, believe me. Ed is going to be impressed. I sure am. Good job, Nan. It looks like you're a natural at this. Maybe in addition to researching pedigrees, you should consider becoming a bloodstock agent."

"Oh, I couldn't."

"Why not? Carla tells me you need something more to do, and that would be right up your alley."

"I've never done anything like that."

"You dealt with people all the time at the ranch, didn't you?"

"Yes, but that was different. I wasn't trying to buy and sell horses."

"No. But you had to sell the idea that your ranch was a good place to have fun. Why don't you think about it? Now that I'm getting back into the training business, I'll be looking up some old contacts. I could put in a good word for you."

"You'd do that?"

"Why not?"

"You hardly know me."

He grinned. "You're a Dunleavy woman, aren't you? It's been my experience that you're a breed apart.

Smart, sharp, determined and competent. What else do I need to know?''

Wade had more confidence in her than she had in herself, but she promised to think about it. She had a lot to think about these days—not the least of which was her reaction to Trent Spencer on the night of the party.

"You've been too long without a man," she tried to tell herself, but she knew that wasn't it. She hadn't even thought about men since the end of that brief affair with Lloyd. So it wasn't men that was the problem; it was *one* man with dark eyes that hypnotized, not to mention a body that made hers ache with desire.

Oh, so you're trying to tell yourself it's just physical, are you? a voice tittered at the back of her mind.

She blushed. Part of the attraction *was* physical. She had to admit Trent Spencer was a very attractive man. But there was more than physical attraction drawing her to him. Right from that inauspicious beginning, when he thought she'd sideswiped his son's bike, something in her had responded to a quality she had sensed in him. It wasn't sadness, exactly; it was...

She didn't know what. Unhappiness? she wondered. Maybe. Resignation? she asked herself. Perhaps. Whatever it was, she identified with it, and that made her vulnerable to him. She wanted to dislike him, but she couldn't. She had tried to put him out of her mind, but it was impossible.

To distract herself, she thought about Done Cryin'. She couldn't keep putting off a decision about the colt; it wasn't fair to the horse or to her grandmother or to anyone else who might be interested in him. The problem was, once she decided, she'd be committed, and she felt so confused about things right now. Did she want to go or to stay? The question went round and round in her mind until she was so tense, pain started up the back of her neck. Sometimes she wished she'd never agreed to come here.

No, she didn't, she thought immediately. No matter what happened, she would always be glad she'd come.

"You seem preoccupied, my dear," Octavia said to her one morning at breakfast. They were alone at the table; Carla and Wade had gone somewhere, and Nan had noticed that Meredith rarely appeared before noon.

"I'm sorry, Grandmother," she said. She put down her fork, having hardly touched her eggs. "I guess I have been in a brown study. I'm trying to figure out what to do."

"About what?"

"Oh . . . about everything. I can't just stay here forever, you know."

"Why not?"

"Because it's not right."

"But of course it is! You're my granddaughter. You have every right to stay as long as you like. I told you, I want you to regard Dunleavy Farm as your home."

"But I'm not contributing anything, don't you see? I know it might not matter to you, but it does to me."

"Of course it matters to me. The last thing I want is for you to be unhappy. And besides, you are contributing something. Carla told me you're researching pedigrees for Wade.''

''But that's not *work*. I'd do that for fun any day. Besides, I can't depend on Wade to give me assignments. He's got enough to do, starting up his own training stable again.''

''Nan, listen to me. From what you've said, you've worked hard all your life. You deserve a rest. You'll have plenty of time to work later. Can't you just think of this as a vacation long overdue?''

Nan knew Octavia was trying to help, but the suggestion didn't solve her problem. Still, she could see that the conversation was upsetting her grandmother, so she forced a smile.

''I'll try,'' she said.

''Good. Now that that's settled, there's something else I want to talk to you about.''

Nan was glad to entertain another subject. ''What is it?''

''I want you to accept Done Cryin','' Octavia said.

Nan immediately protested. ''But I haven't been here a month yet. And I—''

''It doesn't matter.'' Octavia waved away her own terms with a firm hand. ''I saw the way you looked at the colt when you first saw him. I hear the tone in your voice when you talk about him. He was meant for you, and I want you to have him. No strings, no conditions.''

''That's a wonderfully generous offer, Grandmother, and I'd love to accept. You know I've dreamed of owning a racehorse since I was a little girl. But I just can't take him."

"And why not?"

Nan didn't want to upset Octavia again, but she had to say "I don't have any way of paying for him."

"I don't want you to pay. Done Cryin' is a gift. I thought you understood that."

"Please don't be offended. I didn't mean it like that. But it's exactly what we were talking about before. If I can't support myself, how can I support Done Cryin'?"

"Nan, you are the stubbornest woman I ever met!"

Nan smiled. "I think I come by it honestly."

"Hmmph," Octavia said. She looked at Nan again. "I don't suppose it would make a difference if I told you that the colt comes with expenses paid."

Nan reached for one of her grandmother's hands. "No, it wouldn't," she said softly. "But thanks, anyway." Carefully, she squeezed the gnarled fingers. "It was a lovely thought, and it means so much to me."

Octavia harrumphed again. "That still doesn't solve the problem of Done Cryin', does it?"

Trying not to think just how much she would miss the colt, Nan said, "You won't have any difficulty at all selling him. He's such a good horse."

"*Sell* him!" Octavia sounded outraged. "Whatever gave you that idea? I'd never sell him. He belongs here!"

"Then you're going to keep him?"

With a sly smile, Octavia said, "Ah, so you *would* like to own him."

Nan flushed. "You know I would. But I told you—"

"I know what you told me," Octavia said. "Just give me a little time. I think we'll be able to work something out."

"But what?"

"You'll see. Don't give up hope yet."

Nan wasn't sure she could trust that look in Octavia's eyes. She was about to say something more, but her grandmother reached for her cane.

"Well, it's time for my morning visit to Done Roamin'," Octavia said. "Help me up, will you, dear?"

Willingly, Nan helped her grandmother to her feet. "Do you mind if I go with you?"

"Not at all. But don't think you'll get another word out of me about this until I'm good and ready. Besides, just like the evening, this time of day belongs to that old horse. You know how cranky he gets if I don't give him my undivided attention."

Nan laughed, knowing it was true. She'd already seen that Octavia's famous stallion had very firm ideas about how much homage was due him. "All right," she teased, "I promise I won't try to pump you for information while you're paying court."

"Good," Octavia said, ignoring the gentle rib. "Now give me your arm. These old legs of mine are shaky today."

Nan thought of Octavia's heart attack. "Are you feeling all right?"

"Don't you start," Octavia said tartly. "It's bad enough that Carla swoops down on me every five minutes to make sure I've taken all those silly pills. I don't want you fussing over me, too.''

Nan held up her hands in surrender. ''I won't say a word. Do you want me to get some carrots from the kitchen?''

''No need,'' Octavia said, patting the pocket of the apron she wore. ''I've got them right here.''

NAN LEFT her grandmother fussing over Done Roamin', and as she wandered back to the barn she found herself remembering the day she'd met Derry on the motorcycle not far from here. If Trent knew about it, he was certainly keeping closemouthed. Nan had a strong suspicion Derry had not told his father.

Just then, Wade hailed her from his office.

''I want to ask your opinion about something,'' he said, gesturing her to a chair.

''I don't know what help I can be, but go ahead,'' she said.

''All right, it's this . . .''

Nan tried to listen, but now that she was thinking about Derry, her conscience wouldn't let her rest. She knew she should have said something to Trent. If she didn't tell him soon, and her silence contributed to Derry's getting into serious trouble with that big bike, she'd never forgive herself.

She winced. She should have done it when he asked her that night at the restaurant if she'd heard a motorcycle on the hills behind the farm. But she hadn't said anything because she'd hoped Derry would confess. No, that wasn't the whole reason, she thought. She'd known that if she told Trent, the intimate mood that had sprung up between them would have vanished. Selfishly, she had wanted him to herself that night.

Even so, that was no excuse. She knew right from wrong, even if Derry didn't.

Her problem was how she was going to handle the situation now. She could imagine Trent's reaction when he learned that she had been deliberately evasive the other night. He'd want to know why, and she couldn't blame him.

But she couldn't call him out of the blue and say, "By the way, did you realize that your son is riding around on a motorcycle? I know I should have told you before, but for some reason, it slipped my mind." She could imagine his reaction to *that,* too.

"...know it's late in the season to start advertising Done Driftin', but Carla agrees that if we can breed a few mares to him now, we'll have a good idea what he throws by the time the next— Nan, are you listening to me?"

Nan came back to the office with a start. "I'm sorry, Wade," she said. "I guess my mind wandered. What were you saying?"

Looking more amused than exasperated, Wade tossed down his pen. "I was saying," he told her, "that some people think the moon is made of blue cheese, but I happen to believe it's Brie. What do you think?"

Nan said vaguely, "I think that's fine. Whatever you say, Wade."

At that, Wade leaned forward and snapped his fingers under her nose. "Earth to Nan," he said. And when she finally focused, he grinned. "Ah, there you are. Maybe we should do this later. You seem to be having a little trouble concentrating."

Determined to make an effort, she sat up. "I'm sorry. Let's try again. I promise, I'll pay attention this time."

"Maybe it would be easier if you tell me what's on your mind."

The last thing she wanted to do was get into this with Wade. "It's nothing, really. I'm a little preoccupied this morning, that's all."

"No kidding," Wade said dryly. "It wouldn't have anything to do with Trent Spencer, would it?"

"What makes you say that?" she asked quickly.

"Oh, just a feeling... No, that's not right. I have to confess—Carla told me. Men have a tendency to be a little dense about these things, you know."

Nan felt a blush creeping up her neck. "What things? What has Carla been saying?"

"About what?" Carla's voice asked from the doorway.

Nan turned. Her cousin was standing there, her arms filled with file folders. Clearly, *she'd* been working, and successfully, too, if the size of the stack was any indication. But she wasn't going to let Carla get away with anything, so she said, "You know about what. You've been telling stories to Wade about me and...you know who."

Carla came into the office and gave Wade a quick kiss. Then, her eyes sparkling, she perched on the edge of the desk. "Are you talking about Trent Spencer?"

"Well, who do you think? Who else do I know here?"

"I had to ask. You've been so cryptic lately that I wondered if you'd thrown Trent over for a new secret admirer."

"What? That's ridiculous! Besides, there's nothing between me and Trent. We're just friends."

"If you say so."

"I do!"

"Okay, okay." Carla looked at Wade, who hid a smile, then she gestured toward Nan with the file folders she was carrying. "I came to ask if you wouldn't mind delivering these papers to the bank, but if you're busy, I can do it myself."

It was the perfect excuse to escape without attracting notice, Nan thought. She could dash to the bank and then stop by ChangeOver Farm on the way back to rid herself of her burdensome conscience. Trying to sound nonchalant, she said, "I'll do it. I know how much you have to do today to get ready for the accountant." Remembering Wade and the problem he'd wanted to discuss with her, she turned to him. "Unless—"

"No, no, I think you should go," Wade said. "It doesn't seem that I'm making much headway here, and maybe—" he shot a glance at Carla, who twinkled back "—a drive will clear your mind."

"My mind is just fine," she said with as much dignity as she could muster. To prove it, she stood, pulled a crumpled piece of paper from the back pocket of her jeans and handed it to Wade. "Here. You'll see what I mean."

"What's this?"

"It's a list of mares that I think might cross well with Done Driftin'."

"What? Well, I'll be... Why didn't you tell me before I made a fool of myself going over the stud books—or trying to—a while ago?"

"Well, you seemed so eager to show me how to cross pedigrees that I just didn't have the heart to tell you I'd already made a start on it."

"Oh, thanks. I appreciate your not stepping on my fragile ego."

"I didn't mean it like that. Besides, you know Thoroughbred bloodlines much better than I do."

"You could have fooled me."

"No, really. I'm better at quarter horses because I've had more practical experience with them. But don't worry," she added quickly, "I'll study hard every chance I get. Pretty soon, I'll know what I'm doing."

Carla took the list from Wade and looked at it. "I think you already do. This is really something. When did you have time to do this?"

She'd had time last night when she hadn't been able to get to sleep until three. But she didn't want to go into that, so she said, "I worked on it here and there when I had a few minutes to myself."

"A *few* minutes?" Wade shoved his hat back. "This would have taken me three weeks, and even then I might not have thought of some of these names."

"I told you, Wade," Carla said. She winked at Nan.

Nan couldn't prevent a grin of satisfaction. "That's just a start," she said. "I would have done some research on mares for Done Cryin', but I wanted to know what you thought of these first. I could have been going off in the wrong direction."

"No, I don't think so," Wade said. "Judging from this list, you seem to know what you're doing."

Maybe in this area, Nan thought. *But not in others.* "I'll get better, you'll see."

"Well, I'm impressed," Wade said. "I guess the next step is to figure out an advertising approach—"

"Oh, I've got a few ideas about that, too," Nan said.

Carla laughed. "Now, why doesn't that surprise me?"

Wade shook his head. "Maybe we should just leave the new practice in Nan's hands and go live among the palm trees on some sunny faraway island. What do you think?"

"I think it sounds divine," Carla said. "But in the meantime, these papers still have to be delivered to the bank."

"I'm on my way," Nan said.

"Oh, Nan," Carla said as Nan went out. "Give our best to Trent on the way back, will you, please?"

Mortified, Nan escaped. She hadn't fooled them, after all, she thought, and blushed again when she heard their indulgent laughter following her all the way out to the truck.

HER BANK ERRAND completed, Nan slowed to a stop as she approached the driveway to ChangeOver Farm. Now that she was here, she felt reluctant to drive in. Maybe this wasn't such a good idea, after all, she thought. Maybe she should have called first to say she was coming. Maybe Trent wasn't home—or if he was, he might be working and wouldn't want to be interrupted.

What if he was home and had company? He might be entertaining a client or... a woman. That decided it. She put the truck into gear and prepared to go right on by and—

"Why, Miss Dunleavy," said a voice right by her ear. "Is something wrong? Do you need help?"

Nan jumped as though she'd been scalded. She'd been so preoccupied that she hadn't even heard anyone come up to the window. When she turned, George was standing there, gazing at her quizzically. She didn't realize until then that the *putt-putt* she'd been hearing at the back of her mind came from the golf cart he was riding.

"Hello, George," she said, trying to get herself together. "I didn't hear you."

"Is something wrong with your vehicle?"

"Oh, no, I was ... just daydreaming." Hoping that Trent wouldn't be, she asked, "Is Mr. Spencer home?"

"Yes, he's working here today. Go on in. I'll call ahead on the cellular if you like."

"I wouldn't want to interrupt."

"I'm sure he'll be glad of the break."

She couldn't back out now. Releasing the clutch, she drove slowly down the driveway and up to the house. George must have been as good as his word, for as she switched off the engine, the front door opened, and Trent came out.

"Well, this is a surprise," he said.

He seemed glad to see her—at least for now, she thought; he hadn't heard yet what she planned to tell him. "I probably should have called first to see if you were busy," she said. "But I had to make a run to the bank, and—"

"Don't apologize. I was ready to quit, anyway. How about some ice tea?"

"That would be lovely," she said, trying to calm a sudden attack of nerves.

"Come in, and I'll get it."

He smiled, and she followed him to the kitchen, thinking how hard it was to get her thoughts in order when he looked at her like that. She tried not to, but she kept remembering that kiss the other night, and how wonderfully comforting and strong his arms had felt around her. For a second, she wished they could move back in time. At that moment when their lips had met, everything had seemed so...simple.

But nothing was ever simple, and now she was feeling even more confused. Wondering how the mere presence of the man could set all her senses reeling, she tried to concentrate on what he was doing.

"You certainly seem to know your way around the kitchen," she said.

He smiled again. "It's something that ex-husbands have to get used to. We don't have wives to wait on us anymore."

"Well, that's a sexist thing to say," she said pointedly. Then she grinned. "But I have to admit, when I've been overwhelmed with too many chores and errands, I've sometimes thought how nice it would be to have a wife myself."

Laughing, he took two glasses from the cupboard. "Lemon or sugar?"

"Neither, thanks."

She seemed to have run out of small talk. It was now or never, so she said, "If you have time, I do have something I want to talk to you about."

"My time is yours."

He turned to look at her, and the way his dark eyes held hers made her feel dizzy and breathless and thrilled at the same time. She tried to get a grip on herself but her voice was shaky when she said, "I...appreciate that."

Trent obviously sensed how uncomfortable she was. "Why don't we go out on the terrace? I'll follow you as soon as I get this together."

Nan, eager to postpone the confrontation, walked outside. Despite the warmth of the day, her palms felt clammy, and she was just rubbing them down the fronts of her jeans when Trent reappeared. He was carrying a tray, and when she saw the champagne flutes, she looked at him in surprise.

"I thought this would be better," he said, setting the tray down on a shaded patio table. "You look like you might have bad news."

If he only knew, she thought, reaching for a glass. It was made of heavy crystal, encrusted with an intricate pattern, and she was distractedly admiring it when she realized Trent was staring at her again.

"What?" she said.

"I was just thinking how well this worked out."

Cautiously, she asked, "What do you mean?"

"I was going to call you tonight, to ask if I could see you again. But now I don't have to because you're here. Serendipity is a wonderful thing."

"I don't know about that. I've never really believed in luck."

"You don't think it was a stroke of good fortune that we met?"

She started to make a flip comment, but something in his voice stopped her. He was staring at her again, and once more the look in his eyes took her breath away. Slowly, she set down her untouched glass on the table. Unsteadily, she said, "I don't know what to think about that."

"I do," he said. He set down his glass beside hers and reached for her hands. Gently, he pulled her toward him. "Nan, you know as well as I do that there's a reason for this. I can't stop thinking about you. I see your face in my mind, I hear your voice in my dreams." He laughed a little. "I sound like a poetic fool, I know, but I can't help it. I can't ever remember feeling quite like this."

She didn't want him to feel this way now. Struggling to ignore the yearning his words had evoked, she tried to bring them both back to earth by reminding him of his marriage. "But your wife—"

"Sandra is—was—the mother of my son," he said, lifting one hand to touch her face. "We loved each other once, but that was a long time ago. Things changed. *She* changed. The feeling . . . died."

"I'm sorry."

"So was I. I was bitter and angry for a long time. But now—" he pulled her closer to him, his eyes burning "—I've met you."

She felt herself weakening, melting, wanting to flow into him so that their bodies became one. But the feeling frightened her, and she tried vainly one last time. "Trent, I don't—"

"Don't you?" he said, and stopped her protest with a kiss.

The air suddenly took on an electric quality. Nan could almost feel the ends of her hair crackle, and it seemed more difficult to breathe. It was as though Trent had cast some kind of enchantment she was helpless to resist. When his arms were around her like this, and his lips were on hers, she couldn't think of anything else but how much she wanted him—in all ways. Trying to fight the feeling, she pulled away with a gasp.

Trent's eyes were like dark pools. "What is it?"

Nan couldn't explain. She didn't know how. She wasn't ready for this, she thought. Desperate for an excuse, she glanced around and saw a pair of running shoes tossed casually down on the edge of the terrace. She'd seen Derry wearing them, and she was reminded that Trent didn't live here alone. She didn't know where George had gone, but he was certainly around, and she was sure that Derry would be home from school soon. Did she want to be found like this, the two of them wrapped in each other's arms in plain sight on the terrace?

"What about George?" she asked.

Smiling, Trent pulled her closer. Nibbling on her ear, he whispered, "George has been with me a long time. He knows when to leave things alone."

It was difficult to think when Trent was kissing her. From her ear, he'd moved to her jaw, and then to her throat. Trying to keep her mind on other things, she remembered the running shoes. "But Derry—"

"Won't be home from school for hours," Trent murmured. He raised his head, his eyes sparkling like dark stars. "Anything else?"

She tried one last time. "Maybe we should finish our champagne. Don't you want to do that?"

"The champagne can wait. You know what I want. I think you want it, too."

Nan tried again to tell herself that this was going too fast for her, but she knew that wasn't true. She wanted him as much as he wanted her. But if she started something with Trent, she wanted it to last. She couldn't bear a casual fling, not with a man she was beginning to feel she couldn't do without.

"I'm not very good at this, Trent," she said. "I mean, I'm not the kind of woman who drops into and out of affairs—"

"I didn't think you were."

"But neither do I mean I'm looking for an immediate commitment. After all, we hardly know each other—"

"Ah, there you're mistaken. I've known you forever."

She plunged on. "In fact, I don't even know—"

He took her hands. "Nan," he said, making her look up at him. "We agreed we'd take it slow—for both our sakes. But don't deny us the chance..."

She couldn't deny him anything. One of his hands went to the small of her back, and as he drew her toward him, she didn't resist. She lifted her face to his and put her arms around his neck. His body felt lean and hard against hers, and the touch of his lips was like coming home again. She could no more have backed away from him now than she could have flown to the moon.

Almost wonderingly, she felt the warmth that had been glowing inside her burst into heat, and she pressed against him, quivering with need. Their kiss deepened, and when she felt him tremble, she drew back one last time.

"Trent—"

"Let's go inside."

THE BEDROOM was on the second floor, up a flight of thickly carpeted stairs that in other circumstances would have felt luxurious, but which today merely dragged at Nan's feet. Trent stopped on the first landing to kiss her. As their tongues met and sensation flooded her hot body once more, she thought wantonly of making love to him right there. But his bedroom door was only a few feet away, and when they were inside, Trent took her into his arms again and held her tight.

"I've dreamed of this since the first time I met you," he whispered, his lips buried in her hair.

She looked up. Now that it was actually happening, she dismissed all her reservations. Wickedly, she asked, "The *first* time? I thought you looked like you'd rather strangle me."

"I was a fool," he said, kissing her eyelids. "I should have known that instead of being hit by a truck, my son would actually *run into* one."

For a second, her guilty conscience rose like a ghost. Ruthlessly, she shoved it back. *Now* was not the time to talk about Derry and the bike, she told herself. If anything could break the mood, that would.

"Well, it turned out all right," she murmured, reaching up to brush a lock of hair away from his face. His hair felt thick and coarse under her hand, and she tightened her fingers on the strands.

"That it did," he said, gazing into her eyes again. "Nan, I want this to be right..."

"It will be," she whispered. But her voice was shaking with desire for him, and so was her hand when she reached for his belt.

With a shushing sound, the slacks he was wearing fell to the floor. He wore form-fitting briefs underneath, the shorts clearly displaying his burgeoning arousal. She drew in a breath. Almost tentatively, she cupped her hand around him, and he moaned.

His voice ragged, he murmured, "My turn."

She was wearing jeans and one of her customary T-shirts. As though the top were made of silk, Trent gently pulled it over her head. Nan had never been well endowed; suddenly, she was embarrassed.

"I'm not very—"

He stopped her with another kiss. Gently placing a hand over each breast, he murmured, "What you are . . . is perfect."

"But—"

"Shh," he said, running a finger down the inside of her bra to her nipple. She shivered with reaction as he kissed her through the material.

Reaching around to her back, he unsnapped the bra. As the garment fell to the floor, he looked at her, his handsome face expressing his wonder. As her breasts rose and fell with her quickening breath, he closed his eyes.

"You're magnificent," he whispered. He opened his eyes again. "You're so beautiful, I'm almost afraid to touch you."

"Don't be," she murmured, her fingers rapidly un- buttoning his shirt. She pushed it off his shoulders and buried her fingers in the mat of dark hair covering his chest, then tightened her fingers, enjoying the feel of the crisp curls.

She was still wearing her jeans. When Trent slid them down over her hips along with her bikini panties, he cupped her buttocks and pulled her into him. The con- tact of their bodies sent a rush of sensation flooding through her, and before they knew it, they'd kicked away the rest of their clothing. With one arm still hold- ing her, Trent reached down and yanked the bedspread to the floor. Still facing each other, they sank onto soft cotton sheets. It was like falling into a cloud.

This new intimacy aroused them even more. Groan- ing, Trent pulled her with him as he rolled over. Now she was on top, his entire length beneath her. As she straddled him, she looked down into his eyes. It had never happened to her this quickly, but she was ready for him, and, lowering her head to kiss him, she guided him inside.

She had made love before, but nothing prepared her for the feeling that surged through her at this most in- timate union. Eyes closed, she balanced on her arms and threw her head back so that she could feel every sensation. Lost in growing passion, she began to move her hips, drawing him in deeper and deeper until she couldn't take anymore.

Under her, Trent put his hands on her breasts, squeezing them, kneading the flesh until she didn't think she could bear the wild throbbing that pounded within her. Then he lifted his head and began kissing her nipples, suckling them, teasing them with his tongue until her entire being seemed to occupy only three places in the entire universe.

"Oh, Trent," she gasped. "I don't think I can—"

"It's all right," he said hoarsely, reaching for her so he could kiss her mouth. "I'm right behind—"

Whatever else he said was lost, gone in a thundering explosion of pleasure that overwhelmed her. It started at some point deep within and fanned out until every nerve felt on fire. She tried to make sure that he was there with her, but there wasn't time. Her body was no longer her own, but an entity swept into a storm that tumbled her over and over. Just when she thought she couldn't bear it any longer and would have to scream to let go, the intensity of feeling began to abate. Seconds later, she was gently tossed down. When she was finally able to focus, Trent was there with her.

"Lord," he said, looking dazed.

Nan couldn't even say that much. She looked at Trent again, at the sheen of perspiration now drying on his forehead, at his closed eyes, his contented face.

He had aroused feelings and sensations she had never experienced before—had never even known existed, in fact. But as she gazed at him, she knew she had pleased him, too. And that knowledge was the greatest satisfaction she had ever known.

"Trent—" But just then she heard a door slam downstairs. She stiffened. "What's that?" she asked.

Before Trent could answer, a voice shouted, "Dad, I'm home!"

Nan and Trent looked at each other. "Oh, my God!" she exclaimed, leaping off the bed. "He can't find us like this! Where are my clothes?"

"Nan, it's okay," Trent tried to say as she dashed around the room picking up discarded garments and flinging them every which way in an effort to find her own.

"It's not okay!" she said desperately, sliding into bra and panties and grabbing her jeans. She suddenly saw that he hadn't moved. "What are you doing?" she gasped, throwing him a shirt. "Don't just sit there! Get dressed!"

Lazily he grabbed the shirt out of midair. "I don't know if I want to," he said. "I was really enjoying the show."

"Trent!"

He finally took pity on her frantic state. While he hunted for a lost shoe, she quickly remade the bed.

"Now we have to get out of here without being seen," she told him once she'd finished.

"There's a trellis outside," Trent suggested solemnly.

She was so unnerved, she almost took him up on it.

In the end, it wasn't a problem. As Trent had undoubtedly known, Derry went directly to his room when he got home. As Nan tiptoed by the teenager's closed bedroom door, Trent following with a smile, even she could hear the throbbing beat of heavy metal from inside and knew a ruse was unnecessary. She probably could have ridden Done Cryin' down the stairs and through the boy's room, for all the attention Derry paid them.

"You see?" Trent said, his eyes laughing as they safely made it past. "I told you he wouldn't notice. He always hides out in there."

Not always, Nan thought, and felt guiltier than ever. Once more, instead of facing the difficult decision, she had opted for more selfish measures. She had come here to tell Trent about Derry and that bike. Instead, she had spent the afternoon in his bed and in his arms.

Would she pay for it later? she wondered. Almost certainly.

Was it worth it? she asked herself. And without hesitation, came the answer, *You bet.*

CHAPTER ELEVEN

"I'VE BEEN THINKING about it, and you *have* to tell him," Carla said to Nan the next morning. "You know you do. You shouldn't have put it off this long."

Nan didn't answer. She was hunched in one of the chairs in the sun room, wondering if it was possible to feel more miserable. She'd felt so guilt-stricken after that wonderful interlude with Trent yesterday that she told Carla and Wade last night about meeting Derry on the hill with the bike. Now Carla was after her to do something about it.

The first thing she'd done when she came downstairs this morning was find her grandmother and ask if Trent had called.

"Why, yes, he did, dear," Octavia had said. "Several times, in fact. What's it all about?"

Nan had promised Octavia that she wouldn't lie to her, or leave her out of things, but she didn't want to go into all the details. So she said lightly, "Oh, Trent's having a problem with Derry. You know how teenagers are."

"Indeed I do," Octavia said. She paused, then said, "You know what that boy needs?"

"What's that, Grandmother?" Nan asked.

"He needs something to keep him busy," Octavia declared.

Oh, but he has something to keep him busy, Nan thought, wincing as she remembered the motorcycle. Muttering something in vague agreement, she left her grandmother to her reading and escaped. She was in the sun room when Carla came in and started insisting that Nan confess all to Trent.

"Well?" Carla demanded when Nan remained silent.

"Carla, I know you mean well," she said, "but I can't deal with that now."

"Why not?"

Annoyed because her cousin wouldn't leave it alone, she exclaimed, "I never should have told you about that damned motorcycle!"

"Yes, you certainly should have!" Carla retorted. "In fact, you should have told Trent that same day."

"It wasn't any of my business!"

"How can you say that? You know how he feels about Derry riding a bike—"

"Yes, but—"

"For heaven's sake, Nan, what's the matter with you? If you won't consider yourself, think of some other innocent person on the road Derry might hurt!"

"He won't go out on the road," Nan insisted.

"Oh, and how do you know that?"

"Because I just do!" she snapped. "Now, leave it alone, will you, Carla? I have a terrible headache and you're only making it worse."

"Well, excuse me!" Carla said, offended. "And here I thought I was trying to help."

"What would help is if we could just change the subject."

"So you're not going to tell him."

"Not right this minute!"

"All right, if you won't, I will."

"Don't!" Nan cried. "This is my business, and I'll take care of it myself."

"As far as I can see, you're not taking care of it at all. What are you holding back?"

Nan lost patience. "Will you *please* leave it alone! You always think you know everything, Carla, and I admit, most of the time you do. But not this time, so just butt out!"

Carla's face reddened. "How dare you say that to me!"

Nan's temper was hanging by a thread. If she hadn't been feeling so miserably unhappy and guilty, she would have been more careful—or at least, more diplomatic. As it was, she exploded.

"What do you mean, how dare I? Am I not allowed to criticize you, when you've been lecturing me?"

Carla stiffened. "I haven't been lecturing you."

Nan should have been warned by the tone in Carla's voice, but she was suddenly too angry to care. "Yes you have, ever since I came. And you're right, I don't belong here. I'll never fit in!"

"*What?* Are you out of your mind?"

"Do you deny it?"

"I certainly do! We've done everything we could think of to welcome you."

Nan knew Carla was right. Appalled by what she'd said, she jumped up. "I'm sorry, Carla, I didn't mean it, you know I didn't. You have done a lot for me. I'm just so upset, I don't know what I'm talking about."

"Well, *that* part is certainly true!"

"Please forgive me," she pleaded. "I don't know what's gotten into me."

"I do."

"What?"

"You're in love," Carla said, beginning to smile. "It makes hags out of all of us at times, especially when we don't want to be."

"You're right about that," Nan said miserably. "Oh, Carla, what am I going to do?"

Just then, the phone rang. They both looked at it, but before Carla could reach for it, Nan said, "Let Teresa get it, please. I want to straighten this out. I don't want to fight—with you, of all people."

"Neither do I. So let's—"

Before she could finish, Teresa came hurrying into the sun room. Her voice sounding odd, she said, "A phone call for you, Miss Nan." For some reason, her eyes went to Carla before she added, "It's Dwight Connor. I think something's . . . wrong."

Nan drew in a sharp breath. "Where?"

"At the racetrack."

Nan felt rooted to the floor. She looked at Carla, who had gone so pale that Nan thought her cousin might faint. Her heart suddenly pounding so hard it hurt, she asked, "Wh-what did he say?"

Teresa clasped her hands. "He just said he wanted to talk to you."

Carla came quickly to Nan. "I'll talk to him if you like."

"No, he asked for me," Nan said through stiff lips. She was so frightened, she could hardly force her wooden legs to take her to the phone. Willing her numb fingers not to drop the receiver, she picked it up and said, "Hello?"

"Nan? This is Dwight, down at the track."

Nan closed her eyes. *Don't let Done Cryin' be hurt,* she prayed. *Oh, please, don't let it be him.*

"Yes?" she said.

When he hesitated, she knew it was too late to pray. She gripped the phone tightly as he said, "I'm real sorry to have to tell you this, but your colt...well, he... Damn it, I can hardly believe it myself, but he's...gone."

For a few seconds, Nan just stood there blankly, afraid to think what that meant. Then she asked, "What...do you mean...gone?"

"I mean, *gone.* As in vanished, disappeared...not here anymore."

Nan's eyes went to Carla, who was standing beside her. She reached out a hand and Carla grasped it tightly. Nan still didn't understand; she had to say it.

"You don't mean—"

Try as she might, she couldn't say the word, *dead.* But Dwight obviously understood what she meant.

"No, he's not dead. At least we don't think so. I'm sorry, Nan, I'm just so upset, I don't know what I'm saying. I mean, he's gone from his stall. I don't know how the hell it happened. With the security and all the safety checks we have, I would have said it was impossible. But now…" His voice trailed away, as though he was trying to control himself. Then he said, "I think you'd better get down here right away."

CARLA WENT with her. Nan's hands were shaking so badly, she gratefully accepted Carla's offer to drive. They were about to dash out, when they remembered Octavia.

"Shall we tell her?" Carla asked as they halted in the hallway and looked at each other in dismay.

"No," Nan said decisively. She didn't have to think about it. She didn't want to involve Octavia until they knew exactly what they were facing. "Not yet."

"You're right. There's no point in upsetting her now."

"Upsetting whom?" came a voice behind them.

Nan jumped and whirled around. Meredith was standing on the bottom step of the staircase.

Carla's nerves were apparently just as frayed as Nan's. She snapped, "What are you doing up, Mother? It's not even noon yet."

Meredith lifted a carefully sculpted eyebrow. "Why, darling, you're always on about my sleeping the day away. I thought I'd get up early today to see what all the fuss was about." She paused. "I must say, if everyone is so irritable and jumpy at this hour of the morning, I might as well go back to bed.''

"I'm sorry, Aunt Meredith,'' Nan said, shooting a silencing look in Carla's direction. She didn't want to get involved in an argument with her aunt, not when she was in a fever to get going. ''We were surprised to see you. We were just . . . leaving.''

"This early?'' Meredith yawned delicately. ''Whatever the errand is, it must be important.''

"It is,'' Carla said. Her lips tightened. ''Don't tell Grandmother, but something's wrong at the track.''

Meredith's mouth snapped shut. ''What? With whom?''

Nan's warning to her cousin had obviously gone unnoticed. Seeing no option but to confess, Nan said, ''With Done Cryin'. He—'' She couldn't say it, after all. With visions of all the terrible things that could have happened to her colt rising in her mind, she put a hand over her mouth.

Meredith's voice was sharp. ''He what?''

Carla said it for her. ''He's disappeared.''

Meredith gasped. ''That's impossible! How? Why?''

"We don't know,'' Nan said. ''That's where we were going—to find out.''

Meredith gripped the banister so tightly, her knuckles whitened. ''I can't believe it,'' she said. ''No one can just . . . take horses in and out of the track. It isn't possible. It must be a joke.''

Nan couldn't wait any longer. ''Aunt Meredith, would you excuse us, please? We'll call as soon as we know what's going on. And please don't tell Grandmother," she repeated. "We don't want to upset her—"

"Upset me about what?" came another voice.

Nan wanted to scream. Oh, why hadn't she and Carla run out while they'd had the chance?

"It's nothing, Grandmother," she said hurriedly. "Aunt Meredith can fill you in."

"Fill me in?" Octavia came forward quickly. "About what?"

Nan glanced quickly at Carla. Even though she knew it was pointless now to keep the information from her grandmother, she tried to downplay it, anyway.

"Done Cryin' seems to be...missing," she said. "Aunt Meredith thinks it might be a...joke."

"A joke! Nobody would do that for a joke." Octavia turned to her daughter. "You know that, Meredith. What's the matter with you?"

Piqued, Meredith snapped, "For heaven's sake, I merely suggested it. In any case, how would I know? You know I have as little as possible to do with the goings-on at the track."

"Yes," Octavia said thoughtfully, "so you've said."

"And I meant it!"

Nan couldn't be sure, but she thought she saw a flash of fear in her aunt's eyes. Why would Meredith be afraid? And of what? Nan shook her head and dismissed the thought. She was allowing her imagination to run away with her because she was so upset.

Just then, Carla took charge. "Look, we'd love to stay and referee, but we have to get going. Nan is anxious to find out about her horse, and so am I."

"I'm going with you," Octavia immediately announced.

As if on cue, all three women objected. To Nan's surprise, Meredith's voice was the loudest.

"You certainly are not!" Meredith declared. "The doctor said no excitement—although how he imagined we would reduce that element around here, is beyond me. No, don't bother to protest, Mother," she said adamantly, when Octavia tried to object. "You and I will stay here. Carla and Nan will phone when they have news. Won't you, girls?"

Since Carla was staring at her mother in sheer astonishment, Nan answered. "Yes, as soon as we talk to Dwight, and . . . and whoever else might be involved, we'll let you know." She started toward the front door, only to realize that Carla was still standing there. Tugging at her cousin's arm, she said, "Come on, let's go!"

"Just a minute," Carla said. She hadn't stopped staring at Meredith. "Are you all right, Mother?" she asked.

"I'm fine, darling," Meredith replied, giving her a little push. "Go on now, you're wasting time."

"But—"

"We'll be *all right*. After all, your grandmother and I lived together here for years, and we didn't do each other in. I think we can manage some civility now. Don't you, Mother?"

Apparently surprised herself at Meredith's behavior, Octavia murmured an assent. Then she looked at her granddaughters and became more brisk. "Meredith is right. You go ahead. Wait—where's Wade? Maybe he should go with you."

"He can't, Grandmother," Carla said. "Don't you remember? He left for Florida this morning to help bring back Never Done Dreamin'."

"And please don't tell him about Done Cryin' if he calls," Nan pleaded. "He'll rush home to be here, and there's nothing he can do, anyway. We'll tell him when he gets back. Hopefully by then, Done Cryin' will be back where he belongs, and we'll all have a good laugh about it."

THE DRIVE to the track seemed endless. Carla drove with her usual competence, the speedometer needle staying steady at the legal limit. It seemed a snail's pace to Nan, who had to grip her hands tightly in her lap to overcome an almost-irresistible urge to grab the wheel. They were silent the first few miles, but finally Nan couldn't stand it anymore.

"He's all right, don't you think?" she asked.

"Sure he is," Carla said unconvincingly. "Maybe Mother was right. You know how those track people are, always playing practical jokes. They'll probably have him back by the time we get there."

They both knew she was lying through her teeth. People on the backside might play jokes, but no one fooled around with a valuable racehorse. Carla tried to smile at Nan, but when it turned into a frown instead, she looked away.

"It'll be okay," she said.

Holding herself together by a thread, Nan looked out the window. "Is this how you felt when you heard Done Driftin' was hurt?"

"I don't know how I felt. I was too numb to feel anything at first."

"Well, I'm not. I'm mad as hell." Suddenly, Nan erupted. "How could this have happened? What was the groom thinking of? What was Dwight doing? Where was the gate guard? You can't just put a horse in your pocket and walk out with it!"

Sympathetically, Carla reached across the seat and grasped Nan's hand. "I don't have the answers," she said. "But we're going to find out."

"You bet we are!"

Carla gave Nan's hand a squeeze. "We'll know soon enough."

It wasn't too soon for Nan. By the time they pulled into the backside parking lot, she was so tense she felt she might shatter at any second. The car had barely stopped before she was out; when she wanted to run to the barn, she had to force herself to wait for Carla to catch up.

It was almost noon; the backside was quiet. Morning works were over; everyone seemed to be at lunch. A sleepy atmosphere pervaded—until she and Carla arrived at Dwight's barn. When Nan saw the cluster of people gathered outside Done Cryin's stall, she felt a burst of hope. *He's back!* she thought. *It* was *a joke!*

It wasn't.

Dwight was standing outside the stall with everyone else; when he saw them coming, he started toward them, his normally florid face pasty white.

"Thanks for coming," he said. "Let's go into the office and talk."

Nan gestured toward the people by the stall. "But isn't—"

"No," Dwight said grimly, dashing her hopes. "He's not back. He's not at the track, either. I called in everybody I knew and sent them out checking—every stall, every horse. So far, no one has found him."

HOURS LATER, there was still no sign of Done Cryin'. Despite the efforts of track officials, track stewards, grooms, jockeys, owners, trainers, exercise people, the sheriff's department and even the police, the colt seemed to have disappeared without a trace.

"This can't have happened!" Nan cried when she heard the results of the final search. "If he's not at the track, he had to be taken off. What was the gate man doing? Having a nap?"

But exhaustive checks of the gate records proved that all the horses coming in to the track or going out had been passed as legitimate. It was the gate man's job to check all traffic; he hadn't seen or noticed anything amiss.

"But *someone* took him out!" Nan shouted. "Who was it?"

No one knew. Whoever it had been, had had a pass. And, as the guard plaintively stated to anyone within earshot, who would want to steal a horse off the track without papers? He couldn't be raced or sold; it was senseless.

Senseless or not, Nan had to face the awful news that her beloved Done Cryin' had just... vanished.

"Oh, where is he?" she asked uselessly. Visions of killer houses, whose unscrupulous owners accepted anything for slaughter, or rodeo people who might not ask questions about where an animal came from, or bush tracks where the poor horses were run into the ground for pennies, flashed through her mind until she wanted to scream.

No one could comfort her, not Carla, nor Octavia, nor Wade, who had heard the news and rushed home. The only person Nan wanted was Trent, but when she finally called him, he, too, was gone. Not even George was home at ChangeOver Farm. As the phone dropped from her numb fingers, Nan had never felt so alone.

CHAPTER TWELVE

JUST WHEN Nan didn't think she could stand it any longer, Trent called. When she heard he was on the line, she snatched up the phone with a shaky, "Trent?"

He didn't waste time on preliminaries. "I just heard about Done Cryin'," he said. "Has there been any news?"

Trying not to cry, Nan said, "No, not yet. But Dwight is doing everything he can think of. He's turned the track upside down."

Trent obviously heard the hysteria underlying her voice. "Don't worry, we'll find him," he said.

We? That one pronoun was the most comforting word she'd ever heard. "Oh, Trent!" she cried. "Where could he be?"

He couldn't answer that question, so he said, "Hold on, Nan. I'm coming over."

She didn't think that was a good idea. It was late; everyone was exhausted. Octavia had retired to her room, and Nan didn't want her disturbed. She explained briefly, then said, "I think it would be better if we didn't meet here."

"All right. I can come and get you, and bring you back to the house."

She didn't want that, either. She still hadn't told him about the incident with Derry, and she didn't want the teenager's presence to complicate things. "I'm sorry, Trent," she said. "Do you think we could meet somewhere else?"

He barely hesitated. "All right. There's a diner just off the highway called Berta's. Have you see it?"

She had. "What time?"

"As soon as we can get there."

"Fine. I'll see you soon. And Trent—"

"What?"

"Thanks."

"Don't thank me yet," he said. "Wait until we get Done Cryin' back."

In that moment, Nan knew she loved him. She said goodbye, found the keys to her truck and in two minutes was on her way to meet Trent.

To GET to the diner, Nan had to pass a little parklike rest area off the main road. Normally, she wouldn't have given it a glance, but tonight she was so anxious to find Done Cryin' that anything out of the ordinary caught her attention. She noticed two people—a man and a woman—standing by a car at one end of the parking area. There was something familiar about the woman, she thought, and slowed, squinting to see.

It's Aunt Meredith! she thought in surprise. She blinked. What in the world was her aunt doing *here,* at this out-of-the-way rest stop? And who was that with her?

She narrowed her eyes again, trying to make out the man's features before she went by. It was too dark to see his face, but as she watched, he gestured angrily. Meredith responded by chopping her hand hard in the air, as though objecting to what he'd just said.

What was going on? Nan wondered. Before she realized what she was doing, she'd pulled into the parking area. *This is none of your business,* she told herself. But she couldn't pretend she hadn't seen anything and just drive on. What if her aunt was in trouble?

The thought seemed absurd, and her hand hovered over the key in the ignition. If she stopped, Meredith and whoever was with her would be sure to think she was spying on them. But this truck was so recognizable; if she drove off, it would be even worse. The realization that Meredith and her companion seemed to be getting into an argument settled it. She couldn't leave her aunt way out here with an obviously angry man. She would say she'd been going by, had seen them and stopped to say hello. She turned off the engine and reached for the door handle.

"Hello, Aunt Meredith," she said when she came up behind them.

Meredith and the man with her had apparently been too involved in their conversation to notice Nan's presence. They whirled around at the sound of her voice, and they stared at her in surprise. "I was out for a ride, and saw you here, Aunt Meredith. I thought I'd stop and ask if everything was all right."

Meredith was tight-lipped. Without looking at the man beside her, who hadn't yet uttered a sound except for a startled expletive, she said, "Everything is fine, Nan."

"Oh...well, that's good," she said lamely. "I thought maybe you were having car trouble or something, and needed a ride."

"No thank you. That won't be necessary. As you can see, my car is just over there."

Meredith gestured. Nan looked in that direction. She hadn't noticed it before because it was half-hidden by some overgrown shrubbery, but now she caught a glimpse of a silver-colored fender. It seemed obvious that Meredith and her companion had met in this remote place because they didn't want to be seen together. Had she interrupted a liaison? It didn't seem possible, but one never knew.

"I'm sorry," she mumbled. "I just saw you and...I mean, if you don't need..." She turned away, wanting to run back to the truck and disappear. "I'll be on my way now."

She'd gone about five steps, when Meredith called to her. "Wait a minute, Nan."

Nan turned. Meredith hurried over to her. Lowering her voice, her aunt said, "I know this looks awkward."

Embarrassed, Nan said quickly, "You don't have to explain anything to me, Aunt Meredith."

"I know. I just don't want you to get the wrong impression. He's an old school friend of mine. We happened to see each other on the road and pulled in to chat. It's as simple as that."

"Yes, of course," Nan said. "Like I told you, I thought you might need a ride or something."

"No, it's all right. I only wanted to make sure you knew that."

Nan wondered why, if the meeting had been as innocent as Meredith insisted, but she just said, "It's okay. I understand."

Meredith started to say something more, but at that moment she cast a nervous glance over her shoulder. Nan did, too. Clearly impatient at the delay, Meredith's companion had pulled out a cigarette and was lighting it. When the flame from the lighter briefly illuminated his face, Nan caught a better glimpse of his features. It was too dark to tell the color of his eyes, but his hair was blond, worn long, over his ears. The stubble on his face surprised her, for he didn't look like the sort of man her aunt would give the time of day, much less pull over to talk to about old times.

With a start, she realized the man was staring—glaring—at her, and she quickly looked away. His expression disturbed her, and now she didn't know whether or not to insist that her aunt leave with her. She wasn't sure it was safe to leave Meredith alone with him.

Aware of the man's growing impatience, she said hurriedly, "Look, Aunt Meredith, I know it's none of my business, but—"

"You're right," Meredith interrupted, "it's not. Now, you go ahead and don't worry. I'll be right along as soon as I finish talking to my... friend."

Nan knew she couldn't drag her aunt away, so she muttered something about seeing her back at the farm, then she returned to her truck. She looked at them once after starting the engine and backing out of her parking spot and was even more uneasy to see they were staring after her. Unsettled by the whole episode, she turned the wrong way as she left the rest stop. It wasn't until a few miles later, when she was turning around and heading in the direction of the diner again that she realized her aunt had never introduced the man to her.

That's odd, she thought. But then, the entire encounter had been strange. What was her Aunt Meredith doing with a man who was so... unkempt? The more she thought about it, the more inexplicable it seemed.

"Forget it," she muttered. It wasn't her business, so she shouldn't worry about it. From what little she knew about her aunt, Meredith was one woman who could take care of herself.

But still...

Enough! she told herself. She was dwelling on her aunt so she wouldn't have to worry about Done Cryin'. Just the thought of the horse made her feel teary-eyed again, and she blinked rapidly. It wouldn't do any good to cry. She had to think about something else.

But the only other thing she could think about was Derry and the motorcycle. Her mouth tightened. She had to speak to Trent. It was obvious Derry wouldn't—or couldn't—tell his father. From what she'd seen, Trent and his son needed professional help to sort out their differences. She didn't doubt that Trent loved Derry, and she suspected that behind all the rebellious bluster, Derry loved his father, as well. Their difficulty seemed to be that they didn't know how to communicate.

Nan knew how that felt. Her father had been one of the most private people she'd ever met. She had always known, deep down, that he loved her, but for some reason, he'd never been able to say it. It seemed that her grandmother had had problems talking to him, too. She and Nan had discussed Gary soon after she'd arrived at the farm.

"He was a difficult child from the start," Octavia had said with a heartfelt sigh. "So handsome, and so smart—when he wanted to be. He used to frustrate us all with his behavior at school. One term it would be all A's. The next, he'd receive D's and F's in every subject. And the most exasperating thing was that he didn't seem to care whether he passed with flying colors or failed miserably. If he was interested in a topic, he'd be like a sponge, soaking up every little fact. But if he wasn't, he didn't give it a thought. It drove me absolutely mad because nothing I said influenced him."

Octavia's voice had trailed off for a moment before she added sadly, "As I told you, Gary chose to believe I didn't care for your mother, so he bolted before graduation and got married." She focused on the silent Nan. "I'm just glad he was happy."

Happy? Nan had thought. Maybe he had been, once. But Yolanda had told her that he'd changed when Nancy died. It was as though he'd invested everything in the woman he loved and once she was gone, he'd turned to a different kind of companion to help him through.

But she hadn't wanted to burden her grandmother with the knowledge that her only son had had a drinking problem, so when Octavia looked at her hopefully that day, she said as truthfully as she could, "He was happy in his own way, Grandmother. He loved Montana, and the ranch... and my mother."

"I'm so glad," Octavia had said softly, looking directly at Nan. "But I think there's more than what you're telling me. I know he was very bitter toward me."

Chagrined that Octavia had seen through her cover-up, Nan had to say, "Yes, he was. But Yolanda taught me that a person can go only so long blaming someone else for his or her unhappiness. At some point, you have to take responsibility for yourself and your own life."

"Yolanda sounds like a wise woman."

"She is. I miss her a lot."

"Why don't you ask her to visit?"

"Here?"

"Yes, here," Octavia said with a laugh. "Why do you sound so surprised? Lord knows, we've got plenty of room."

"That would be wonderful," Nan said, trying not to get too excited at the prospect. Then she slumped. "But

I don't think she will. She said she'd never leave Montana.''

"Not even for a visit? Besides, what's that saying? Never say never?''

"Yes, but you don't know Yolanda. She can be very stubborn when she chooses.''

"It sounds like she'd fit in here just fine,'' Octavia said. "And who knows? She might even stay. From what I hear, as time goes on, those Montana winters don't get any easier.''

Tonight, as she drove back down the road toward Berta's diner, Nan was wondering if Yolanda would come for a visit, when she realized that the headlight of the car behind her had been blazing in her rearview mirror for some time. Squinting against the glare, she tried to see who was behind her, but the light was too bright.

"Okay, if you're in such a hurry, go ahead and pass,'' she muttered, rolling down the window and sticking her arm out to gesture the tailgater around her. To her annoyance, the light stayed just where it was.

"Well, damn it, make up your mind,'' she said, and didn't realize until then that she was seeing one headlight, not two. There was something eerie about the way it was following her, practically on her fender, and now that she was aware of it, she suddenly realized that the sound of the engine behind her didn't belong to a car, but came from a motorcycle. A big one.

Like the one Derry had been riding in the hills behind the Farm?

She felt a chill. The road was empty on both sides, and despite herself, her heart jumped a little. *Stop it!* she commanded. She wasn't in danger. Whoever was back there had no reason to harm her.

She squinted again, trying to peer through the glare in her rearview mirror to see the driver. But whoever it was had come up even closer. Now the light was so blinding that she had to put up a hand to shield her eyes.

It didn't seem that she had any choice. Hoping the old truck would take it, she increased her speed and had the momentary satisfaction of seeing the headlight recede a little. But before she could congratulate herself, the bike speeded up, swinging in behind her again. It was so close that if she'd been in the back, she could have touched it.

The thought that maybe the driver was deliberately trying to scare her made her angry. If he wouldn't pass her, maybe she could outrun him, she decided, and increased her speed once more. This time, the bike stayed right with her.

"What's *with* this guy?" she exclaimed. She glanced down at the speedometer and saw the needle hovering at sixty, then sixty-five, then . . .

She never made it to seventy. She was starting to feel the vibration in the steering wheel that indicated the old engine was straining, when she saw the bike swing up alongside. Was he trying to force her off the road?

"What are you doing?" she cried, the wheel bucking like a wild horse in her hands. She felt, more than heard, gravel from the side of the road spray up under her spinning tires, and knew that she was dangerously close to the edge of the pavement. "Stop it!"

Relentlessly, the biker pressed her over. One of the truck's back wheels slid in the soft shoulder, swinging the bed of the vehicle out behind her like a pendulum. She tried to correct, but the wheel wouldn't answer her. Frantically, she glanced over at the other driver, but she couldn't see who was behind the helmet's dark visor.

"Why are you doing this?" she screamed just as the right front wheel lost purchase and the truck spun completely out of control. With a sickening lurch, it began to pitch to one side, and Nan realized with horror that it was going to roll. She barely had time to brace herself before the world turned over.

TRENT WAITED over an hour for Nan at Berta's diner. When he glanced at his watch for what had to be the hundredth time, the waitress looked at him sympathetically. She was new to the area and didn't know him.

"Can't believe a guy like you has been stood up," she said, bringing over a carafe to pour him yet another cup of coffee.

"How did you know I was waiting for someone?" he asked.

"It's pretty obvious," she said, shrugging. "Coffee, but nothing to eat, stares out the window—when he's not looking at his watch. All the classic signs."

He made himself smile. "You seem to be an expert."

"On waiting for guys that don't show up?"

"On reading people."

"It comes with the job, sugar. When you've been doing this as long as I have, you realize early on that some things never change. In fact—"

She stopped as an ambulance with lights flashing went by. Moving over to the window, she followed its progress for a few seconds before she nodded with satisfaction and proclaimed, "Can't be too serious."

Now he was curious. "How do you know that?"

"No sirens. Can I at least get you a piece of pie? We got some real good key lime. Or wait, I know—pecan. You look like a pecan pie kind of man."

He didn't want to be rude, but he was too worried about Nan to join in the woman's banter. Getting up, he tossed a couple of bills on the table and said, "Not tonight, thanks."

Trent drove slowly home, his unease about Nan mounting. What had happened to her? he wondered. Maybe he should swing by Dunleavy Farm and find out. After a moment, he decided against it. Maybe Nan had decided she wanted to be alone. He couldn't blame her. He knew she was distraught about Done Cryin'. If he arrived at Dunleavy looking for her and she wasn't there, he'd upset Octavia. He decided to go home. Maybe Nan had left a message with George.

His jaw tightened. If he ever got his hands on the son of a bitch who took Done Cryin', the guy would be sorry, he thought. Worrying Nan like this wasn't something he was going to suffer lightly. If that horse wasn't back in the next day or so, there would be hell to pay.

Which reminded him, he thought with grimace, Derry had better be there when he got home. His son had come in after school, apparently thrown his books—unopened, of course—onto his bed and taken off. He still hadn't appeared by dinnertime, and if he wasn't in his room studying hard when Trent got home, being grounded for the rest of his life was going to be the least of his problems.

George didn't come to the door when Trent arrived home. He knew it wasn't a good sign that the houseman hadn't appeared. It probably meant that Derry wasn't there, and that George didn't want to be the one to tell him. But just to make sure, Trent went immediately to his son's room. Sure enough, the door was not only unlocked, it stood wide open, the books exactly as they had been before. Trying to control his anger, Trent stared at the sight for a moment. Then he went to find George.

He located the houseman in the kitchen, studiously frosting a cake. "Oh, there you are," George said. "Did Miss Nan have any word about the horse?"

Obviously George hadn't heard from Nan. Trent's anxiety went up a notch. If she'd changed her mind, she'd surely have tried to call.

As he did so often, George seemed able to read his mood, if not his mind. As the houseman placed the frosting bowl and spatula in the sink and ran hot water over them, he said, "Derry will be home soon."

Trent wanted to believe that, but real dread was growing inside him now for both Nan and Derry. *Take it easy,* he admonished himself. *Deal with one problem at a time.* Throwing himself down on one of the bar stools ringing the high counter, he said, "I wish I could be as sure as you are."

Calmly, George poured him a cup of coffee and set it before him. "He's only doing this to worry you."

Trent pushed the mug away and got up again. He was too agitated to sit still; the last thing he needed was a jolt of caffeine. "Well, he's succeeding. Where *is* he?"

"Any one of a hundred places, I imagine. Teenage boys have a way of disappearing at times. Surely, you remember."

"I'm too old to remember. And I never pulled this type of thing, anyway."

"How quickly we forget."

"I'm not in the mood for this, George," Trent said just as the back door opened. They both turned as Derry appeared in the doorway. Startled to see George and his father staring at him, the teenager stopped in his tracks. Immediately, a guilty flush spread over his handsome features.

Trent didn't waste any time. "Where in the *hell* have you been?"

Derry's flush deepened, this time with temper. Defiantly, he said, "Out."

"That's not good enough."

"Well, it's going to have to be."

Trent had had it. With no clear idea of what he was going to do, he advanced on his son. Derry flinched, but stood his ground. They were only inches apart when the phone rang. Trent ignored it, but George snatched up the receiver. He listened a moment, then held it out to Trent.

"I'm sorry, but it's Miss Dunleavy from Dunleavy Farm," George said. "She says it's an emergency."

Thank God! Trent thought. Nan was obviously okay if she was calling him. To Derry, he said, "This isn't finished. Go to your room until I cool off enough to meet you there."

"I'm not a—" Derry stopped midsentence after another dark look from his father. Scowling, he slouched off down the hallway.

Trent waited until Derry had disappeared. Then, taking a deep breath, he said into the receiver, "Nan, what happened—"

"Trent, this is Carla Dunleavy."

"Oh . . . Carla, I'm sorry. I thought that Nan—"

She interrupted, her voice high. "I had to call you. There's been an . . . accident."

"An accident?" he repeated blankly. What was she talking about? Derry was home—safe and unharmed despite all his father's nightmarish projections—but home. She must be mistaken.

"Yes," Carla said shakily. "It's Nan. Her truck went off the road tonight, and they took her to the hospital. That's where I'm calling from now. The police notified me and I came right away. Grandmother doesn't know yet," she added hastily. "I didn't want to upset her until I knew . . . what the situation was."

This couldn't be happening, he thought. Nan was supposed to meet him tonight at the diner. She'd changed her mind; that was all. Nothing could have happened to her!

He realized that his hand was shaking. Gripping the phone more tightly, he said, "How... is she?"

"I don't know." Her voice shook again. "She's got a head injury, and they're doing tests."

Trent closed his eyes as the room began to reel. When he opened them again, he saw George staring at him in concern, and behind him, a white-faced Derry, who'd come into the kitchen once more. He wondered fleetingly why his son looked so frightened, but he didn't have time to dwell on it. Trying not to think of anything else, he said, "I'll be right there. What hospital is it?"

Carla told him. Two seconds later, he was on his way.

CHAPTER THIRTEEN

TRENT DROVE to the hospital as fast as the law allowed. The entire way there, he sat like an automaton, his hands clenched on the wheel. He was so frightened, he couldn't even pray. All he could think, over and over and over again, was: *She'll be all right. She has to be.*

But when he finally arrived and drove around to the emergency entrance, his heart lurched. Several ambulances were strewn about, their back doors wide open, no one in sight. Quickly, he pulled into the nearest parking space and ran inside. His dread increased when he saw all the activity. Nurses in uniforms and doctors in lab coats were rushing around, tending, examining and taking care of the throng that seemed to fill the entire space.

Trent had never seen such a sight. People were everywhere—sitting, lying, leaning against the walls. Some had bloody bandages wrapped around them; others were gingerly holding arms or legs or just sobbing quietly. As he stood there in the center of the floor, a scream erupted from behind one of the curtained-off areas.

What the hell was going on? he wondered. Where was Carla? He looked frantically over the crowd, but he couldn't see her. He grabbed the arm of a harried-looking nurse who had just emerged from behind a screen. She was holding a pan of some kind and was obviously in a hurry, but Trent didn't care.

"I want to see Nan Dunleavy," he said. "Where is she?"

The nurse looked at him as though he'd lost his mind. "I haven't the faintest idea," she snapped. "We've been too busy with this bus wreck to log everybody in."

She tried to pull away, but he held her fast. He sympathized with these other people, but none of them were Nan, and he wasn't leaving until he found her.

"Who would know then?" he demanded.

The nurse jerked her head toward the desk. "Ask the charge nurse—if you can find her. Now, mister, as you can see, we're a little busy here. If you don't mind, please let go of my arm."

Trent released her. She rushed off, and he was turning toward the main desk, when an orderly rushed by with a gurney. Trent had to jump quickly out of the way, and as he did, he caught a glimpse of a dark-haired woman behind one of the curtains. He knew it was Nan, and he practically fell over someone in his haste to get to her.

"Nan!" he shouted, shoving the curtain aside.

It wasn't Nan. The dark-haired woman who had been sitting on the bed looked at him, first in surprise, then in consternation.

"You're not Dr. Hergenberger!" she exclaimed.

Backing out as quickly as possible, Trent mumbled, "No, I'm not. I'm sorry I disturbed you."

Once outside the cubicle, he looked around wildly. If he didn't find Nan soon, he'd start bellowing.

"Hello, can I help you?" someone said.

He turned. A petite woman with snow-white hair and a pink-and-white striped apron was standing behind him.

"I'm looking for Nan Dunleavy," he said frantically. "She was in a car accident tonight and—"

"Oh, yes, such a *nice* young woman. Are you her husband?"

"No, I'm a...friend. Where is she? Is she all right?"

"Well, you'll have to talk to the doctor about that. But she's out of X ray, and I believe they've taken her to a room."

"Do you know which one?"

"Well, let me check the register."

With a fierce effort, Trent controlled his impatience and followed the woman across the seething emergency room to a desk. He wanted to rip the register out of her hand, but he forced himself to wait while she slowly ran her finger down all the names until she came to Nan's.

"Room 203, on the second floor," she said finally. "The elevators are just through—"

Trent had already seen the elevators. Two groups of people were waiting, so he quickly thanked the woman and sprinted for the stairs.

Carla was coming out of Nan's room when Trent dashed up. She took one look at him and stopped in her tracks.

"You look terrible," she said.

He didn't care how he looked. "How's Nan?"

To his relief, she said, "She's going to be okay. The bump on her head was apparently just that. But they want to keep her here tonight to make sure. Would you like to see her? I don't think the medication they gave her has taken effect yet."

He took a deep breath and pushed open the door.

He didn't know what to expect. Maybe a hushed, dimly lit room with a wan figure lying in the bed. What he saw was a blaze of light, the television on but turned down and Nan sitting cross-legged on top of the covers. Now that he could see that she was all right, the knot of tension that had been growing inside him began to loosen, and he wanted to take her in his arms. Emotions that he'd thought long dead—or at least buried—were working their way up to the surface, and as he stared at Nan, he had to admit he liked these feelings. But he wasn't ready to discuss them yet, so he asked, "What happened?"

She avoided his eyes. "Carla told you, it was an accident. I wasn't watching where I was going, and I went off the road."

"You . . . went off the road?"

"Well, I didn't do it on purpose," she said, irritated. "It just happened."

"It just *happened?*"

"Yes. I guess I wasn't paying attention."

He seemed unable to control his anger. The woman that he was beginning to really care about could have killed herself tonight, and all because she wasn't paying *attention?*

"What kind of excuse is that?" he demanded.

"It's not an excuse. Do you mind if we don't talk about it? I feel stupid enough."

He couldn't let it go. "Something must have been wrong with you. Were you feeling sick? Were you in pain? Had you had anything to drink?"

Really annoyed, she snapped, "No, I hadn't had anything to drink! I'm insulted that you'd even ask."

"You're right. I'm sorry. I'm just trying to figure out how this could have—"

"Yes, well, so am I," she interrupted. "So if you figure it out, let me know, all right? In the meantime, we've got other things to talk about."

She was right. Maybe she'd been so worried about the horse that she hadn't been paying attention to her driving. "Yes, I know," he said. "But as I told you, we'll—"

Abruptly, she asked, "Was Derry home tonight?"

Startled by the question, he started to say, "As a matter of fact, he—" He stopped. "Why?"

Nan didn't know what was happening to her. Without warning, the room seemed to shift, and she grabbed on to the side of the bed for balance.

"Nan, are you all right?" Trent asked in concern.

She looked at him. To her surprise, he seemed to have a halo around him. Belatedly, she realized the medication she'd been given was starting to take effect.

"Yes, I'm fine," she said. "Why?"

"Nan? Why did you want to know about Derry?" he asked.

She tried to think. Vaguely, she said, "I don't know. I just wondered."

"But why?"

Suddenly, a vision of that helmeted biker tonight flashed behind her eyes and despite herself, she cringed. *Could* it have been Derry?

No! She was crazy even to consider it. Why would Derry try to hurt her? Or even to scare her? She hadn't done anything to him...

Except, perhaps, given him cause to wonder if she'd told Trent about their meeting on the hill behind the farm. But even in a confused teen's eyes, was that a sufficient reason for him to terrorize her?

No, no and no! she thought. The bump on her head must have knocked out her good sense. She *knew* Derry hadn't had anything to do with what had happened tonight; she wasn't even going to consider it.

"It's not important," she mumbled. "I don't even know why I asked."

But Trent had obviously heard something in her voice, for he persisted, "You must have had a reason for mentioning him."

The medication wasn't doing much for her headache; the pain made it hard to concentrate. "No reason," she muttered. "It was just something I thought of..."

"What do you mean?"

But Nan couldn't think what she had meant. Dizzy again, she put a hand to her head. "I...don't know," she said. She looked at him helplessly. "I'm sorry, Trent."

"That's okay. Look, you're not well. You need to rest. Maybe I should go."

"Yes, maybe..." She waited until the room stopped shifting. Then she asked, "Did you tell me about Derry?"

He looked bewildered. "What about him?"

She knew she had something important to tell him, but she couldn't think of it. Bowling balls were beginning to roll around behind her eyes, and over the thunder they made, she said, "You should keep your eye on him, Trent."

"Nan, you need to rest."

She almost had it. It was right there, at the edge of her mind. But just then, the heavy rolling balls crashed together behind her eyes, and she said, "Maybe it doesn't matter."

"Nan, please, try to relax."

Whatever she was trying to think of was gone. "Never mind. I knew I shouldn't have mentioned it."

The crashing in her head was getting louder, but she heard him clearly when he said, "Nan, you need to rest now. Don't worry about Derry. He's not your concern."

His tone irritated her. Before she could stop herself, she said, "Then maybe you should start acting like he's yours. You're so set on turning him into the perfect son that you can't see what you're doing to him."

He stiffened. "Are you telling me how to raise my own son?"

"No, but someone should," she said. Why were they talking about this now? She didn't know. But she couldn't stop herself from saying, "Because I'm not sure you know so much about it. If you did, would Derry want to ride around on a big bike he has no business riding? Who knows what could happen?"

Trent went still. "Nan, what are you talking about? Have you seen Derry riding a motorcycle?"

"No. Did I say that?" She couldn't seem to follow the conversation; everything he said was confusing her. "I told you, I don't know *who* it was. It all happened so fast."

Trent's face paled in sudden comprehension. "What do you mean, you don't know *who* it was? Are you telling me that someone was responsible for your accident tonight?"

Why couldn't she get through to him? She felt as if they were shouting at each other through a curtain of gauze. And what in the hell had the doctor given her? She felt woozy and dizzy and the wrong words kept coming out of her mouth.

"Nan, sweetheart, just tell me one thing. Did someone try to force you off the road tonight? Was *that* why you had an accident?"

She tried to focus on him. "I didn't say that. I told you, I'm not sure what happened."

"It wasn't an accident, was it?"

"What difference does it make?"

"What *difference?*"

Her voice beginning to shake—with fatigue, and the effects of whatever pills she'd been given—she said, "I don't want to fight about this."

"I don't want to, either. But I have to know. If you were forced off the road, why didn't you tell the police?"

"Because I—" She stopped. That was a good question, she thought. Why hadn't she told the police?

"Nan?"

She tried to focus on him again. "I don't know, all right? Can we discuss this tomorrow? I don't want to get Derry in trouble—"

"What does Derry have to do with this?"

"Well, what do you think, Trent? What have I been trying to tell you all this time?"

He looked at her as though she'd suddenly sprouted a Medusa head. Incredulously, he asked, "Are you trying to say that *Derry* had something to do with your accident?"

"I didn't say that. I don't know. But he's been on and on about this motorcycle business, and—"

Trent stood up so suddenly that she blinked. "And whoever ran you off the road was driving a motorcycle? Is that what you're saying?"

Nan didn't know what she was saying. All she wanted to do was to go to sleep. She closed her eyes.

NAN CAME HOME from the hospital the next day. Carla picked her up, and on the way back to the farm, they didn't say much. There had been no word about Done Cryin'. Carla was worried about Nan's pallor, and Nan was still trying to make sense of her discussion with Trent.

There hadn't been time the night before to tell Carla much about the accident, so after reassuring a worried Wade that she was all right, she gave her cousin a much-expurgated version when they were alone. After her talk with Trent, she'd learned her lesson, and she side-stepped reminding Carla about having seen Derry on a motorcycle up in the hills behind the farm. Instead, she concentrated on the fact that someone had forced her off the road.

Carla listened with increasing horror. When Nan finished the tale, she exclaimed, "I don't believe it! We have to call the police right away!"

She started to reach for the phone, but Nan stopped her. "Not now," she begged. "I don't feel up to it at the moment."

"But—"

"Please, Carla. All I want to do is take a shower and climb into bed. Can't we deal with this later?"

"What are we going to do about Grandmother?"

Nan winced at the thought of her grandmother. "We'll have to tell her something. I can't hide my face, and I think she'll be more upset if we try to avoid explanations than if we tell her."

"Yes, but tell her what?"

"Let's just say I . . . I ran off the road while trying to avoid hitting an animal. She'll believe that, won't she?"

Carla looked at her. "Yes, but it will be a lie."

"I know. But I don't want to worry her."

"All right," she said. She gave Nan a gentle hug. "I'm so glad you weren't really hurt."

Grateful for her cousin's support, Nan returned the hug. "I wish I could say the same for my truck. If it's not a total loss, it's close to that."

"Don't worry about it," Carla said at once. "You can borrow one of the farm trucks if you need it. It's still so unbelievable. Are you sure you didn't get even a glimpse of the driver?"

Nan started to shake her head, then thought better of it when the balls began crashing around inside again. "No, it was too dark. And besides, he was wearing one of those helmets with the dark-tinted visors. It's impossible to see through those."

"So you don't have *any* idea?"

Nan was too tired to think. "No."

Carla helped her up the stairs. At the door to Nan's bedroom, they stopped and Carla said, "It's so strange."

"Strange?"

"Remember I told you that a man on a motorcycle was responsible for scaring Done Driftin' that awful day?"

In all the confusion and turmoil of last night, Nan had forgotten. Or maybe she just hadn't wanted to make the connection, she thought. "You don't think it could be the same person, do you?"

"No, it can't be. Why would someone want to hurt my colt, and then come after you? It doesn't make sense."

"Nothing makes sense about this," Nan said wearily. She reached for the doorknob, longing for a nap. Just before she went in, she thought of something and turned back to Carla. "By the way, I saw your mother last night."

"You did?" Carla said, surprised. "Where?"

"In that rest stop off the main road. I was going by, and there they were."

"They?"

"She was with some man. I don't know who because she didn't introduce him when I stopped to see if everything was all right. But he didn't look like her type. In fact, I was surprised to see her with a guy like that. He was sort of . . . scruffy."

"Scruffy?" Carla's eyebrows rose.

"You know, unkempt. Hadn't shaved for a few days, needed a haircut."

"Why on earth would my mother be with someone like that?"

"You tell me. She said it was an old school friend she happened to run into, but—"

"What?"

Nan tried to think, but her headache was starting again. "I don't remember. It probably wasn't important. If I think of it, I'll let you know. Meanwhile, I've got to lie down."

"Are you sure you're all right?" Carla asked anxiously.

Nan tried to smile, but it turned into a grimace instead. "I'm fine. They wouldn't have released me if I wasn't, would they? Don't worry, I'll take a short nap and be like new."

Inside her room, Nan went to the bathroom to take one of the pain pills the doctor had sent home with her. As she ran a glass of water, she looked at herself in the mirror. Her face was whiter than the bandage on her forehead; her pallor contrasted with the bruise under her right eye.

But it wasn't her injuries she was thinking of as she stared at her reflection. She was thinking again of the biker who had forced her off the road last night. With all her heart, she didn't want to believe it had been Derry. But she couldn't forget something else she'd seen. As she'd told Carla, the motorcyclist had been wearing a helmet that completely masked his face. But what she hadn't said to anyone was that she'd recognized the leather jacket he'd been wearing. That day up in the hills, she'd seen an identical jacket on Derry.

CHAPTER FOURTEEN

NAN WAS still in a daze the next morning. She spent fifteen minutes in the shower, trying to think of nothing at all. Set on massage, the faucet pelted her body with hot needles of water, easing her bruises, making her feel a little better by the time she turned off the water.

She knew she couldn't avoid the rest of the family for long, so she dressed, went downstairs for coffee from the breakfast sideboard in the dining room and walked right into the middle of an argument between Octavia and Meredith. They were so preoccupied that they didn't hear her until she came into the room; by the time she realized that she had intruded, it was too late to back out without being seen.

"I'm sorry," she said when they both turned to look at her. "I didn't mean to interrupt."

Meredith poured herself more coffee from the sideboard, where Teresa kept breakfast hot until about ten in the morning. She brought the cup back to the dining-room table, set it down with barely a rattle and reached for her cigarette case. "It's all right," she said. "Mother and I were just having words. You know, the usual thing."

As much as Nan longed for a cup of her own, the last thing she wanted was to get involved in a disagreement between her grandmother and her aunt. "Well, I'll leave you to it," she said weakly, and began to back out.

"Nonsense," Octavia said. "There's no reason you can't stay, Nan. We weren't discussing anything of substance, anyway, were we, Meredith?"

"Of course not," Meredith said, exhaling a long plume of smoke that made Nan feel a little faint. "But then, we never do, do we, Mother?" She looked at Nan. "Please, come in. It will be a relief to have a referee."

"There's no need for melodrama," Octavia retorted. "If you want to be secretive about your whereabouts, Meredith, that's your business. You're a grown woman."

"I'm glad you've finally recognized that fact," Meredith said, taking another drag from her cigarette. Nan nervously poured herself a cup of coffee and brought it to the table as Meredith added, "And I wasn't being *secretive*. I simply forgot that around here, one must sign in and out, like at a college dormitory."

"Don't be absurd. It was a simple question, not—as you're inferring—an interrogation."

Abruptly, Meredith stubbed out her cigarette. "We're being rude, Mother. Don't you see that we're making Nan anxious? I think we should talk about something else. I—" Meredith stopped abruptly. "For heaven's sake! What happened to your face, Nan?"

Involuntarily, Nan's hand went up to touch the bandage on her forehead. She'd tried to hide it with her bangs, but apparently she hadn't been successful. Avoiding Octavia's eyes, she said, "It's nothing. I had a little . . . accident last night."

"An accident!" Octavia exclaimed. "What happened?"

Nan knew her grandmother was going to find out, anyway, so she said, "I ran off the road."

Octavia put a hand to her throat. "Good heavens!"

"It's not serious," Nan assured her quickly. "At least, not for me. I'm afraid the old truck came out of it worse than I did."

"The truck! Who cares about that? Oh, Nan, are you all right?"

"I'm fine," Nan said. "Please, don't get upset, Grandmother. It was a stupid accident. I—" She stopped. She had intended on staying with the story she had concocted last night, about her swerving to avoid an animal, but now that the moment had come, she couldn't lie. Octavia deserved more, she thought, and she said carefully, "Some other driver tried to pass me, and came just a little too close. I tried to avoid him, and overcorrected the wheel. That's all there is to it."

"That's all!"

"But that's terrible!" Meredith said. "It must have happened after I—"

She stopped so abruptly that Octavia looked at her. "After you what?" Octavia asked.

"Never mind, it's not important," Meredith said dismissively. She turned to Nan again. "Did you see who it was?"

Nan thought she saw a flash of fear in her aunt's eyes. But then, it was gone so quickly that she was sure she'd imagined it. Besides, she thought, Meredith couldn't possibly blame herself for the accident; she hadn't been anywhere near the place where the truck had gone off the road.

"No, unfortunately," she said. "I didn't even get a license-plate number."

"Why wasn't I informed of this?" Octavia demanded.

Nan looked at her. "I didn't want to upset you."

"I'm not as delicate as you all like to believe," Octavia said tartly. "In future, I would appreciate knowing these little details. I can't believe it! What is this place coming to!"

"I'm sorry." Nan reached for Octavia's hand. "I didn't mean to leave you out. It's just that ... well, I'm sorry. I won't do it again, I promise."

"Let's hope there won't *be* a next time," Meredith muttered.

"I'm sure there won't," Nan said. Then, as much to comfort herself as to reassure Octavia, she said, "It was just one of those things, Grandmother. Some motorcycle rider was out joyriding, and—"

Meredith had just taken a drag on her cigarette. She started to say something, but began to choke on the smoke. Nan jumped up, but, red-faced and coughing furiously, Meredith waved her away. Finally, after a few agonizing seconds, she caught her breath and gasped, "You didn't say it was someone on a motorcycle!"

"I didn't?"

"No, you only said something about a driver."

"Well, it doesn't matter. Whoever it was—"

Meredith took a quick drink of water from a goblet on the table. Her eyes still teary, she said to Nan, "Are you *sure* you didn't see the driver?"

"No, it was dark, and he was wearing a helmet with a tinted visor."

"Was there anything special about the motorcycle? Anything at all that you can remember?"

Wondering why Meredith was interrogating her like this, Nan said, "No, it just looked like a motorcycle to me. But then, I don't know much about that kind of—" She stopped. "Why?"

Her hand to her chest, Meredith reached for the water glass again and took another sip. When she set the glass down, she seemed to have herself under control, for she said, "I was curious that's all."

"Curious?" Octavia repeated.

"Yes, Mother. Don't make a big deal out of it—like you always do about everything."

"Well, don't blame me if you seemed so upset a moment ago," Octavia said. She gazed keenly at her oldest daughter. "Are you sure you're all right? You look as if you've seen a ghost."

"Don't be ridiculous," Meredith snapped, and then contradicted herself. "And why shouldn't I be upset? Nan could have been seriously hurt!"

Nan didn't want Octavia to begin dwelling on that. Quickly, she said, "Yes, but I wasn't. Now, if you'll excuse me—"

She started to go, but Octavia said, "Don't leave, Nan. In light of what you've just told us, I'm not sure this is the right time, but I would like to talk to you for a moment."

"This is *my* cue to leave, then," Meredith said. Gathering her cigarettes and lighter, she stood and said, "I'm glad you weren't seriously hurt, Nan." Then she looked deliberately at Octavia and added mockingly, "Don't hold dinner for me, Mother. I won't be back until very late—if at all."

Octavia sighed as Meredith waggled her fingers at them and sauntered out of the room. "Sometimes I wonder why she comes back here if she dislikes it—and me—so much."

Nan had wondered the same thing—until now. Her expression was thoughtful as she watched Meredith depart, and she said, "I think I know why. I haven't been here that long, but even I can feel the farm's pull. It's almost as if it...as if it gets into your blood—" She stopped, embarrassed. "I sound silly, don't I?"

Octavia smiled tremulously. "No, you sound like a Dunleavy." Then her smile disappeared and she reached again for Nan's hand. "I'm so glad you weren't badly hurt, my dear. I don't know what I'd do if anything happened to you."

Octavia sounded so lost and forlorn that Nan put her arms around her. "Nothing's going to happen to me, Grandmother."

Octavia patted her arm. "If we keep on this tack, you'll have me blubbering in no time, and before that happens, I did have something I wanted to talk to you about."

"What's that?"

"Well, I've been thinking about this problem you and I have about you wanting to earn your keep," Octavia said as Nan sat down again. "And I believe I've come up with a solution."

"What is it?"

"You know that as soon as Wade fills up his new training barn, he's not going to have much time for the farm, don't you?"

"I hadn't thought about it, but I suppose you're right. Unless he trains horses here, that is."

"As much as I'd like that, I can't ask him to be my barn manager and run his own stable. He needs to concentrate on his business, not mine. And a race trainer needs to be at the track. So, while I wish him the best, I'm still left with a problem."

"A problem?"

"Yes. Who's going to be my barn manager when Wade is gone?"

Nan laughed. "Oh, Grandmother, I'm sure there are dozens of people who would be eager for the job! Especially when Done Driftin' starts his breeding season." Forgetting her problems for the moment in sudden enthusiasm, she added before she thought, "And don't forget Done Cryin'. He's going to be a valuable—"

She stopped, tears welling up. Octavia patted her arm and said, "We'll find him, my dear. Don't you doubt that for a minute."

Reaching for a napkin to wipe her eyes, Nan said, "I hope you're right."

"I am. I know it. And in the meantime, I can't have a stranger in charge of the barn."

Nan tried to focus on what Octavia was saying. "But Wade was a stranger when he first came, and look what a wonderful job he did..." She trailed off as she realized what Octavia was getting at. "Grandmother, are you offering *me* the job?"

"Who's better qualified? You know horses, you know pedigrees, and best of all, you're family. So, what do you think, Nan? Would you like to try it?"

Nan didn't have to think about it. With visions of all those beautiful horses under her care, she said, "Oh, Grandmother, it's something I've always wanted to do. I'd love the chance to try!"

"You'll have to do more than give it a try," Octavia said with satisfaction. "With the plans Carla has for improving things, and with what I know you can do in the barns, soon the farm will be humming again."

"And," Nan added, "when we get Done Cryin' back, everything will be perfect."

"Only if you'll finally accept him as yours," Octavia said.

Nan didn't have to think twice. "I will," she said, hugging Octavia again. "Yes, Grandmother. Thank you. I certainly will!"

THE FIRST THING Nan did after she accepted Octavia's offer was to call Trent.

"I'm so sorry I upset you," she said when he answered the phone. "I don't know whether it was the bump on my head, or the medication they gave me. But whatever it was, I didn't mean to offend you. Can you forgive me?"

Trent didn't hesitate. "There's nothing to forgive. I admit you scared me when you hinted that someone—possibly Derry—forced you off the road. I should have realized you weren't yourself. How are you feeling this morning?"

"Aside from a few aches and pains, I'm fine," she said. "In fact, I'm going to the track today to talk to Dwight about Done Cryin's disappearance. I hope there's something he's forgotten, or overlooked."

"I don't think you should drive right now. Why don't I pick you up?"

"Don't you have work to do?"

"Nothing's more important than you."

Nan was glowing when she replaced the receiver. She was turning to go upstairs and freshen up, when she realized Carla was standing in the doorway.

"Well," Carla said. "I see by that fatuous look on your face, you've been speaking to Trent."

Nan could feel her grin spreading and couldn't stop it. "Is it that obvious?"

"About as obvious as it gets," Carla said with a grin of her own. "But that's okay, I understand. The same thing happened to me with Wade."

"When did you realize you were in love with Wade?" Nan asked suddenly.

Carla didn't seem to find the question outlandish. "I'm not sure," she said. "I think it just crept up on me."

"But you knew it when it happened, right?"

"You don't know that about Trent?"

"I don't know what I feel. I'm scared, Carla."

Carla laughed. "Well, join the club. I felt that way, too."

"Oh, no, not you!"

"Yes, me. In fact, I was downright terrified. Sometimes I still am. I look at Wade and wonder, who *is* this man? Every time I start to plan our wedding, I go clammy. Committing yourself to one person for the rest of your life is an awesome thing."

"Yes, but that's you and Wade. Trent and I haven't even talked about—"

"The dreaded C word?" Carla said with another grin. "Isn't it all about commitment? What else is there between two people who love each other? And don't try to tell me that Trent isn't in love with you. All anyone has to do is watch the way he looks at you to know he's boxed, wrapped and tied up with a bow. And, I can say the same about you."

"But I didn't want this to happen!"

"I know," Carla said sympathetically. "But aren't you glad it did?"

Nan didn't get a chance to answer, for just then they heard the sound of a car pulling up in front. Carla looked out the window and smirked, "Well, that was certainly fast. I'd say your man is a little anxious to see you, my dear."

Nan was anxious to see him, too. Flying out the door, she ran down the steps and threw herself into his arms. "Oh, Trent, I'm so glad to see you."

"Me, too," he said, and gave her a kiss that swept her right off her feet.

A WHILE LATER, after they'd arrived at the backside parking lot and were walking together toward Dwight's barn, Nan looked covertly at Trent and wondered how this had all happened. She'd come to Kentucky to visit a grandmother she'd never known existed and to have a firsthand look at a real Kentucky racing farm. She hadn't intended to fall in love, either with the place, the horse, or, most important of all, the man beside her. And yet...

"I'm glad we're together," she said, snuggling against him.

He smiled at her. "So am I."

"Trent, be honest. Do you think maybe we're moving too fast?"

"Too fast?"

She couldn't meet his eyes. "Maybe we should take this one step at a time."

He stopped. "I thought that's what we were doing."

"Yes, but I think we need to talk about this—"

"This? You mean, *us?*

"Yes, I mean *us,*" she said stubbornly. "We haven't known each other for very long—"

Trent took her hand. "Nan," he said quietly, "don't make it sound as though we're both going to need seconds for a duel. If we're going to discuss our future—" He saw her face change again and stopped. "That *is* what we're going to discuss, isn't it?"

She looked away. How could she tell this man that she was scared?

Scared of defining her involvement and committing herself to a man she hardly knew; scared of the life-style he led, the house and farm he had, the things he owned. But most of all, she was leery of Derry's reaction when he found out that she and Trent were developing a relationship—*had* developed a relationship. She knew Derry resented his father, so how would he regard *her,* a stranger who might take his mother's place? She remembered the times she'd seen him. He'd acted as if he hated her.

No, she was being absurd: Derry didn't *hate* her. He was just being a teenager and feeling entitled to act as if the entire world were against him. The fact that he'd been skipping school and pestering his father for a motorcycle didn't have anything to do with her; he'd been doing that long before she'd come into the picture.

"What about Derry?" she said.

Trent's expression hardened. "What about him?"

"Well, he's part of this, too, isn't he? Maybe before you and I make plans, we should hear what he has to say."

"My son is not going to run my life. I won't let that happen."

"I didn't think—"

But she didn't have a chance to finish the sentence, for as though she'd conjured him, she suddenly glimpsed Derry walking down the shedrow in their direction.

"Why didn't you tell me Derry was here?" she asked.

"What do you mean? Of course he's not here. He's in school—or should be."

"Well, you'd better check again. If that's not Derry, it's sure his double."

Trent turned. At the same time, Derry looked up and saw them. He was too close to pretend he hadn't seen them, and just far enough away so that he could turn on his heel and start off at a run. He hadn't taken two strides before Trent shouted, "Derry!"

Nan could practically see the teenager debating how far he could sprint before his father caught up to him. He obviously decided prudence was called for because he stopped reluctantly and turned around. At glacial speed, he came over to them. He couldn't have looked more sullen if he'd tried.

"What?" he said.

Trent's voice was already beginning to vibrate with anger. "What are you doing here? And, more to the point, *how* did you get here?"

"I hitched a ride."

"You *what!*"

"All right, I didn't hitch," Derry said sulkily. "I know how you feel about that."

"Well, I'm glad to see you still have some common sense!"

Nan could see where this was leading. Trent's face was turning red, and the more furious he looked, the more sullen Derry became. She started to say something, but Trent held up a hand to silence her. Harshly, he said, "I'm waiting, Derry."

Derry's blue eyes flashed at his father's tone. "All right, since you *have* to know, I rode a bike, okay? Does that make you happy?"

"Are you trying to tell me that you rode a bicycle all the way from home to *here?*"

"Oh, come on, Dad," Derry said with that long-suffering tone that meant all adults were idiots. "You know damned well I was talking about a motorcycle."

For a few seconds, there was only silence as Trent digested what his son was saying. Nan saw Derry look at her as if this were all her fault, and she bit her lip. Trent looked ready to explode, and she put a hand on his arm. The muscles below her fingers felt like granite.

"Trent," she said hesitantly, "maybe you should discuss this when you're calmer."

He didn't even look at her. Tight-lipped, he said, "I'm as calm as I'm likely to be. Don't try to protect him, Nan. He knows how I feel about this."

"Yeah, yeah, you're right, Dad!" Derry suddenly erupted with anger of his own. "I know how you feel about this, and that, and everything! You've made it very clear that I can't do anything right!"

Before the enraged Trent could answer, Derry turned to Nan and shouted at her, "You had to go and tell him, didn't you? You couldn't *wait* to get me into trouble! Well, fine. Don't think I'll forget it, *Ms*. Dunleavy. One of these days—"

"That's enough, Derry!" Trent thundered. He grabbed his son's arm so hard that Derry winced. Trent didn't even notice as he commanded, "Apologize to Nan this instant! She didn't have anything to do with getting you into trouble. You did that all by yourself!"

Derry wrenched his arm away. "Oh, yeah? You think I'm trouble now, well, just wait!"

And with that, he whirled and started to run. They could see him heading for the backside parking lot, and Trent bellowed, *"Damn it!"*

"Maybe you'd better go after him," Nan said hurriedly. She didn't want Derry riding that powerful bike onto the freeway, too angry to watch where he was going.

"You're right. I'm sorry—"

"Don't worry about it. Just go!"

TRENT HAD NO TIME to think about Derry's accusation about Nan. He spent hours looking for his son, but there was no sign of the boy, either on the freeway, or on any of the side roads. By the time he parked the car in front of the house, he didn't know whether to be angry or worried.

George met him at the door. Trent had called several times from the car phone, but as soon as their eyes met and he saw the worry in his houseman's expression, Trent knew that Derry hadn't come home.

"Damn it, where is he?" he shouted, as though George could conjure the boy out of thin air.

"I don't know. I've called all his friends—"

Trent was too livid to listen. "I didn't know he had any."

Wisely, George ignored the comment. "But no one has seen him," he went on. "I've also been in touch with the police—"

"The police!"

"I have a friend on the force, remember? I asked him to check—discreetly, of course—and let us know if there are any... incidents."

"And?" Trent's heart jerked into his throat.

George shook his head. "Nothing so far."

"Thank God!"

"Maybe you would like a drink."

Trent ran a hand through his hair. "No, I'd better keep all my wits about me—so I can strangle that kid when he finally decides to come home."

"May I say something?"

They were still in the entryway. Heading into the living room, Trent said over his shoulder, "You need permission? Go ahead, you will, anyway."

George followed him. "I think he's just testing you."

"Testing mc!" Trent spun around. "What kind of psychobabble is that?"

"Think about it. He wants to see how far he can go."

"Well, he's going to find out," Trent said, his jaw tight. "I've had it. I've threatened before, but now he's going to go to the strictest military school I can find."

"You don't mean that."

"Indeed I do. But first, I'm going to find out where he got that bike."

George obviously knew when it was time to leave well enough alone. "I don't suppose you're hungry," he said.

Food was the last thing on Trent's mind. "No. All I want is a cigarette."

"You gave up smoking years ago."

"You see what this boy is doing to me?" Trent threw himself down on a chair, only to get up immediately. "I'm going out again to look for him."

"Do you think that's wise?"

"No, but it's better than sitting here wondering where the hell he is, or what he's doing. Call me on the car phone the instant you hear anything."

"You know I will."

Trent was just starting the car, when he suddenly remembered a snatch of the conversation he and Nan had

had with Derry at the track. He stopped, his hand in midair.

You had to go and tell him! Derry had shouted at her. *You couldn't wait to get me in trouble!*

He frowned. *You had to go and tell him!*

What did that mean, exactly? Surely if Nan had known about Derry riding a motorcycle she would have told him. She knew how he felt about his son and bikes.

So what had Derry meant? Trent drove out, dialing Dunleavy's number as he went. He'd talk to Nan, he thought, and get this all straightened out.

NAN WAS WAITING by the phone when Trent called. The instant she recognized his voice, she asked, "Did you find him?"

"Not yet. I called to ask you something."

Nan heard something in his voice and tensed. "What is it?"

"Did you know about Derry's riding a bike?"

This was it, Nan thought. She couldn't evade or avoid the subject any longer. Miserably, she said, "Oh, Trent, I meant to tell you a hundred times. The truth is, I saw Derry with a bike that day I went riding up in the hills behind the farm."

Trent was silent. Then all he said was, "I see."

She couldn't bear his coldness. "Please try to understand," she begged. "At first, I didn't want to tell you because I thought Derry should do it himself. Then, as time went on, it became more and more difficult. I'm sorry. I know what I did was inexcusable."

"Yes, it was," he said.

She felt chilled to the bone. "I'll do anything to make it up to you. Please, let me—"

"There's nothing you can do, Nan," he said. "I have to look for my son."

"I'll look with—" She stopped as she heard the dial tone.

CHAPTER FIFTEEN

AFTER A SLEEPLESS NIGHT, Nan came downstairs the following morning with a heavy heart. The knowledge that Trent was hurting and didn't want her help was almost more than she could bear, and she was just passing by the living room when she heard voices and paused. Octavia and Carla were talking softly, and there was a third voice...Trent! she thought, and rushed into the room in time to hear him say—

"Derry's disappeared."

Disappeared? Nan thought blankly. The room seemed to spin. This was her fault, she knew. She should have gone to Trent the moment she'd discovered that Derry was defying his father's wishes.

"Oh, Trent..." she whispered.

He turned to her. She had never seen him look so awful. Dark shadows circled his eyes and his face was white and pasty. His hand shook when he reached to push back his disheveled hair.

"He's vanished," Trent said. "No one has seen him since you and I talked to him at the track."

"But that was twenty-four hours ago!"

His face crumpled, and to Nan, nothing was more important at that moment than comforting him. She flew across the room to him, and to her relief, he swept her up and hugged her tight.

"Oh, Nan," he said brokenly.

Carla and Octavia exchanged quick glances. Then Carla said, "Come on, Grandmother. Let's you and I go into the den."

"Good idea," Octavia said, getting to her feet. "Trent, Nan, let us know if there's anything we can do."

Nan hardly noticed when the two women went out.

Trent's body trembled against her, and she knew he was close to tears. She pressed against him with all her might, trying to infuse some of her strength into him, telling him without words that everything was going to be all right. They stood like that for almost a full minute. Only when she was sure he could speak again did she pull away and look up into his face.

"We'll find him," she whispered, her eyes burning with conviction. "We will."

She knew that the words sounded as hollow to him as they had earlier, but she couldn't think of anything else to say. All she could do was to hold him close.

"Have you spoken to the police?" she asked.

"About filing a missing persons report?" His voice shook. "I tried, but even though they took the information, they said they'll probably treat him as a runaway for now. They know that Derry and I had...words at the track."

"How do they know that?" Nan asked.

"Because I told them. Because it's true. I know I've been hard on the boy. Especially about the motorcycle business. You see, I used to ride one and I'm afraid for his safety. And because...damn it! I want my son back!''

"You look exhausted," Nan said. She led him to a chair and forced him to sit down. "Can I get you some coffee?"

He shook his head. "No, I don't want anything. You go ahead."

Nan didn't want anything, either. Carefully, she sat on a chair beside Trent, who had his head against the backrest, his eyes closed. He looked, she thought, at the end of his rope.

She took his hand and held it tight. "What can I do?" she asked.

Wearily, he squeezed her fingers. "Nothing. Just sit here with me while I get myself together." He was silent a moment, then his hand tightened even more. "Has there been any news of Done Cryin'?"

She didn't want to talk about her horse, but she sensed that he needed, however brief, a change of subject. "No. Dwight and I went over every possibility we could think of, and he's talked to anyone who even went *near* the track."

"They'll find him in time to train for the Derby."

When Nan thought about Done Cryin', it wasn't in connection with the Kentucky Derby. The only thing that mattered to her was that they get him back. She didn't even care if he ever raced again, as long as he was found, safe and sound.

"Oh, Nan," Trent said, his eyes still closed. "I'm sorry. I know how you feel about that horse."

"It's not over yet," she said. "We'll find him, and when we do, we'll prosecute whoever is responsible." Her lips tightened. "I'll make sure of that."

She waited, then said carefully, "But in the meantime, what are we going to do about Derry?"

He opened his eyes. Turning his head, he looked at her. "We?"

"Yes," she said firmly, gazing right back. *"We."*

He smiled for the first time that morning. "I know this isn't the time to talk about it, but...I'm glad you're here, Nan."

She laced her fingers with his. "So am I. Now, let's try and figure out again where he might have gone."

"Be my guest. I've gone around and around in my mind about it, but haven't come up with a thing. I just don't know what to believe about him anymore."

"He's been going through a tough time, Trent," she said. "You both have."

"And so have you," he said. "I can't help thinking about your accident. If Derry is responsible for trying to hurt you—"

"He isn't."

"How can you be so sure? He could be doing these awful things to get back at me. God knows, he hates me enough."

"He doesn't hate you, Trent. I told you that. He's just angry and confused and—"

"But what if he *did* try to run you off the road?" Trent said, shuddering. "And why has he disappeared now?"

Something was at the back of her mind, something she couldn't quite pin down. It kept nagging at her, telling her there was a connection to be made, something to put together that she hadn't thought of yet. She tried hard, but she couldn't catch it.

"I don't know, but we'll find him."

"I hope you're right. I'm not sure I could choose between my son and the woman I love."

The woman I love. The words wrapped her in a warm glow. She loved him, too. And seeing him like this made her realize just how much he meant to her. All the quarrels and arguments and disagreements in the world couldn't change that.

She reached for him, cradling his head on her shoulder and stroking his hair. "We'll find him," she whispered. "I know we will."

They were still sitting there when Carla came in and said, "George just called."

Trent sat up at once, the look of hope on his face fading when Carla saw it and shook her head. "No, he hasn't found Derry. But two detectives are at your house and they want to talk to you." Sympathetically, she looked at Nan, as she added, "Alone."

Trent said to Nan, "I won't go without you."

"It's all right," Nan said. She summoned a smile. "You go ahead. Call me when they leave."

"I want you with me," Trent said, gazing at her. "I never want to be apart from you."

Gently, she touched his face. Her feelings for him plain in her expressive eyes, she said simply, "I know. And I'll be there. But right now, Derry is more important. Go on now, talk to the detectives. I'll come over when you call."

He was still reluctant to leave. "Promise?"

"With all my heart."

It wasn't the time for a passionate kiss, but Nan knew the depth of his emotion when he stood and pulled her to him in an embrace. She hugged him in return, then pushed him resolutely toward the door. It was one of the hardest things she had ever done—standing by as she watched him drive away. Carla came out and stood with her, and they waited until the car disappeared down the driveway.

"Is he all right?" Carla asked.

"I hope so," Nan said. "Do you know what the police want with him?"

"George didn't say much, but I gathered that they wanted to talk to him about the missing persons report. Do you think they might have found Derry?"

"I hope not," Nan said.

Carla looked startled. "What?"

Hurriedly, Nan explained. "I mean that it would be simpler and better for both Derry and Trent if they could resolve this for themselves."

"Oh, yes, you're right, of course. Somehow, though, I don't see that happening."

"You never know."

"That's for sure. Listen, I know you have a lot on your mind, but I wanted to tell you what Wade told me."

"What's that?" Nan asked, her mind still on Trent. Suddenly, something occurred to her, and she looked quickly at her cousin. "Don't tell me there's something wrong with Never Done Dreamin'!"

"No, no, it's not that. Not yet, anyway."

"Not *yet?*"

"Well, Nan, we've got to face the likelihood that *someone* has a grudge either against the Dunleavy horses, or the farm itself. How else can we explain all the awful things that have happened?"

Nan hadn't had time to think about it. Or maybe, she thought, she just hadn't wanted to consider the awful possibility. But now that Carla had brought it up, she had to admit, "You're right. First, there was Done Roamin'. Then your colt was hurt. Now Done Cryin' has been stolen. It's all too much of a coincidence, isn't it?"

"It certainly is."

"So, what are we going to do?"

"I don't know. Maybe we should call the police again."

"And tell them what? That we think there's some kind of conspiracy?"

"We don't have any proof," Carla said glumly. She was silent a moment, then she said, "You don't think that Derry is involved in—"

"No, I don't," Nan said sharply. "And frankly, Carla, I'm surprised you'd even ask."

"I know, I know. I'm sorry. I don't know why I said that. I don't believe for a minute that Derry had anything to do with . . . well, you know. But *someone* is responsible."

"So all we have to do is figure out who before Never Done Dreamin' gets hurt."

"Oh, Nan, I couldn't bear it if someone hurt that beautiful filly, could you?"

"Do you think we should hire someone to guard her? It sounds ridiculous, I know, but—"

Carla shivered. "It doesn't sound ridiculous to me. I don't think I can go through this again. And there's no doubt that if someone doesn't want Dunleavy Farm to have a winner, he'd have to do something about Never Done Dreamin'. The way she's been running, Wade thinks she might be able to take the Derby—if not the Triple Crown itself."

"If she even makes it to the first race," Nan said sadly. "Your colt didn't. And unless a miracle happens, it seems that neither will Done Cryin'." Her voice shook and she bit her lip. *Where is he?* she wondered. And then, even more fearfully, *Where's Derry?*

They were silent a moment, then Carla said, "Wade told me something else. He thinks he knows where to find Honey and Seth."

"What? Where?"

"Well, he talked to someone who talked to someone who thinks he remembered that they were staying at some layover farm in Arizona. I was just waiting until Trent left so we could call the place. Are you with me?"

"You have the number?"

"You know Wade, thorough in every way."

Relieved to have something to do, Nan said, "Let's go."

In the front room, they debated about which one of them should call.

"You do it," Nan said. "I'm too nervous."

"But what will I say?"

"You didn't have any trouble convincing me to come."

"That was different."

"Why?"

"I don't know. It just was."

Nan reached for the phone. "Give me the number, then. I'll do it."

As Carla handed her the paper with a phone number on it, she said, "You've changed so much since you arrived here."

Nan was already dialing. "I have? How?"

"I don't know. You're more confident, less... prickly."

"I was *never* prickly!"

"Oh yes you were. When you first came, you were like a porcupine, all spines."

"And now?"

"Now, being in love has made you softer."

"Well, I hope—" Someone picked up the phone at the other end, and she broke off. "Hello?" She crossed her fingers. "May I please speak to Seth Dunleavy?"

"He's not here," said a harried feminine voice. "Who's calling?"

"Well, er... this is a little awkward, but I'm Seth's cousin. We've never met, but my name is Nan Dunleavy, and I'm calling from Dunleavy Farm in Kentucky."

"Yes?"

Nan couldn't tell from that single word if she was making any progress. She looked at Carla, who silently mouthed, *"What's going on?"* Nan shook her head and tried again.

"Do you know when he'll be back?" she asked. "It's really important that I talk to him."

There was a definite freeze in the voice this time. "About what?"

Nan decided to go for it. "Do you know if he received a letter from Octavia Dunleavy?"

"And if he did?"

"Well, if he did, Octavia Dunleavy is our grandmother—his and mine, that is—and Carla's, too. She's here with me—Carla, that is. She's Seth's cousin, too. Would you like to talk to her?"

Without waiting for an answer, Nan shoved the receiver into the startled Carla's hand. *"You* talk to her," she whispered. "I'm not making any headway at all. She sounds mad, or something. Maybe we shouldn't have called."

"Hello, hello?"

Hastily, Carla put the phone to her ear. "Hello," she said. "This is Carla Dunleavy. And you're...?"

"Honey Dunleavy. Look, is this a joke? Because if it is, I don't have time for it. I've got stalls to clean, and horses to feed, and—"

"I understand," Carla said. "I won't take much more of your time, I promise. But Nan and I would like to get in touch with Seth, if it's at all possible. You see, Seth is Octavia Dunleavy's only grandson, and she's anxious to see him. She sent a letter too, explaining everything, but I gather you never received it?''

"Oh, Seth got it, all right," Honey said, sounding angry. "He just didn't do anything about it."

"Oh, I...see." Carla shifted the receiver slightly away from her ear so Nan could come close and listen, too. "Does that mean that he's not interested in accepting Grandmother's invitation to visit the farm?"

The voice turned bitter. "You got that right."

"That's too bad," Carla said, signaling Nan with a what-shall-I-say-now? look. Nan responded by pretending to ride a horse. Carla nodded and said, "Did you know that Grandmother wants to give him one of her horses?"

"Yes, she mentioned it in the letter."

"But he's not interested in that, either?"

"Look, Karen, we've got enough problems right now—"

"It's Carla, and I understand. But I promise, he—or rather, both of you—won't be disappointed if you accept Grandmother's offer. You're acquainted with racing, aren't you?"

"Yeah, a little," Honey said sarcastically. "We *do* run the fair circuit with a string of our own."

"Then you're familiar with the filly Never Done Dreamin'?" Carla said, crossing her fingers so Nan could see them.

Nan could hear the gasp that came over the line. "N-N-N-Never Done Dreamin'?" Honey stammered. "Who isn't? What about her?"

Looking satisfied, Carla winked at Nan. "That's the horse that Grandmother would like Seth to have—if you and he can take the time to visit."

There was a silence. Then Honey said unsteadily, "Are we talking about the Never Done Dreamin' who just won the Florida Derby? The one they're comparing to Ruffian?"

"That's the one."

Another silence. Then, "Look, I'll have to get back to you."

"That's fine. Here's our number. But I do ask that you get back to us as soon as possible. We're bringing the filly up from Florida as we speak, and you know the Kentucky Derby isn't far off. Grandmother would love to have you here by then. So would we," Carla added. "Do you think you might be able to come?"

"I don't know." Honey sounded harried again. "Things are a little . . . difficult right now. I don't know if you're aware of it, but Seth broke his leg a while ago, and it hasn't been . . . easy for him."

"This is a wonderful place to recuperate," Carla told her. "And if you don't mind my saying so, you sound like you could use a little vacation."

"What I could use is a permanent furlough—no, I didn't mean that. Look, I've got to go now. I'll tell Seth you called."

"Please do. And, it was nice talking to you."

When Carla hung up, Nan immediately asked, "Well?"

"I don't know. It didn't sound too promising. She seems to have a lot on her mind."

"Don't we all."

"Well, we tried. The rest is up to Seth and Honey. Hey, wait, where are you going?"

An idea had come to Nan while she'd listened to Carla talking about how great the farm was as a place to recuperate. Nan agreed. There were so many peaceful spots where one could go to think things out. Suddenly Nan knew what she had to do.

"I'll let you know," she said cryptically as she turned and headed out.

THIS TIME, Nan didn't saddle a horse for the trip up the hill behind the farm. She took it on foot—at a fast clip. The entire time she was climbing, she hoped that she wasn't mistaken. If she was, she thought, she didn't have another plan.

She wasn't mistaken. A familiar figure, dirty and disheveled and a bit tear-stained, huddled in the grove atop the hill. Panting from the exertion, Nan stopped, and for a few seconds, woman and boy just looked at each other. Nan hoped her unexpected presence wouldn't scare him away, but she needn't have worried. Even though the motorcycle was parked a few feet off, the helmet hanging from one of the handlebars, the runaway was obviously too tired to go anywhere.

"Hi," she said when she had enough breath to speak. "Are you and your father having a contest? You look almost as awful as he does."

"Yeah, well, you should talk," Derry said. "What did you do, get into a fight?"

She'd forgotten about the bandage on her face. Right now, it didn't seem important. She said, "No, I rolled my truck."

"No kidding? That was a clever move."

"Yes, I know. Do you mind if I sit down?"

A curtain came down over his face again, and he shrugged. "Suit yourself."

Trying to believe that this was going well, she sat. "You know, if I hadn't been in such a hurry, I would have brought sandwiches or something. You look hungry."

He shrugged again. "How did you know I was here?"

"I didn't. I guessed."

"It was a pretty good guess, then."

"Well, I've had some practice, remember?" she said lightly. "All those teenagers at the Saddleback who resented their parents for dragging them along had to go somewhere. And when I remembered that we'd met up here that day, I thought you might come back. I was right. You did."

"Bully for you."

She ignored that. "Have you been here all night?"

His lip curled, he said, "Since you know so much, what do you think?"

"I think that it probably got pretty cold up here, and you wished you were in your own bed, that's what I think."

His eyes shifted to ChangeOver Farm, spread out below them on the other side of the hill. "Yeah, well, I'm not going back there."

"What are you going to do instead?"

"It's none of your business."

"That's true. I was just making conversation."

"Don't bother."

She imitated his shrug. "Okay, I've got enough problems of my own."

He glanced down at his portable radio. "Yeah," he said. "I heard Done Cryin' is still missing. Too bad."

"Yes," she agreed. "It is."

"You sound pretty calm about it."

Calm? she thought. If she had time, she'd be out of her mind with worry. But she had learned you could only worry about so many things at once, and even then, they all had to take a number. There were priorities, and Derry and Trent came first.

"There's nothing I can do," she said. "People are looking for him." She paused. "Just like people are looking for you."

"Yeah, well, pretty soon it'll be too late, 'cause I'm out of here."

"I sort of figured that. But you'd better be careful when you go."

"Yeah? Why?"

"Because they're looking for someone on a bike. A big bike, like that one."

Derry glanced uneasily at the gleaming motorcycle. "Why like that one?"

"Because it's just like the one that forced me off the road the night I rolled the truck."

He stiffened. "And you think *I* did it?"

"Did you?"

He got up suddenly, kicking the radio so that it flew about ten feet, hitting a rock and smashing into a hundred pieces. Nan gazed at it for a second, then said, "Feel better?"

He glared at her, his fists clenched. "You think I did it, don't you?" His expression turned even uglier. "Does Dad think I'm responsible?"

"You'll have to ask him," she said neutrally.

"I'm not going to ask him anything!" he yelled, and turned away before adding, "He wouldn't believe me, anyway."

"He'd believe you if you told the truth. He's worried about you, Derry."

"Oh, yeah, right. He's so worried that he's probably calling up some military school right now—if he isn't talking to the police."

"As a matter of fact, at the moment, he's talking to two detectives about you."

Derry whirled again, his face whitening under the dirt. "He's going to have me arrested?"

"Well, I don't know. Can you be arrested for driving a motorcycle without a license?"

"I'd *have* a license if he'd let me!" Derry said fiercely.

"Why won't he? You're sixteen, aren't you?"

"Yeah, but it doesn't make any difference. He has to sign, and he says he won't do it until I bring my grades up."

"That seems like a pretty good incentive to me."

"What do you care?" he shouted suddenly. "Why should anyone care about me? All I do is screw things up!"

Careful to keep her voice calm, Nan asked, "What things?"

He made a savage gesture with a grubby hand. "Everything! Everything I touch!"

"That's a little broad. Can you be more specific?"

Angry tears welling in his eyes, he glared at her furiously. Abruptly, he sat down again. "Everything... I told you! I've let everybody down."

"No, you didn't, Derry."

"Yes, I did. I did!" He looked at her wildly, tears spilling over and making two lines in the dirt on his cheeks. "Dad told me to take care of Mom, but I...but I...but I couldn't!" He started to choke, to sob, and he put his head in his hands. Shoulders heaving, he spoke through his tears, "I tried, but I couldn't. She died, and there wasn't a damned thing I could do about it!"

As she had done for his father, Nan gently put her arms around him. Burying his face in her shoulder, he clutched her and cried—hoarse sobs that seemed to come from some deep untouchable place inside him. The sounds were agonizing, the violent trembling of his young body no less so. But Nan held on with all her strength and let him cry until he had no more tears in him. Then, knowing he'd be embarrassed, she let him go and looked away as he scrubbed at his eyes with his T-shirt.

"I'm s-sorry." He hiccuped, mortified. "I shouldn't have done that."

"Why not? Tears are a release. Heaven knows, I've shed enough of them. Buckets, in fact, during the time that my father had cancer and I had to watch him die."

She could feel him staring at her. "Just like my mom."

She nodded. "Yes. And it was awful and painful and there wasn't a thing I could do about it except watch." She turned to him. "So you see, Derry, I understand. It's the worst thing in the world to be helpless when someone you love is suffering." She grabbed his hands and forced him to look at her. "But it wasn't your fault. You were there for her, and that's all that counts."

"But I—"

Holding his eyes, she said intensely, "*People die, Derry.* That's the way it is. And sometimes all we're allowed is to sit by and hold that person's hand. It's not enough—it's never enough—but that's all we get. Until something more comes along, we'll have to make do with that."

"But Dad—"

Nan took a chance. The moment was here, and she wasn't sure they'd ever get it back again if she didn't take advantage of it. Praying that Trent would forgive her for relating something so personal, she said, "Your dad doesn't blame you, Derry. In fact, he blames himself. He was the husband, the father…the *man.* He feels he should have done something, too. But just like you, he couldn't."

In Derry's blue eyes, Nan could see disbelief warring with his intense longing to believe. He said, "Dad feels that way?"

"He's your father, Derry. Do you think he feels any less than you?"

"But . . . but he never said anything."

"Neither did you."

For a long moment, he stared down at the ground. Then he said, "You never told my dad about seeing me up here on the bike, did you?"

"No, I was waiting for you to do it."

He kept staring down. Finally, he sighed. "I guess I'd better do it, then." He looked up. "Will you come with me?"

"If you want me to."

He glanced over at the bike. "I guess you don't want to—"

"You guess right," she said. "Come on, get your helmet. We'll walk. Someone else can come back for the bike."

Derry got his helmet and tucked it under his arm. Then they started down the hill on foot. He was silent for a moment, then he stopped. Nan took a step or two beyond him before she looked back.

He shuddered. "I didn't do it," he said. "I didn't run you off the road."

"I know," she said, and started walking again.

His legs were so long that he caught up with her in one stride. "How do you know?"

She kept walking. "Well, I admit . . . at first I was thrown off by the similarity of the leather jackets. They all look the same to me. But then I realized . . . Derry, put your helmet on."

"What?"

"Just put your helmet on."

He looked perplexed, but he complied. "Now what?"

She stopped and looked at him. "I can see your eyes," she said. "They're blue."

"So?"

"So your helmet visor isn't tinted, it's clear. The person who ran me off the road was wearing a helmet with a dark-tinted visor. I couldn't see who it was. No one could have."

Derry took off the helmet and put it back under his arm. Disappointed, he asked, "What if by some chance, *my* visor had been tinted? Would you have suspected me *then?*"

She didn't hesitate. "No."

"Why not?"

"Because," she said, "even though both you and your dad can ride a motorcycle, neither one of you is a coward who hides behind a mask—or a tinted visor. That's why."

She began walking again. Derry stood where he was a moment. Then, in a couple of ungainly bounds, he caught up to her again. "Dad can ride a bike?"

Smiling to herself, Nan said, "Now, why do you think he didn't want you on one? He knows all about the trouble young men can get into on motorcycles."

Derry looked at her incredulously. *"Dad?"*

She laughed. By this time, they had walked far enough so that she could see a beloved figure standing alone on the terrace at ChangeOver Farm, watching them. At the sight, she stopped and pointed.

"There he is," she said. "Why don't you go ask him yourself?"

Derry gazed at her for a long moment. Even with blue eyes instead of Trent's brown, he looked so much like his father that Nan felt a pang. Then he smiled, and the resemblance became even more pronounced.

"I've got an idea," he said.

"What's that?"

Shyly, he took her hand. "Why don't we go ask him together?"

TRENT MET THEM at the gate to the back paddock. As he looked at Nan, she was elated to see that the shadows were gone from his eyes. Then, when he transferred his gaze to his son, and she saw his expression soften even more, she smiled. They still had a long way to go, she thought. But that look in Trent's eyes told her they were halfway home.

At the thought that she was home with them, tears filled her eyes. Derry, who had awkwardly embraced his father, and who had been tightly hugged in return, stepped back and saw the glitter on her eyelashes. In fake alarm, he said, "Hey, don't cry now! Everything's going to work out just fine."

Nan tried to hold back her tears, but it was impossible. "I . . . know," she blubbered. "And I couldn't be h-h-h-happier . . ."

Derry looked in consternation at his father. Trent smiled as he put his arm around the weeping, ecstatic Nan. "Don't ask," he said to his son.

Nan tried to smile through her tears. "Give a girl a break, will you? It's not every day that I get to witness a family reunion. I just wish..."

Trent understood. Holding her tightly, he said, "We'll find your colt, Nan. If we have to move heaven and earth to find him, that's what we'll do."

Derry came to her side. Clumsily, he hugged her, too. "You bet," he said. "We're in this together now."

Nan looked from one to the other, loving them both so much she could hardly speak. "I know we are," she said. "And once we find that horse, I promise you, I'll be done cryin' for good."

EPILOGUE

THE SUN WAS GOING DOWN, the sky already streaked with pale golds and mauve, when Octavia came out of the house and started slowly toward the paddocks. When she thought of her granddaughters, sophisticated and temperamental Carla, and sensitive and impatient Nan, she smiled. They were so different, she mused, and yet, she loved them both equally. Together, they'd brought life and excitement into her life, and, except for the fact that Done Driftin' was still recovering from his injury, and Done Cryin' hadn't been found yet, Octavia had never enjoyed herself more.

Now, if only, she thought with a sigh, she could come to terms with her oldest daughter. She and Meredith were getting along a little better these days, but Octavia knew they had a long way to go. Still, the fact that they were at least *speaking* to each other was more than she'd dared hope only a few months ago. So, even though her step wasn't light, tonight her spirits certainly were as she went to give Done Roamin' his carrot.

From his usual position high on the hill, Done Roamin' saw her and whinnied. As the sound carried down to her on the light breeze, Octavia stopped a moment to look at him.

You and me, old man, she thought, *we've done ourselves proud.*

Carla and Wade hadn't set a date yet for their wedding, but from the looks on their faces and the way they couldn't keep their hands off each other, Octavia didn't doubt it would be soon. And Nan had just returned from visiting the Spencers at ChangeOver Farm. She'd told them that she thought Trent and Derry might actually work things out. At the recollection, Octavia chuckled to herself. Nan wouldn't mention it, but Octavia knew that her granddaughter had played a big part in any reconciliation that might come about.

Nan was like her father in that way, Octavia thought, sobering at the thought of her only son. Gary had always been kind and generous to a fault. But he had also worn his heart on his sleeve, which was why he'd been so easily hurt. That wouldn't happen to Nan now—or at least, Octavia thought, not so often. That's why she was so pleased about Trent and Nan. Trent would help buffer her sensitive granddaughter against the hurts of the world. Not too much, she mused, but enough.

And now, Octavia reflected, all she had to do was wait. Nan and Carla had contacted Honey and Seth, and while Honey hadn't said they'd come, not yet, Octavia was hopeful. If things worked out, the timing would be just right. Soon it would be Derby week, and then the big race. Never Done Dreamin' was coming back from Florida where she'd been racing; if all went as planned, they might soon have a Derby winner in the barn.

As though to remind her that he, too, was a winner, Done Roamin' whinnied impatiently again from the hill. As he stood there silhouetted against the sky, Octavia felt a pang. He looked as he had so many years ago, she thought, fleet and strong, and oh so proud.

"... and it's Done Roamin' pulling away all by himself!" the loudspeaker had blared that day of the Belmont, the final leg of the Triple Crown. Done Roamin' had won the Kentucky Derby and the Preakness that year; all that was left was this last contest. As the horses rounded the final turn, the announcer's voice had soared. *"Done Roamin' by three lengths, four... by ten lengths now! It's Done Roamin' driving to the wire... Done Roamin' all alone...! Ladies and gentlemen, Done Roamin' has just won the Triple Crown!"*

Ah, those were the days, Octavia thought, coming back from the past. But the cheers were long gone, and the thundering hoofbeats stilled. Tonight, she was an old lady hobbling along with her cane, and her famous stallion was just an aged horse, waiting by the fence for his treat.

"So how are you, old son?" she murmured when Done Roamin' put his head over the railing.

The venerable stallion took the carrot she offered, and as Octavia stood there listening contentedly to the crunching sounds he made, she looked up at the glowing sunset and sighed.

"I guess things never turn out exactly the way you plan, Roamy," she said. "But I think Nan and Trent are made for each other, don't you?"

Done Roamin' snorted.

Octavia smiled. "I believe Nan's Yolanda is going to think so, too. Nan called her, you know, and finally persuaded her to visit. I'm looking forward to meeting her.''

Octavia's smile faded.

''We still don't know who hurt Done Driftin','' she went on. ''And now Done Cryin' has been stolen. If I weren't a lady, I'd curse at the injustice of it all. Nan had such plans...''

She paused a moment, then looked determined. ''But when we get him back—and we will—he'll still have some racing in him, then he can join Done Driftin' in the stallion barn. You'll be proud of them, Roamy. After all, they're your last sons.''

Done Roamin' snorted again.

''You know,'' Octavia said thoughtfully, ''I still think Meredith knows more than she's saying about all this. There was something in her eyes when she heard about Nan's colt. But maybe I'm just imagining things. Old ladies tend to do that, don't they?''

This time, Done Roamin' didn't answer. It was time for both of them to go in. Octavia gave the horse a pat on his still-glossy neck. But just as she started back to the house, she saw a taxi pull in.

''What in heaven's name...?'' Surprised, she stopped where she was and watched as a tall, slender young woman got out of the back of the cab. The setting sun shimmered on the woman's pale blond hair, and Octavia drew in a breath.

Could it be? she asked herself. Could it possibly be?

Just then, Carla and Nan came rushing out of the house and down the steps. The three young women conferred excitedly, with many gestures and startled exclamations. Then, as one, they all turned in Octavia's direction. Carla waved at her, and Nan tugged the newcomer along. Completely forgetting the hapless cabdriver, the three of them rushed over to where Octavia was standing.

"Grandmother, you'll never guess . . . !" Nan cried.

"Grandmother, look who's come!" Carla exclaimed.

Together, they pushed the newcomer forward.

"Hello, my dear," Octavia said, trying to be calm. But her heart was pounding. "You must be . . ."

"Honey Dunleavy," the young woman said in a voice that matched her name. She was wearing a denim dress with a white belt. The evening breeze blew her hair across her face, and as she pulled the long strands back with one hand, she held the other out. Eyes the dark blue of a mountain lake met Octavia's, and in that gaze was a world of hurt. Octavia took the work-worn hand in her own as Honey said, "It's so nice to meet you after all this time . . . Mrs. Dunleavy."

"Please call me Grandmother, dear. And let's go inside. I want to hear all about it."

Honey looked startled. "How . . . did you know?"

Octavia smiled tenderly. "You came alone, didn't you?"

Honey's full lower lip trembled. She started to say, "Seth would have come, but—" She stopped at the look in Octavia's eyes. With a heavy sigh, she finished, "It's a long story."

Octavia glanced at Carla on one side, and at Nan on the other. Briskly, she said, "Well, we've got plenty of time, don't we, my dears? Now, Carla, please pay that patient cabdriver, and tell Teresa that Honey is here.

And Nan, please show Honey to her room in case she wants to freshen up. I'll be in presently, and we'll have a cup of tea and a nice, long talk.''

With Honey casting a grateful glance over her shoulder, the three young women started toward the house, but Octavia held back. Done Roamin' was still at the fence, and she turned to him before she followed the others inside.

''Well, Roamy,'' she said. ''It looks like our story isn't quite finished.'' She paused, a faraway look in her eyes, then added, ''I guess the end is going to depend on Honey and Seth and Never Done Dreamin'.''

* * * * *

Be sure to look for Honey and Seth's story in
NEVER DONE DREAMIN',
by
Janis Flores

The final title in the Dunleavy Legacy.
Available next month wherever Harlequin books
are sold.

HARLEQUIN SUPERROMANCE®

WOMEN WHO DARE
They take chances, make changes
and follow their hearts!

Kate
by Patricia Armstrong

Kate Bainbridge is hopping mad. Someone has set fire to the
old logging mill her grandfather won in a game of gin rummy
and bequeathed to his only granddaughter. And the man in
charge of the mill is being singularly unhelpful.

Locke Martyn has no time to teach the new owner—*a city
woman,* who knows nothing about logging—how to run a mill
or how to deal with the eccentric locals who work there. He
thinks Kate should simply stay where she belongs.

Of course, Locke has never *met* Kate....

**Watch for Superromance #665 *Kate*
by Patricia Armstrong**

**Available in October 1995 wherever
Harlequin books are sold.**

OFFICIAL RULES

FLYAWAY VACATION SWEEPSTAKES 3449

NO PURCHASE OR OBLIGATION NECESSARY

Three Harlequin Reader Service 1995 shipments will contain respectively, coupons for entry into three different prize drawings, one for a trip for two to San Francisco, another for a trip for two to Las Vegas and the third for a trip for two to Orlando, Florida. To enter any drawing using an Entry Coupon, simply complete and mail according to directions.

There is no obligation to continue using the Reader Service to enter and be eligible for any prize drawing. You may also enter any drawing by hand printing the words "Flyaway Vacation," your name and address on a 3"x5" card and the destination of the prize you wish that entry to be considered for (i.e., San Francisco trip, Las Vegas trip or Orlando trip). Send your 3"x5" entries via first-class mail (limit: one entry per envelope) to: Flyaway Vacation Sweepstakes 3449, c/o Prize Destination you wish that entry to be considered for, P.O. Box 1315, Buffalo, NY 14269-1315, USA or P.O. Box 610, Fort Erie, Ontario L2A 5X3, Canada.

To be eligible for the San Francisco trip, entries must be received by 5/30/95; for the Las Vegas trip, 7/30/95; and for the Orlando trip, 9/30/95.

Winners will be determined in random drawings conducted under the supervision of D.L. Blair, Inc., an independent judging organization whose decisions are final, from among all eligible entries received for that drawing. San Francisco trip prize includes round-trip airfare for two, 4-day/3-night weekend accommodations at a first-class hotel, and $500 in cash (trip must be taken between 7/30/95—7/30/96, approximate prize value—$3,500); Las Vegas trip includes round-trip airfare for two, 4-day/3-night weekend accommodations at a first-class hotel, and $500 in cash (trip must be taken between 9/30/95—9/30/96, approximate prize value—$3,500); Orlando trip includes round-trip airfare for two, 4-day/3-night weekend accommodations at a first-class hotel, and $500 in cash (trip must be taken between 11/30/95—11/30/96, approximate prize value—$3,500). All travelers must sign and return a Release of Liability prior to travel. Hotel accommodations and flights are subject to accommodation and schedule availability. Sweepstakes open to residents of the U.S. (except Puerto Rico) and Canada, 18 years of age or older. Employees and immediate family members of Harlequin Enterprises, Ltd., D.L. Blair, Inc., their affiliates, subsidiaries and all other agencies, entities and persons connected with the use, marketing or conduct of this sweepstakes are not eligible. Odds of winning a prize are dependent upon the number of eligible entries received for that drawing. Prize drawing and winner notification for each drawing will occur no later than 15 days after deadline for entry eligibility for that drawing. Limit: one prize to an individual, family or organization. All applicable laws and regulations apply. Sweepstakes offer void wherever prohibited by law. Any litigation within the province of Quebec respecting the conduct and awarding of the prizes in this sweepstakes must be submitted to the Regies des loteries et Courses du Quebec. In order to win a prize, residents of Canada will be required to correctly answer a time-limited arithmetical skill-testing question. Value of prizes are in U.S. currency.

Winners will be obligated to sign and return an Affidavit of Eligibility within 30 days of notification. In the event of noncompliance within this time period, prize may not be awarded. If any prize or prize notification is returned as undeliverable, that prize will not be awarded. By acceptance of a prize, winner consents to use of his/her name, photograph or other likeness for purposes of advertising, trade and promotion on behalf of Harlequin Enterprises, Ltd., without further compensation, unless prohibited by law.

For the names of prizewinners (available after 12/31/95), send a self-addressed, stamped envelope to: Flyaway Vacation Sweepstakes 3449 Winners, P.O. Box 4200, Blair, NE 68009.

RVC KAL